DISCARD

Lyons, Nan
Sold!

Sold!

Sold!

Nan and Ivan Lyons

Coward, McCann & Geoghegan ❧ New York

Library of Congress Cataloging in Publication Data

Lyons, Nan.
    Sold!

    I. Lyons, Ivan.   II. Title.
PS3562.Y449S6   1982   813'.54   81-19576
ISBN 0-399-90127-2   AACR2

Printed in the United States of America

ACKNOWLEDGMENTS

The authors wish to thank
Lorna C. Kelly, auctioneer, Sotheby Parke Bernet,
for sharing her wealth of auction expertise,
and
Peter L. Schaffer, of A La Vieille Russie,
for spinning flax into gold.

This book is dedicated to the memory of
Tony Godwin

The old truck filled with old furniture and old trunks bounced along the dusty road. There were no cars in sight as it wheezed its way past Farmer Jessup's alfalfa field. Across the road, as flat and square as a primitive painting, stood the black-and-white and brown-and-white cows from Kennert's Dairy. The last flashes of a late July sun burst like flames from between the trees.

Emmett took one hand off the steering wheel and reached for the can of beer pressed between his knees. After a long drink, he poured some onto his sweat-drenched hair. "Can't be."

Chip nodded Yes as he gulped down all the beer. After belching long and loud, he threw the can out the open window. He picked up the book in his lap. "Is," he said, belching again.

"Damn."

"One more time," Chip insisted.

Emmett sighed. "Han, Sui, T'ang, Sung, Yüan, Ch'ing, Ming."

"Shit! You did it again. Ch'ing comes after Ming." Chip waved a worn copy of *The Antique Dealers Friend*. "Ming is 1368 to 1643. Ch'ing is 1644 to 1912, you asshole!"

Emmett made a screeching left turn at the Adirondack Park boundary that skirted the town of Perry Falls, New York, where they were born during Eisenhower 1952 to 1956. Emmett was the handsome brother: bright blue eyes, curly brown hair, and a wiry six-foot frame. Chip, two years younger, was paunchy and had features made of pudding. "Goddamn!" Emmett shouted.

Chip was wide-eyed as he held onto the rattling door. "Slow down! You're gonna kill us." He belched again.

Emmett shook his head. "Only thing's gonna kill us is Lorraine's fancy French cuisine. Why the hell does she have to make *soupe du jour* and *plat du jour* and *dessert du jour* every goddamn day? Didn't you ever tell her it's quality that counts, not quantity?"

Chip smiled. "You're just saying that 'cause you got a smaller pecker than me."

"Never figure out how God made a mistake like that."

"Only mistake God made was letting Duffy be the oldest."

"Doesn't matter anymore," Emmett said. "Duffy's through running my life. I'm gonna quit."

Chip sighed. "Whole afternoon was a big waste. All the old lady had was garbage."

"This time I mean it," Emmett yelled.

"That's what you always say."

"You'll see!" Emmett pushed the gas pedal to the floor. "I'm gonna tell her soon as we get back to the barn."

The Nickel Man Barn sat on the edge of the property still known as the Ryerson farm though all the Ryersons had long since died. The farm had withstood nearly a hundred bitter New York State winters before Ezra Ryerson faced the bitterest winter of all. In January of 1944, his son was killed in the war. Then, just before spring, his wife died. Not even his daughter Georgina spared him grief. Within the year she was pregnant and had to marry the icebox salesman who came through the war without a scratch.

Georgina and Red Patterson lived with Ezra, who, in his despair, forgot the fields and tended only his sorrow. He gave up on everything. Finally, when the milk trucks stopped coming, there was nothing to do but sell the cows. Georgina asked Red why he kept going back to the county auction every week even after all the livestock was sold. He told her it was a good place for a salesman to make contacts. The truth was Red had fallen in love with the auction business.

One Arm Henry was the county livestock auctioneer. He was a bearded, ugly man whose right arm had been ripped off and plowed under the soil at Miller's Farm. But to the icebox salesman, One Arm Henry was a croupier, a clown, a magician, the voice of God. No one had ever slammed a back door in *his* face.

Georgina was shocked by Red's decision to auction off the Ryerson farm equipment himself. Not even the success of his first sale changed her attitude. She was embarrassed when local farmers began asking Red to sell their surplus machinery in her father's barn. And she was ashamed when their wives began sending over broken sets of dishes and old attic furniture.

But Red needed more merchandise than he could coax out of his neighbors. As he traveled upstate peddling iceboxes, he searched for things to sell at the barn. The other auctioneers called him "the nickel man," a junk dealer who bids a nickel on things no one else wants.

Once a month, Red held an auction. Once a month, Georgina kept the children in the house with the shades drawn. Out of respect for the Old Man, Red waited until he died before painting THE NICKEL MAN on the side of the barn. Georgina said he should have waited until she died, too.

Red stopped selling iceboxes. He was determined to have the biggest auction house in the county. He made room for cars by graveling over the grass all around the barn. He built wooden bleachers six levels high across the whole north side. When the Lyric movie house closed down, he bought ten rows of bright red velvet seats as a reserved section for his regulars. And, for himself, Red bought a pulpit from a church near Elmira. With an old black bowler angled across his curly orange hair, a starched white shirt, green elastic armbands and a smile for everyone, he sat high above the crowd. Red Patterson was on top of the world.

Georgina died in 1966. Free from the shadow of her disapproval, Red worked night and day to make the business grow. He even went back on the road. He was gone for days at a time. When he returned, he was no longer greeted by Georgina's bitterness. Instead, the family was reunited in a burst of expectation. The three honks of his horn on Friday night heralded the arrival of a new treasure. Red described his latest acquisitions as though they came from the fabled courts of Europe. His children listened in awe. They laughed and hooted from the sheer joy of each new adventure.

Emmett was with the army in Germany, and Chip was at Fort Dix in 1975 when Red died. They came home on emergency leave and after the funeral locked themselves in the barn with Duffy. They cried softly and they cried aloud. They cried together and they cried alone. They couldn't stop crying until Duffy recalled the lawyer's wife who bid on her own dishes by mistake. As soon as they all began to laugh, Duffy unlocked the barn door.

". . . T'ang, Sung, Yüan, Ming, and then that little sucker, Ch'ing!" exclaimed Emmett.

"Ah, so," Chip nodded, closing the book. "Number One Son gets laid tonight."

Emmett frowned. "Only two things you ever think about. Food and fucking."

Chip began to giggle and then belched again. "What the hell else do you think about?"

"I think about having my own shop, that's what."

"Oh, shit. Not that again."

"I think about selling *real* antiques. And about going to an auction to *buy* instead of to *sell*."

"Will you slow down?"

"Most of all, I think about having one of those reserved dealer seats for my reserved dealer ass."

Chip sighed. "Must be Saturday night."

As they neared the bright red barn, Emmett slammed his foot on the brakes. There were more cars in the parking lot than ever before. "What the hell is going on?"

Chip moved his lips as he counted the number of trucks. "Boy, Duffy sure was right to put those ads in the Albany paper!"

"It's time she was right about something." Emmett parked on the side of the barn that still read

THE NICKEL MAN
Red Patterson, Auctioneer

as the signature of an artist remains after his death. They had once asked about changing it to "Duffy Patterson, Auctioneer." But from the look she gave them, they might as well have suggested murder.

The back door to the barn opened into the kitchen. It was a hot windowless room with a noisy overhead exhaust. Stoves and refrigerators were on one wall. Large tubs of ice were filled with cans of soda. Slices of homemade pie and bags of potato chips lined the counter near the service area.

Lorraine looked up from a steaming pot. "Where've you been?" she asked. "Duffy's going to kill you."

Chip slapped her on the behind and leaned over to see what kind of *soupe du jour* she was making. He inhaled deeply and stamped his feet like an excited child. "Bouillabaisse!"

Lorraine, her plump face framed by rings of honey-colored braids, smiled a big toothy grin. "My first!"

Emmett's wife, Rita, shook her head while turning hamburgers on a spitting grill. "I don't think Julia Child's going to lose any sleep."

Ann Marie, the dentist's daughter, was taking orders at the

window. "That's six burgers I got workin'," she called to Rita. "And two grilled cheeses. One with bacon."

Emmett put his hand on Rita's cheek. She sighed and nestled her angular face in his palm. He kissed her silken black hair. "Duffy's going to kill you," she said.

"Another burger well!" Ann Marie yelled.

"Another survivor," Rita muttered.

"And just what is that supposed to mean?" Lorraine asked.

"It means that if you didn't make dumb things like bouillabaisse everyone wouldn't be ordering burgers and I wouldn't be grilling myself into an early grave."

"The deal is you are the grill man," Lorraine reminded her.

"That's six workin'," Ann Marie shouted, "and now I need three more!"

Emmett grabbed Rita and pulled her away from the grill. "Are you crazy?" she asked. "I got nine working!"

He took the greasy spatula and handed it to Lorraine. "I have to talk to Rita."

Lorraine rolled her eyes. "Must be Saturday night. Emmett's quitting again."

"Two more cheeseburgers!"

Emmett's voice grew tense. "I'm goddamn tired of being a garbage man."

Rita sighed. "And I'm goddamn tired of being a grill man. But what's that going to do for us or the baby? How do you expect to feed Louis Comfort after you walk out of here?"

"Damn it, Rita, I've got to get out of this barn!"

She put an arm around him. "We will. We just can't do it now."

"You can't do it now," Lorraine snapped, "because the grill man is supposed to keep the burgers moving!"

"Can't I even talk to my own wife in peace?"

"Not while she's in my kitchen." Lorraine handed the spatula back to Rita. "We all got our jobs to do right now."

"Where are my grilled cheeses?" Ann Marie pleaded.

Emmett pushed Chip away from the soup pot. "That means you, too," he said angrily. "We all got our jobs to do."

Old Mrs. Jackson's patchwork quilts hung from the cross-beams, the colors of war above a battlefield. There were nearly two hundred people beneath the barn's vaulted roof. They swarmed like bees. Bodies wedged themselves in front of other bodies. Impatient hands reached out toward the display tables. Everything had to be touched, as though touching made things suddenly visible.

Five Limoges teacups nestled against six saucers. A black duck decoy peered through an empty ornate gilt picture frame. Cranberry glass, depression glass, and pressed glass mingled with satin glass, milk glass, cut glass, and pieces of art glass. A tin Edison phonograph horn, a Popsicle-stick jewelry box, and an Occupied Japan bisque teapot occupied the top of an oak dresser. Boxes of old buttons and cartons of green glass insulators hid under a cherry wood drop leaf table on which rested silver-plated corn holders and a 1953 calendar plate. An old toy fire engine, a green-and-orange Bakelite radio, a Kodak folding camera, and a rusted wire egg basket sat on the shelves of an oak cabinet with serpentine glass doors. Lamps with frayed cords lit the faces of Meissen figurines with chipped noses. A Pepsi-Cola sign leaned against a Hudson River scene painted on black velvet. Two white wicker chairs perched atop a water-stained library table with massive claw feet. Milk bottles from the 1940s sat inside an 1840 pine storage cupboard. New York State stoneware jugs lined the open space beneath a blanket rack. A collection of paperweights and a straight razor filled the top of a maple candle stand. A glass case protected old wedding rings and cameos and watches and picture-filled lockets. But nothing protected Duffy Patterson.

Wearing a long white Victorian dress, with a wide peach-satin sash fitted to her narrow waist, she was as much a part of the crowd as their high hopes. Duffy chatted, advised, confided, and encouraged. Although she played the role of guardian angel, no one would have mistaken her for a celestial being at that moment. No matter that her delicate features were framed by a halo of orange curls worthy of the most heavenly cherub. Duffy's bright blue eyes gave her away. They flashed with the sin of wrath. As Emmett came toward her, she leaned close as though kissing his cheek. "I ought to tear you limb from limb! Where the hell have you been?" Before he could answer, Duffy grabbed hold of his arm and pushed him up the stairs to the pulpit. "How do you expect me to handle a crowd this size myself? We got three new dealers and a pair of decorators from Philadelphia."

"I'm quitting, Duffy."

"They've been asking me more questions than the tax man. They must think I made the stuff."

"This time I mean it."

"Damn it, Emmett! Not again! Not tonight!"

"I'm through being a garbage man. All you sent me out for was a truckload of openers. Nothing you can put up once you're past the dollar bids."

Duffy felt someone tug at her sleeve. Mrs. Davis stood at the foot of the steps. She pointed to the jewelry case. "That Elmer Hartwell's watch in there?"

"I'll show it to you," Duffy said. "Emmett thinks it's turn of the century."

"I know what it is. Used to see him fiddling with it in church. How much you think it'll go for?"

"Probably go cheap," Duffy whispered. "Doesn't look like a jewelry crowd."

Mrs. Davis shook her head. "That's what you always say."

Duffy turned back to Emmett. "What did you expect to find? An old lady dies. No family. Lives off some kind of small pension. What did you think she had? The crown jewels?"

"Duffy, you got a minute?" It was John Parker.

"Just about. We've got to start."

"Those Windsor chairs."

"Best we ever had," Emmett nodded. "Except for those hoop backs two years ago."

John shook his head. "I never should have dropped out at forty-five. Never. You don't know how often I think about that."

"Might go cheap tonight," Duffy said. "Doesn't look like a furniture crowd."

"Doesn't matter. I won't go above fifty."

Duffy smiled. "You better, unless you want to spend another two years saying I-should-have."

"Fifty bucks. I know my limit!"

As soon as John walked away, Emmett narrowed his eyes. "I have a limit, too. You own one-third of this business. That doesn't mean you own one-third of me."

"I don't want one-third of you. I need all of you."

"Hey, Duff! How'd you get these?" It was Seth Moore who fixed old clocks. He held up a box of motel-room keys.

"Not the way you think!" She turned to Emmett and took his arm. "You know the first rule of estate sales. You take the small ones, you get the big ones. I took Miss Natalie's house because I wanted to protect our relationship with the bank."

"Like hell. All you wanted to protect was your relationship with the banker."

Duffy spoke very slowly. "Emmett, I am doing the very best I can to keep this family together."

"Maybe that's the problem. Maybe this family's been together too long."

She took his hand. "Try to hold on. Look at the crowd we have tonight. Once the barn really gets going you'll have enough money to open the best shop in the county." She smiled. "You better! I expect you to be my biggest customer."

He stared at her, anger melting into love. That's the way it always ended. What was the use? He put his arm around her. "Sell one for Papa," he said.

"Duffy!" It was Mrs. M, the cashier. "It's getting late." Mrs. Matts took names and addresses in return for paper plates with bid numbers marked in black crayon. She handed Duffy the registration sheet. "Emmett quit again?" she asked.

Duffy nodded. "He wants that shop so badly."

"Maybe he'll change his mind when things pick up."

"What have we got?" Duffy asked, looking at the sheet.

Mrs. M shook her head proudly. "No less than six Manhattan trucks with resale numbers."

Duffy smiled. "Come to steal the pants off us hicks."

Mrs. M pointed to a name. "There's a guy with a blue hat and a moustache. He looks bouncy-bouncy to me. And that young girl with the baby. In the third row. Couldn't get a loan at the bank. Better be careful."

"Anything else?"

"Yes. How do you spell boo-ya-bayze?"

"Good evening, folks. Welcome to the Nickel Man Barn." Whatever else Duffy said all week long, nothing was as important to her as those few words. They were the magic phrases that made a problematic world suddenly more controllable. Once she sat in the pulpit on Saturday night, Duffy Patterson became a dealer with a brand-new deck of cards.

"You buy everything as you see it," she explained, looking to see where the new faces were. Red taught her it was a business of faces. How many bids in that kisser? How much desperation in those eyes? Old ladies in the front row always went one bid higher. A man with a tie was hard to budge. But women with hats were just begging to have another bid pulled out of them. What everyone had in common was they wanted to win. They wanted to be lucky. They all wanted something for nothing.

"You see something you like, just raise your hand. If I don't catch it, my brothers will. I want you all to relax, have a good time, and spend a lot of money. We're gonna begin tonight with a carton of mixed pleasures." Emmett pointed to a carton of dishes. Chip took out a platter. "Let 'em see that platter. Any marks on the back?" Duffy asked.

"Says 'Made in England.'"

"That's what the Queen says on Saturday night. All right. What else we got there, Emmett? A Made in England white platter . . ."

"Some pretty teacups," he said.

"They got saucers?" she asked.

"Don't need 'em," Emmett shouted. "Nice for the porch."

"Who's got ten dollars for the carton? Ten is all. Just ten. C'mon, raise your hands. I won't send you to the bathroom. All right, somebody start at five. Somebody? Anybody? Folks, there's a lot to sell tonight. Who'll give me a dollar?" Four hands shot up. "There you are. Thought you were all in strait-jackets. Okay. I got one all over the house. Two? Three? Four? Five? Now that's where we should have started. I have five down front. Where's the six? Make it six. Bid the six." Her tongue raced through the words.

"Says made in England," Chip reminded.

"All right. Gonna let it go for five? Fair warning. Sold! Number 14. We gotta wake these people up. Emmett, show them the candle molds." He held up two tin molds, and gave a pair to Chip. "We got only four of these. Come out of a house in Maine. You know what they're getting for twelve-tube candle molds. They show a little wear but so would you if you'd been around as long as these have. I'm selling them all for one money. Who's got two hundred? Should be. Somebody open. Start it with a hundred." One of the new people raised a hand.

"Yes!" Emmett yelled.

"Yes!" Chip yelled.

"A hundred, I got. Who's got the twenty-five?"

A man from the bleachers called out, "Hundred and five."

Duffy smiled. "Didn't ask your temperature, mister. I'm asking for bids. Who's got the quarter?" She nodded. "I got the quarter. Hundred and a quarter."

"Yes!"

"Yes!"

"Hundred and a half?"

The president of the Perry Falls Savings and Loan didn't have to be handsome in order to be the town's most eligible bachelor. But he was. Ben Perry was six foot three, with deep-set eyes and straight black hair. Unlike the boys he grew up with, Ben had an air of melancholy that everyone attributed to wealth. Having inherited the bank from his father, Ben Perry fulfilled the prediction in the Perry Falls High School yearbook that he was the boy most likely to succeed.

It was nine-thirty. He had been sitting outside in his car for nearly half an hour. Ben wanted to be sure the sale was nearly over before coming in. The crowd had thinned out considerably. Dry sinks, rugs, and oak tables were being loaded into vans as Duffy sold the last lots.

"Listen, people, you know what Windsors are going for these days?" Duffy shook her head. "I can't let these go at fifty bucks apiece. In the city you'd pay two hundred for one." John Parker raised his hand. "Right, John. Sixty." Leonard Gray nodded. "Seventy." John nodded. "Eighty." Leonard. "Ninety." John. "Hundred. Got the hundred. Now the ten. Fine quality. Won't see 'em again." Leonard nodded. "Got the ten. Where's the twenty?" Duffy looked at John. "Might not see these again for years." John stared angrily at her and then nodded. "Hundred and twenty. One hundred and twenty apiece for these beauties. What do I hear? Hundred thirty?" Leonard shook his head No. Duffy looked out at the house. "Hundred thirty? Should be." In a burst of passion, John raised his hand. Duffy smiled. "You're the hundred twenty, John. Don't bid against yourself. Any more? Anybody? Hundred thirty? Sold!"

John stood up excitedly. "I don't know my number. I lost my plate!"

"Don't worry, John. I'll sell you a new one."

Ben walked toward the kitchen, eager to turn his back on Duffy the Auctioneer. That wasn't the Duffy he came to see. The auctioneer was the one who always got in the way.

"Now here's a piece good enough to be Lady Godiva's dresser. It's solid oak, got three swell-front drawers. The handles are brass, and you got a nice bevel mirror," Duffy said. "She's clean and ready to go. Who's gonna start her at a hundred and a half? Worth twice that. Jason, you got a better chance of owning it if you bid. Where's my hundred and a half? Anybody out there still alive? How about a hundred?"

Marjorie Michaelson called out "Fifty."

Duffy smiled. "Marjorie, you want everybody to know how old you are that's your business. I got fifty."

Ben leaned over at the kitchen window. Ann Marie's face brightened. "Hi, Mr. Perry."

"Any coffee left?"

Lorraine pushed Ann Marie aside. "Coffee? Didn't you see the sign? I made bouillabaisse."

"Hundred seventy!" Duffy shouted.

"Yes!"

"Yes!"

"And still under the money! Emmett, you take one of those drawers and show it. Where you people gonna find that kind of flare-wedge jointing?" Leonard nodded. "Hundred eighty." Marjorie put up her hand. "Hundred ninety."

Ben took his coffee and sat in the last row. Damn barn, he thought. There was no way to control it. Not the way he could control the rest of his life. He paid all his bills upon receipt and renewed his magazine subscriptions after the first notice. He had standing appointments for his monthly haircut, his annual physical, and even his ten-thousand-mile tune-up. Aside from the barn, the only other debit in Ben's well-ordered existence was the fact he had been adopted.

"You people make me work too hard! I'm getting old before my time. For two ten I'll take it myself." Duffy smiled as she sighted Ben. "Two twenty!" she yelled, pointing at him. "New bidder in the back."

"Yes!"

"Yes!"

Ben tensed. Goddamn. Why didn't she use the house number? Why did she have to use him to jump the bid? The barn again.

"Got two twenty from the man at the bank." Duffy was staring right at Leonard. "If the banker's spending money you know it must be good." Leonard nodded. "Two thirty."

"Yes!"

"Yes!"

"Now forty from the banker," Duffy called pointing toward Ben, but looking at Leonard. "Fifty and it's yours! Trust me. The banker only bids twice. Don't lose it for the ten. Don't lose it for movie money. You know it's worth it. I got two forty. Looking for fifty. Fair warning." Leonard nodded. "Fifty. I got two fifty."

"Yes!"

"Yes!"

"Fair warning." She slammed down the gavel. "Sold! Number 98." Duffy stood up. "That's the evening, folks. Thank you. Be sure to come back next week with a full wallet and an empty stomach."

Duffy stretched as she turned off the microphone. Ben walked over and held out a hand. "They're going to catch you jumping bids one of these days," he said, kissing her. "Maybe if I'm lucky, they'll close this place down."

Duffy leaned over and whispered. "That dresser belonged to Jimmy's wife. He's still got hospital bills to pay."

Ben shook his head. "I suppose Robin Hood told Jimmy she wouldn't take any commission from him either."

"For God's sake, don't tell Emmett. He's steamed enough." Duffy pulled back as Ben put his arms around her. "No. Not now. I need a shower."

Ben smiled. "Thought you'd never ask."

The south porch had been enclosed to give Duffy her own room and bath. The brothers shared the rest of the sprawling farmhouse. The living room, dining room, and kitchen were common ground on which Ryerson and Patterson furniture styles clashed as consistently as the sisters-in-law themselves. There was no mortgage, and even though each wanted to move away, the price was right. The only consolation was the house offered enough privacy in which to sulk about the lack of privacy.

Duffy's room had three walls lined with unsold books. She joked about how they were good for insulation. More than that, they saved her the trouble of decorating. She had floor-to-ceiling books, a large brass bed, and Red's old rocker. A silken, still shiny Tabriz that she had bought in with the house number covered the floor.

Ben and Duffy stood in the shower holding one another. "Hotter," she whispered.

"Hotter?" Ben turned the faucet. "Too hot," he complained.

Duffy moaned. "Now cold."

"Nooooooo," he pleaded. "Heart attack."

"You don't have a heart," she growled.

"I do. But it's broken."

"Doesn't count."

"You can fix it."

"How?"

"Marry me."

"Marry someone your own size."

Ben lifted her up in his arms. "Okay."

"That's cheating." Duffy slid down, gently rubbing her thigh between his legs. "Don't bid on the house. Marry someone else."

"I did that once."

"What happened?"

"Can't remember."

"Why?" she asked.

"Brain melted."

"Cold. We need cold."

Ben shook his head. "No!" He reached out and stopped her from turning the faucet.

"Why not?"

"My hard-on."

"You have one of those again?"

"Don't know what to do."

She smiled. "Take two aspirin and call me in the morning."

"I know a better treatment."

The shiny Tabriz was a magic carpet on which Duffy and Ben made love. It was a matter of honor, Duffy's honor, that they never made love in a bed. Whenever Ben came home from college, through four years of holiday sex, they had met near the lake or in the barn. Ben proposed to Duffy by asking her to make love in a proper bed, a bed befitting a future bank president's wife. But that wasn't Duffy's idea of love or marriage or life. She wouldn't go from being The Auctioneer's Daughter to being The Bank President's Wife.

It had been ten years since Ben married Susan, the perfect candidate for the position. They had a perfect son and lived in a perfect house, no doubt having perfect sex in a perfect bed.

The divorce shocked Duffy as much as it shocked Ben. Neither was prepared to accept that he, too, rejected the bank president's wife. Susan had custody of Bobby, who was now nearly nine, and for the past three years Duffy had had custody of Ben, who never again suggested they make love in a proper bed.

They sat naked in the center of the rug, cross-legged on either side of a Victorian wicker picnic basket. The wine goblets were mismatched Baccarat crystal. Duffy's plate was black Wedgwood rimmed in gold, Ben's was Japanese Imari porcelain. The forks, knives and spoons were sterling, each in a different pattern, no two with the same monogram. The napkins and tablecloth were from broken sets with other people's embroidered initials.

Duffy liked listening to Chopin during dinner. Dinner, which always followed sex, was always provided by Ben. And Ben always provided a dinner of cold lobster with spicy sauce, or else spareribs with spicy sauce. They drank an appropriately colored wine and, for dessert, always had a birthday cake.

"You're going to make someone a wonderful wife," Duffy said, taking a piece of lobster.

"Is that a proposal?"

Duffy gasped and put her hand to her throat. "Aaaaaaaah," she groaned. "The sauce!"

Ben handed her a glass of white wine. "Glad you like it," he coughed.

Duffy put a hand to her forehead. "My sinuses. Oh!" She took a deep breath. "It's wonderful." Then, after having enjoyed the full effect of the sauce, she took a sip of wine. "Mmm. Insolent, but drinkable. What is it?"

Ben held his glass to the light. "About six bucks a bottle."

Duffy took another sip. "Doesn't taste more than four." She reached for another piece of lobster and swirled it in the sauce. "You should get married, Ben."

"Now that's a proposal! You can't fool me."

Duffy put her hands to the sides of her head as she swallowed. She sniffed and exhaled loudly. "Goddamn, that's good!"

"Marry me."

"You think I marry every guy I go to bed with?"

He leaned over and took hold of her hands. "I'm the guy you won't go to bed with. Remember?"

"I remember."

"Let's face it. We couldn't make our separation work."

Duffy put her arms around him, their bare bodies adhering to the contours of flesh and feelings. "I've never loved anyone else," she said.

"I have." He smiled. "You didn't miss much. What we've got is better."

Duffy leaned her head against his shoulder. "Then let's keep what we've got. I don't want to lose it."

He kissed her gently on the neck. "I don't want to settle for better. I want best."

Duffy reached for the box. "I want cake." He sighed and lay back on the rug. She watched him, feeling his hurt. "Ben, don't go home tonight. Stay with me."

"No."

"Everyone knows about us," she said. "It's no secret."

"You expect too much of me. I'm a boring banker in a small town. I can't live my life the way you live yours." He sat up. "Don't you understand? I live for more than just Saturday night. What am I supposed to do Monday through Friday?"

She put her hand to his cheek. They stared at one another waiting for something wonderful to be said. But there was nothing to say. Duffy opened the box. The cake was frosted pink with yellow and green flowers. The red jelly message said, "Happy Birthday, Duffy." She looked up at Ben. "That's wrong. It was my week last week."

"No, it was *my* week last week. This week it's yours."

"Ben, I had the lemon frosting with the purple flowers. That was last week. This one is supposed to be yours. This week it should say 'Happy Birthday, Ben.'"

He got up and walked across the room to his clothes. He reached into his jacket and took out a small appointment book. Duffy watched in amazement as he checked through the pages. "Today's the twenty-fifth. Duffy. Last week, the eighteenth, Ben. The eleventh it was Duffy. The fourth . . ."

"You keep it in a book?"

"Why not?"

Duffy began to laugh. "I do love you."

"Don't be so damn condescending. I'm a banker. I keep records."

"You do more than keep records. You keep score. The Grim Reaper of Perry Falls."

Ben took a white envelope from the book. "And what about you? Our Lady of the Auction Block! Going, going, but never getting anywhere. Is all you want this secondhand room and that goddamn barn full of junk? Why don't you want more?" He turned away from her. "Why don't you want me?"

"I thought I had you."

He shook his head. "On consignment. One used husband." Ben started to get dressed. "Everything you have is used. You even have your father's used dreams. They didn't do much for him. And they're not going to lead you anywhere."

"Dreams don't have to lead anywhere. It's having them that's fun."

He handed her the white envelope. "Enjoy yourself," he said angrily.

"What's this?"

"Another one-way ticket to nowhere. The contract for Miss Natalie's estate."

"Contract?" Duffy's voice began to rise. "You had a contract made out for that load of garbage?"

"I like contracts. They let you know where you stand." He put on his jacket. "It's not as easy to walk away if you have one."

"The way you're doing now."

"The way I'm doing now."

"And if we were married? What would you do then?"

"I wouldn't be leaving. I'd honor my contract."

Duffy took the envelope from him and crumpled it in her hand. "I don't need contracts, banker. I do what my heart tells me."

Ben walked to the door. "I can't."

"Why not?"

"I told you. It's broken."

There was no use trying to sleep. Duffy put on her robe. She didn't need to know what time it was. It was night. That was all that mattered. It was night and she was alone.

There had been other lonely nights. Lots of them. They had passed, one no different from the others. But that night she was afraid she would always be alone.

Not that she had to be. There was always someone who would love her—if she made up or gave in. But what kind of love was that? Where was great love, unconditional love, love that stood fast despite failure and anger and even contracts? One thing was sure, it wasn't birthday-cake love.

Duffy looked up at the sky as she walked to the barn. A crescent moon. Bright stars. Definitely Art Deco. No sign of wear. Good as the day they were made and they didn't make 'em like that anymore.

Duffy unlocked the door and stepped into the darkness,

wanting to call out "Papa?" She turned on the lights and looked around the empty barn. There was a loud meow from the pulpit as Fat Cat scolded her for interrupting his sleep. She walked past the tables that next week would display the last of Miss Natalie. When would they display the last of Miss Duffy? She stared at the row of empty tables. There it all was, she thought. Nothing. The estate of Miss Duffy. Someday an auctioneer would spin the tale of Old Lady Patterson and her slightly used but highly collectible dreams.

Standing in front of the furniture brought in from Miss Natalie's house, Duffy felt a sudden sorrow for the dead woman. Amid the litter that masqueraded as an estate there was one kitchen chair. A sagging, faded sofa. A single bed. Some plates. A vase. Small framed pictures of stern people who looked as though they never smiled. A few pieces of unmatched silverware. Four forks. Six knives. Two spoons. The signposts of a lonely life. Familiar. Frightening. They might have come from Duffy's picnic basket.

Garbage. It *was* all garbage. No wonder Emmett was angry, she thought, as the tears began to fall. He had every right to be angry, she sobbed. Duffy picked up the dead woman's cane and smashed it against the plates, shattering them. "What the hell kind of life is this?" she cried out.

Fat Cat skittered across the barn and out the open door. Duffy dropped the cane. She sighed deeply, as one does after acknowledging yet another permanent scar.

Duffy sat on the floor and opened one of the trunks. She piled up the books next to her, thinking she would have to make room for them on her shelves. It was a puzzling collection for an old lady—a library of fear and rage. *Why the Government Must Be Overthrown! Workers' Rights! How the Church Steals Your Faith! Is American Justice for Millionaires Only?*

Duffy reached deep into the trunk and felt something that was not a book. Something soft. She lifted out a small oval box covered in a pale yellow velvet. It had a latch with a bright red stone. On the stone was a small enamel figure of a two-headed eagle. Duffy pressed the latch and lifted back the top.

Fitted into the white satin lining was an egg-shaped object of brilliant strawberry enamel. It was decorated with carved golden ribbons and arrows made of glistening white stones. Duffy stared at it, her senses dazzled by the unmistakable reality of gold and diamonds.

She explored the egg cautiously. It opened to reveal a small white enameled rosebud with a bright green stem. As though it were a fresh flower, the petals separated gracefully. Inside was a miniature gold crown set with diamonds and rubies. A tiny ruby egg hung from the center of the crown.

Duffy sat staring at the pieces in her lap. She felt a momentary panic, thinking she must put it back together quickly. She began fitting the pieces within the egg, overwhelmed by guilt at having uncovered someone's secret. She closed the box and set it on the floor. Don't touch it. Don't even think about it. Just take out the rest of the books.

She leaned over to look inside the trunk and gasped. Fitted together neatly were dozens of boxes of different sizes and shapes. Duffy took out a pink velvet square. She held her breath at the sight of a diamond necklace with an enormous emerald pendant. The next box held a carved agate owl with sapphire eyes. And the next, a double-heart picture frame set with hundreds of rubies. The two photographs—on one side a baby, on the other, a woman wearing a crown—were encircled by diamonds. She opened box after box until the trunk was empty.

Duffy Patterson sat on the floor of the Nickel Man Barn in Perry Falls, New York, surrounded by ninety-six velvet boxes containing ninety-six jeweled masterpieces made by Peter Carl Fabergé for the Court of Imperial Russia.

ᴥ

Everything had a price, thought Peter Carl Fabergé. Everything but the weather. He shivered as he stood in front of the Winter Palace waiting for his carriage. He had just seen the richest man in the world, but not even the Czar himself could do anything about the piercing cold.

Fabergé looked up at the cloudless gray sky over St. Petersburg and folded his arms to keep warm. The weather was the price he had to pay for his artistic freedom. Had the climate been less hostile there might have been no dearth of local talent. There might have been time for Russians to use their imaginations on more than how to survive the cold. Since the days of Peter the Great, artists and scientists had been welcomed and rewarded handsomely for their efforts to Westernize so backward a country. So cold a country! Where was that moujik with his carriage?

It was that same relentless, dreary weather that was responsible, in part, for the success of the House of Fabergé. After leaving France, his father had eased into the eager hospitality of a society starved for elegance and susceptible to whim. While the rest of Europe inhaled breathlessly the first scent of art nouveau, *Russian aristocracy was being suffocated by* nouveau riche.

When the House first opened, jewelry in St. Petersburg was as cumbersome as clothing. Fabergé brought beauty measurable by brilliant design and superb craftsmanship rather than by hundreds of carats per stone. He brought fantasy. He brought eternal spring.

In April of 1895, Peter Carl Fabergé was forty-nine years old
and had been running his father's business for a quarter of a
century. Czar Nicholas II was twenty-seven years old and had
been running his father's business for less than six months.
Fabergé had nearly seven hundred employees, the Czar had over
one hundred and thirty million.

He put his hands into his pockets to keep them warm and felt
the velvet pouch Nicholas had given him. Fabergé shook his
head and sighed. He stared at his frozen breath and wondered
what in the world he was going to make with three hundred
rubies.

"Three hundred rubies?" Perchin asked.

Fabergé sat behind his desk and emptied the pouch. "He
made me count them. One by one."

Mikhail Evlampievich Perchin was his chief workmaster. Of
peasant stock, a moujik, the thirty-five-year-old Perchin served
his apprenticeship with various goldsmiths before opening his
own shop. He worked exclusively to produce pieces for the
House of Fabergé. His workshop was located in the four-story
building at 24 Bolshaya Morskaya Street in which Fabergé lived
and had his salesroom. "He took them from the Royal Trea-
sury?" Perchin asked. "Or from the Romanovs?" He shook his
head. "The stones are not very good. Perhaps the Czarina
brought them with her from Germany." He smiled and put a
hand to his mouth.

Fabergé stood up and walked to the blackboard. He took a
piece of chalk and held it poised over the slate. "We have three
hundred rubies . . ."

"Excuse me, Carl Gustavovich, but what happens if we need
three hundred and two, or only two hundred and ninety-nine?"

"When the Czarina gives birth to a son, the guns will be fired
three hundred times to welcome the new Czarevitch. Not three
hundred and two, or two hundred and ninety-nine."

"And if the Czarina has a daughter?"

"One hundred and one."

Perchin looked at the rubies on the desk. "The Czar expects a son."

"And therefore we must expect a son." Fabergé raised an eyebrow and turned back to the board. "If the Czar gave you three hundred rubies . . ."

"My heart would burst!" Perchin exclaimed, putting a hand to his mouth.

Fabergé smiled. He drew a heart and then looked at Perchin. "Your heart, dear Mikhail Evlampievich, would burst in two." He drew another heart overlapping the first. Within each heart he drew an oval. "A picture frame. Mother and child. Three hundred rubies to salute the heir to the throne." He scooped up the rubies and put them back into the pouch. "A lovely gift. From the Czar to me." He handed the pouch to Perchin. "To you."

"And, as always, back to the Czar."

ϨА

"Good afternoon, madam." A doorman with great white muttonchop whiskers helped Duffy out of the taxi. She walked across the pavement and pushed on the gleaming brass door to Wyndham's. It wouldn't move. "It wants to be pulled, madam," the doorman said. His gloved hand opened it for her.

Duffy nodded a nervous thank you as she stepped into the lobby of the former Bennington mansion, now New York's leading auction house. She looked up at the marble staircase that swept dramatically around a huge crystal chandelier. Not that she hadn't been inside Wyndham's before. That wasn't what stopped her. It was her reflection in the glass-covered bulletin board. How much she had changed since she and her brothers first ogled their way through the Manhattan auction scene. How much she had changed since just last Monday when they picked up consignment pieces at the firehouse. She wasn't wearing a green velvet blazer, silk pants and high heels then.

"May I help you?"

"I'm just looking." The security guard nodded. Then Duffy admitted, "Yes," as if confessing to a crime. She took a deep breath. "I have something. A friend asked me . . . my friend . . . wants to sell."

"At the desk, madam."

"That desk?"

"Yes, madam," he said, pointing to the only desk in the lobby.

It was a large mahogany circle within which were three aggressively fashionable debutantes, pretenders to the throne who answered inquiries with equally fashionable boredom. Where are the Impressionists?/The East Gallery. Do you have a catalog for the English Silver sale?/Eleven dollars. Are Tibetan tankas included in Oriental Art?/Yes.

"Can you tell me where the Ladies' Room is?" Duffy whispered.

"The Ladies' Room is on three," was the crisp reply.

Duffy winced. "Excuse me, again. I have something to sell."

"Do you have it with you?"

"Yes." She reached into her bag. "Actually, it belongs to a friend . . ."

"Three," the girl said. "Our Appraisals Desk is on three."

"Three," Duffy repeated. Our Appraisals Desk is on three. Must be next to Our Ladies' Room. Despite the pounding of her heart, Duffy smiled as she walked to Our Elevator.

A crowd had gathered, bristling wth unspoken impatience as they watched the indicator above the door. Duffy tugged at her shoulder bag, as though adjusting her life-support system to the hostile atmosphere of a city in which people waited in silent groups like pillars at Stonehenge.

Perry Falls seemed more than miles away, longer ago than just that morning. Duffy had left Emmett a note saying she'd gone to Albany to handle a tag sale for Janie Dodge. Instead, she drove to the railway station and waited nearly an hour for the train to New York.

Throughout the ride Duffy relived the events since Saturday night as though looking at snapshots. Her fight with Emmett. The sale. Making love with Ben. Arguing. A barn full of junk. Used dreams. Crying as she unpacked the books. That first touch of velvet.

It was almost dawn by the time she finished carrying the treasure to her room. She locked the door. Like a thief. She stayed in all day Sunday. Behind the locked door, Duffy searched her books for clues. What were they? Were they real?

They looked like Fabergé. She found a picture of an enameled cigarette case. The enamel looked the same. Fabergé. Fabergé. Fabergé. She whispered the name over and over as though it were an incantation. The spell began to work. If each box were worth a hundred dollars, she had found a ninety-six-hundred-dollar treasure. A thousand dollars each would be ninety-six thousand. Ten thousand dollars each would be nine hundred and sixty thousand dollars. Nearly one million. Fabergé. Fabergé. Fabergé.

Duffy held tight to her bag as the elevator door opened. The army of the chic paraded silently past her. The women in Saint Laurent dresses, Dior hats, Hermes shoes, Gucci bags. The men in Saint Laurent suits, Dior shirts, Hermes ties, Gucci shoes. As though attesting to their own authenticity, everything they wore had to be signed. Signed, sealed and delivered.

A woman stepped into the elevator and said, as coolly as if asking for the housewares department, "The Impressionists!"

The doors closed and Duffy prepared for liftoff. It was out of her hands. They might be real and they might not.

Almost everyone got off at two. The operator looked back at Duffy. "Madam?"

They couldn't be real. They couldn't! Why were they in the trunk? Had Miss Natalie known they were there?

"Impressionists?" he asked.

Why not? Duffy needed more time. She followed the others through the double doors into the sale room.

There were fewer than fifty people on metal folding chairs. Duffy would have been embarrassed to draw so small a crowd at the barn. The side walls of the rectangular room were hung with ornately framed paintings. On the rostrum, surrounded by a supporting cast of department heads, clerks, and bid spotters, was the auctioneer.

Charles Wyndham, in his early forties, was beginning to reap the benefits of the boyishness he had never outgrown. He had unruly brown hair, full lips posed in a half-smile of expectation. Charles had an exuberance, a compelling sexuality that challenged the confines of his very proper British accent.

"Are we through, then? At one hundred and thirty thousand?" he asked. "Is that to be it?" He smiled. "One hundred and thirty-five. The bid is one three five. One hundred and thirty-five thousand dollars." Charles banged the ivory gavel on the rostrum. "Sold! Yours, sir."

The conversion board overhead translated $135,000 into six currencies. A young woman handed the man on the aisle a bid form to sign. Two porters removed the painting from the easel as two others brought in the next lot. The conversion board cleared. Duffy leaned against the wall, as awed by the sum of $135,000 as by the smoothly choreographed transition.

"Lot One Four Five," Charles announced. "We have a number of order bids." He turned to one of the clerks on the telephone. "We'll begin at seventy-five thousand." The clerk nodded. "Eighty," acknowledged Charles. Then he looked at the audience, finding another bidder. "Eighty-five." He turned to the clerk. "Ninety." Back to the audience. "Ninety-five." The girl on the phone shook her head No and hung up. "I have ninety-five on my left." One of the spotters pointed to the center. Charles followed quickly. "One hundred in the center. One hundred thousand dollars."

Wyndham & Sons was founded in the early 1800s as a bookstore in Cambridge, England. Although his shop was a prime resource for university students and faculty, James Wyndham's weekly gambling debts exceeded his weekly sales. In an effort to raise cash, he held book auctions at which volumes were sold for less than shelf price.

To his surprise, and relief, professors and spendthrift students recognized the auctions as a source of funds. They brought in enough books to keep both James and the roulette wheel spinning. His son, Richard, later enlarged the business to feature special sales of maps and illustrations. Richard's sons went on to open branches in Oxford and London.

It was Melton Wyndham, in London, who expanded sales to all areas of fine art. Melton drew upon university personnel to evaluate consignments and Wyndham & Sons (London) became internationally respected for its expertise. The business grew despite wars, depression, devaluation, and inflation. The male heirs of James Wyndham succeeded to the directorship of the firm.

In 1970, Wyndham & Sons bought the Bennington mansion in New York, planning to renovate its splendid public rooms into their American branch. The only son of Nigel Wyndham was sent to New York to keep an eye on the budget. But Charles fell in love with the old Victorian mansion and overspent by twice the original allocation. A public battle among father, son, and shareholders was resolved after much bitterness. In return for his stock in Wyndham & Sons (London), Charles was given the renovated mansion on East 67th Street. He had permission to use his own name, provided he did not claim any affiliation to the London branch. At thirty, Charles Wyndham sat without a penny in the most elaborately designed and well-equipped auction house in the world. That was more than ten years before Duffy watched the Renoir exceed its presale estimate in six currencies and on open telephone lines across eleven time zones.

Charles was able to bring Wyndham's to its present stature because he was in the right recession at the right time. A better educated, more widely traveled generation of Americans were seeking refuge from a sluggish economy. Instead of money as the traditional vehicle for art and antiques, art and antiques became the vehicle for money. The stock market was lackluster, outperformed by tangibles such as gold, diamonds, Old Master paintings, coins and stamps. It was a time to take the money and run.

Americans were moving more frequently and divorcing more easily. Nuclear families had no place to store the fallout from their community property. Selling at auction became an increasingly popular pit stop as the former upwardly mobile struggled to keep their feet on the ground. For those who lost the battle, Charles had an elite corps of ambulance chasers reading obituaries across the country and sending letters of condolence offering to assist the bereaved with disposing of everything but the body.

The energy crisis, inflation, and the decline of the dollar emptied the cafés in Paris and filled the auction houses in New York. Emigrés from emirates descended upon the new Mecca with open purses. Germans and Japanese invaded the sale rooms to recapture the spoils of war. New York became a glittering international oasis for thirsty connoisseurs.

Charles danced at the right parties with the right people. He was smart enough to know with whom not to sleep. He was good copy in a media-mad society. He challenged museums by touting presale exhibits as free cultural events. People could touch things the museums made them view from a distance. He turned his most important sales into exciting theatrical events by dressing the staff formally, restricting admittance to ticketholders only, and filling the room with people whose faces were as familiar as the works on which they bid. A battalion of photographers kept the bulbs popping. Charles had accomplished his own cultural revolution: the Saturday crowd marched north from Bloomingdale's.

"At two hundred thousand dollars, then. Sold at two hundred thousand." And then, suddenly, he smiled. "Two hundred and ten thousand. Just in time. Two ten. Two twenty now. Two hundred and twenty thousand. Two hundred and thirty thousand. Two forty thousand. Two fifty thousand. Two hundred and fifty thousand dollars. At two hundred and fifty, then. Two hundred and fifty thousand dollars." Finally, Charles brought down the gavel. "Sold!"

The tension was broken by a spontaneous round of applause. Everyone began talking and strained to see the buyer. As inquisitive eyes searched the room, Duffy felt they were looking at her, that they could see what she had in her purse.

She rang for the elevator and mumbled, "Three, please." What if they weren't real? Even more frightening, what if they were?

The appraisal area reminded Duffy of a clinic. A dozen or so people afflicted with terminal optimism sat clutching paper bags, portfolios, or items wrapped in newspaper. Others paced nervously. Behind a long counter three young women interviewed patients before summoning an appropriate specialist. One woman was on the phone while the man in front of her pointed repeatedly to the signature on his small painting. "Tell him it's a listed artist," he insisted. In the middle, an old lady excitedly unwrapped a porcelain figurine she had bought at a flea market. The well-dressed man on the end shook his head forlornly as he stared at a pair of earrings. "But they can't be glass," he protested. "They were my mother's!"

Duffy sat waiting her turn as other people's expectations were valued as worthless, fifty dollars, three hundred and fifty dollars. She had ninety-six expectations.

"Yes?" The woman smiled joylessly at Duffy.

"Hi. I'm not sure who I need to see."

"What is it you have?"

"I don't know. But it feels fatal." The girl waited impatiently. Duffy smiled. "Is there someone here who knows about Fabergé?"

"That would be Russian Art." The girl reached for a

clipboard. "Would you like to make an appointment?"

"No. I need to see someone now. Right now!" Neither of them was prepared for Duffy's intensity. "I'm from out of town," she offered, as an excuse.

"I'll try." She picked up the phone and dialed. "Is Greg there? Old Masters?" She raised an eyebrow as she redialed and muttered, "What's he doing in Old Masters?"

Gregory Konstantinovich Rosenko was startlingly handsome. He was Alexander Nevsky crossing the ice, a square-jawed young lieutenant leading the *Potemkin* mutiny, the Prince in *Swan Lake*. He was tall, with heroic blond hair, and blue eyes filled with the heartbreak of Mother Russia. He was the son of a cultural attaché at the Soviet embassy in Washington, and his parents divorced to avoid public scandal over the major affairs his mother had with minor diplomats. After his father was recalled, the boy was dependent upon public assistance for food and upon his mother's private assistance for a place to live. They moved from lover to lover as she kept pace with his growing adolescent needs. There was a dentist when he needed braces, a psychiatrist during his rebellious years, and an admissions director when he needed a scholarship. Gregory studied Art History and worked summers for a Russian art dealer.

The Old Master Paintings Department had floor-to-ceiling shelves that were stacked with millions of dollars' worth of ornately framed portraits and landscapes. Uniformed porters wheeled ten-foot ladders across row upon row of pictures to find lots needed for cataloging. On the other side of the room, Gregory leaned on the desk as he vowed, "I'll pay you back on Friday."

"No."

"Thursday."

Ann Meadows, ten years his senior, shook her head and tried to ignore the stares of the researchers who shared her office. "It's only Monday," she whispered, "and you're broke again."

He laughed, the chameleon color of his eyes brightening. "Annuschka, make a poor peasant happy. I have never before seen such a silk shirt. It is not for myself that I ask, but for my glorious Russian body. *Tovarich*, Wednesday!"

Ann sighed. "You know as much about money as you do about art." She reached for her purse.

Gregory narrowed his eyes. "What is there to know about art? Old Master Paintings—big tits! Impressionist Paintings—small tits that look like big tits! Modern Paintings—three tits!"

The phone rang. Ann picked it up and handed him the receiver. "There's an emergency on Sesame Street."

"Rosenko," he proclaimed imperiously. He kissed Ann's fingertips as she handed him the money. Then he frowned. "Shitskii! Tell her to come back Friday." He rolled his eyes as he held the receiver away from his ear. "Da. Da. Da." He sighed and hung up. Gregory opened the door. "If I forget to pay you back, remind me."

Once past the racks of paintings, he walked down a narrow corridor lined with offices that overflowed with experts and their researchers. Behind every closed door, desks were piled high with catalogs, books, and reference files as everyone played detective and then press agent for the fine and not-so-fine art they authenticated. Miniatures and Paperweights. Rugs and Carpets. Antiquities. European Furniture, an open door to the sound of strident voices arguing ball-and-claw versus talon-and-claw. Chinese Art. Coins. He turned the corner and stopped, as he always did, in front of the chain-link grillwork that surrounded the Silver Department. Open shelves glittered with sterling candelabra, bowls, platters and plates, goblets and tea services, coasters and salvers. The tables were covered with trays of knives and forks and spoons.

Gregory reached out for the fencing and shook it noisily. Lisabeth Goslin glanced at him from the corners of her eyes. He smiled and asked, "What are you doing for dinner?"

She shook her head. "May I turn to stainless steel. Never again."

"Lizochka, while you sit here tarnishing with your tureens, civilization moves on. It is perfectly acceptable for a woman to take a man to dinner."

"The Communist Manifesto, Part Two."

"*Tovarich*," he appealed, stretching his fingers through the metal mesh. "I have found the most beautiful beef Stroganoff in all of New York."

"That's what I thought you were."

He withdrew his hand. "I told you, I had a headache. Is that all you wanted me for? My beautiful body?"

"Leave me alone. I have work to do." He started to go. Without looking back, she said, "I'll pick you up at seven."

Gregory turned the corner to the Appraisals Desk, the "teacup" as it was known. He hated going there to tell the fortune of some ignorant peasant who had found a kopek and thought it was a crown.

"Madam, may I help you?"

Duffy took a deep breath. Surely, he was too handsome to give her bad news. "A friend asked me to get some information."

Gregory nodded. Always a friend. "Information on what?"

She reached into her bag and took out the box. "On this."

Gregory stared at the velvet box. Betraying himself, he glanced up at her. As a match bursts into flame, Duffy felt herself grow flush. Even if she didn't know it from the box, as Gregory did, she knew it from his face. Even if she couldn't read jeweler's marks, Duffy could read Gregory's expression when he saw the strawberry enamel. It had to be real.

He closed the box. "My name is Gregory Rosenko," he said, extending his hand.

"My name is Dorothy Patterson."

Gregory nodded and pointed toward the open door of a small room with a table and two chairs. "Please."

Duffy's heart was racing. She sat down and watched as he closed the door. Without saying a word, he opened the box again and gently removed the brilliant strawberry enameled egg from its white satin nest. His fingers moved slowly across the contours of the carved golden ribbons as though reading braille. He rubbed his forefinger on the hinges and then across the engraved markings on the bottom. He smiled.

"The miracle of a Fabergé piece is the attention given to the smallest, seemingly the most inconsequential, of details." Gregory knew exactly which stone to press in order to open the egg. "The tradition was begun by Czar Alexander the Third. Each Easter he would give a jeweled egg to his wife, the Czarina Marie." Gregory sighed as he lifted out the white enamel rosebud. "After Alexander died, Nicholas continued the tradition by commissioning two eggs each year, one for his mother and one for Alexandra." He opened the petals and removed the miniature gold crown. "Most of the eggs have been accounted for. There are only seven that have never been found."

Duffy stared at Gregory. "Seven?" She had found seven.

He opened the crown to catch the small ruby pendant. "One of those missing is the egg Nicholas gave to his mother in 1905. The Rosebud Egg."

She nodded. "I see."

Gregory stared at her while he spoke. "The gold carving is of the finest craftsmanship. It is the work of Fabergé's master goldsmith, Perchin." He paused and looked at the egg. Softly, as a medium would call out to a spirit, he repeated the name. "Perchin." Suddenly embarrassed for having shared his dream with a stranger, he asked, "Who are you?"

"You're sure it's real?"

"What else have you got?"

"How much is it worth?"

"Where did you get it?"

Duffy reached for the egg. She held it nervously in her lap as she repeated her name, rank and serial number. "I am here because a friend of mine wants to know what this will bring at auction."

Gregory spoke slowly, as though challenging her by merely reciting the facts. "The last egg sold in 1978. It was the one Nicholas gave to Alexandra in 1900. The winning bid was over two hundred thousand dollars."

Duffy froze. "For one egg?"

"For one egg." Gregory reached out and touched her hand. "You have all seven, don't you?"

She nodded her head several times before daring to say, "Yes."

There was a long silence. Gregory watched Duffy put the egg back into the box. "I know about the Silver Jubilee Egg. It is the only other one for which we have records. It is gold, enameled pale blue and white. Isn't it?"

"Yes."

"Tell me about the others," he asked softly.

Duffy hesitated. "One is that famous church in Moscow."

"St. Basil's."

"There's one with a big green-and-white building."

"The Winter Palace."

"One has a sleigh with two diamond horses."

"The Troika Egg."

"One is broken, or there's a piece missing. It's a gold bell . . ."

"It's not broken. There is such a bell in the Kremlin. It was made for Ivan the Great."

"There's one filled with miniature icons."

"Tell me . . ." Gregory hesitated. "Do you . . ." he smiled. "Does your friend also have a necklace? A diamond necklace with a large emerald pendant?"

She thought her heart would burst. "How did you know?"

Duffy sat bolt upright in Gregory's office as he examined the egg under a magnifying glass. She stared at the ceiling-high bookshelves crammed with well-worn volumes on all aspects of the art and history of Russia, scrapbooks bulging with torn yellowed clippings, and piles of catalogs from Russian art sales and exhibits held over many decades throughout the world.

But nowhere amid that profusion of recorded knowledge was the answer Gregory sought. He turned off the lamp and looked at Duffy. "Where did you get this?"

"I told you. A friend."

He smiled. "Miss Patterson . . ."

"A friend," she repeated firmly. "It's real, then."

"That depends upon your definition of reality. It is here. That makes it real. It exists. The stones are real stones. The gold is real gold. The markings are perfect. The workmanship is classic. But is it perhaps a brilliant forgery?"

"Is it?"

"Where did you get it? A record of previous ownership, a provenance, is needed to establish authenticity."

"And if it were just a copy? Would it still be worth money?"

Gregory shook his head. "Yes. But, Miss Patterson, it could be worth much more than money. More than money," he repeated. "That is the privilege of art. And the curse of it."

"Is it a copy?"

"No." He pronounced the final judgment. "This is the Imperial Easter Egg that Czar Nicholas the Second gave his mother twelve years before the Revolution."

"How do you know?"

He handed Duffy the magnifying glass. "Look at the signature on the gold rim. Feel it. It's smooth, actually part of the metal. Fabergé pieces were signed before they were assembled so the stamping would be polished and given the same care as the most delicate of carving."

"What does fifty-six mean?"

"The Russian standard mark for gold. Fifty-six *zolotniks*, corresponding to fourteen carats. You see there, the imprint of the scepter and crossed anchors? They were the marks for the St. Petersburg workshop. All the Imperial pieces were made in St. Petersburg."

"And the letters in the rectangle?"

"M. P. for Michael Perchin."

Duffy put down the magnifying glass. "But that's not how you know it's real. I've seen beanpots that say Elmira on them but I know . . ."

Gregory smiled. "You're right. It is simply 'I know.' No books, no tests, no special equipment, just, 'I know.' That's my job. To know." He shrugged. "The marks are the last things to look at." He leaned toward Duffy. "The piece itself tells me it's real. The proportions. The angles at which the stones are set. The incredible quality and design. The marks don't mean a damn unless everything else is right." Gregory smiled. "I can spot Fabergé at a glance, the way other people spot friends in a crowd. It's not hard once you know what you're looking for." He opened a book, turning the pages quickly. He showed it to Duffy. It was a photograph of Alexandra wearing the emerald necklace. "It's been missing for nearly seventy years."

"Who is she?" Duffy asked.

"The Czarina. The last Czarina."

Compulsively, as though a witness to some horrible accident, Duffy reached out for the book. She turned the pages. Alexandra. Nicholas. The children. "They killed them all. The whole family. Didn't they?" She turned the page and put a hand to her mouth. It was another picture of Alexandra. She was sitting in a chair. On the table next to her was the double-heart ruby frame.

"Miss Patterson, are you feeling ill?"

Duffy closed the book. "No."

"What is it?"

"The picture frame."

His eyes widened. "You have the ruby frame as well?"

"They killed the little boy, too."

"Rubies. Diamonds. Overlapping hearts," Gregory prompted.

"Yes."

"Miss Patterson," he began accusingly, "do you know how many people have been searching for these pieces?"

"No."

"Curators. Dealers. Collectors. The Soviet government. Me!" Gregory spoke slowly, circling her chair like a predator. "Miss Patterson, what else do you have?"

The pressure was overwhelming. She was losing control. Duffy couldn't help herself. She exploded with laughter. "I have ninety-six pieces." Gregory reached for the telephone. She stopped laughing. "Who are you calling?"

"Charles Wyndham." He looked at his watch. "The sale must be over."

Duffy stood up. She put the egg back in her purse. "I'd like to powder my nose."

"Of course." He opened the door. "On your right, opposite the stairs."

"Thanks."

Gregory walked back into his office. There were so many people to call. But first Charles. He picked up the phone and dialed. Busy. He dialed again and then shouted, "Holy Mother Russia!" He dropped the phone and ran into the hallway. Without hesitating, he opened the door to the Ladies' Room. It was empty. He ran back to the office and dialed Security.

"Lobby," a voice responded immediately.

"A redhead in a green jacket. Follow her! Find out where she's going!"

Gregory raced down the stairs. How could he have been so stupid? By the time he reached the lobby, the unmarked security car had pulled away in pursuit of Duffy's taxi. He walked outside, crossed the street and turned the corner. He stepped into a phone booth and dialed.

"Yes?" It was a man's voice.

"This is Rosenko," Gregory said.

"Where are you calling from?"

"A phone booth on Sixty-eighth near Park."

"One moment."

Gregory waited for them to check the line. He looked at his watch. It was midnight in Moscow.

Duffy sat in her room at the hotel. On the table at her side was the velvet box. She had checked in after leaving Wyndham's. She needed a place in which to be alone, a place in which to multiply over and over again seven times two hundred thousand dollars. One million four hundred thousand. Nearly one and a half million without even counting the other eighty-nine lots. They could be worth millions, too. She lost track of time as she sat in the chair.

There was a knock at the door. Duffy grabbed the box and put it into her bag. "Yes? Who is it?"

"Room Service."

She hesitated and then she opened the door. "I didn't order anything . . ."

Charles Wyndham smiled impishly. "But I did." He held a champagne bucket in one hand and two glasses in the other. He walked into the room. "May I?" he asked as an afterthought.

Duffy leaned back against the open door. "You look different."

"You don't," he said.

"You saw me?"

"I saw a Renoir walk in to buy a Renoir. Or so I thought. But you never even bid." He handed her a glass of champagne. "To the sale."

"To what sale?" She glanced into the hallway, half hoping someone would come by.

"According to Gregory, you and I are about to make a great deal of money. Not to mention history."

"And if I don't want to make history?"

Charles shrugged. "Then we'll just make money." He clinked his glass against hers.

"How did you find me?" she asked.

"A bit of cops and robbers for my security people. That was the easy part."

"What's the hard part?"

"Convincing you to have dinner with me."

Duffy smiled. "Which one are you? A cop or a robber?"

He laughed. "That depends. Which are *you*, Miss Patterson?"

"You want the truth?"

Charles raised his glass. "In vino veritas."

"The truth is, Mr. Wyndham, that I am very hungry."

A uniformed chauffeur met them as they came out of the Howard Johnson lobby. He took the champagne cooler from Charles. He walked over to a white Rolls-Royce and opened the door. Duffy hesitated a moment and then stepped in. Charles sat on the red leather seat next to her. The chauffeur pulled down a burled walnut tray for the champagne.

Charles shrugged. "Not bad for a used furniture dealer."

Duffy laughed. She was thrilled by the presence of Charles Wyndham, not because he was attractive or because he had a devastating mix of self-confidence and self-mockery. His being there was all the evidence she needed. Incredibly, wonderfully, magically, someone wanted Duffy for her money.

Still smiling, she turned to him. "How much of a cut do you take?"

Charles slapped his forehead. "Miss Patterson," he moaned. "How can you talk money at a time like this?" Then he added in a businesslike tone, "Ten."

"And what does the competition take?"

"I have no competition," he said simply. "There's no other house that can handle a sale like this."

Duffy leaned back in her seat. Charles refilled her glass. She spoke softly, daring to ask, "If the eggs are worth over two hundred thousand dollars each . . ."

"Two hundred thousand?" Charles began to laugh. "Wherever did you get that ridiculous figure?"

"From Gregory Rosenko."

"He must be mad!"

"I don't understand." Duffy put down her glass. She felt sick.

Charles poured more champagne. "I must apologize for Gregory. I don't see them going for less than half a million apiece."

"What are we doing here?" Duffy asked.

They were in front of Wyndham's. Charles jumped out of the car and held the door open. "Welcome to the Patterson Collection of Czarist Treasures," he announced with great bravado. "The sale of the century!"

Duffy took his hand as he stepped onto the pavement. "Mr. Wyndham . . . my friend only wanted . . ."

"We'll have an Imperial flag, the double-headed eagle, lit with kliegs from below." Charles walked ahead, pulling Duffy along as she stared up at the empty flagpole. "It will, of course, be an evening sale," he called over his shoulder. As the doorman stood at attention, Charles whispered to her, "Perhaps we'll even dress old James as a Cossack."

Charles pointed to a row of Chinese ancestral portraits on exhibit in the lobby. "We'll cover that whole wall with photographs of Imperial Easter Eggs." He paused for a moment. "Definitely a black-tie preview. Blinis and martinis. Miss Patterson, have you any idea how many Russian collectors have been dreaming of a sale like this?" He led her around the corner to his private elevator. Charles smiled as he held the door open.

"They'll crawl out of the woodwork for this one, Miss Patterson! They'll come from every corner of the globe!"

It was a tiny elevator, the walls paneled in black walnut with etched glass mirrors. Duffy wondered whether "they" would come from all corners to Perry Falls. Charles pressed up against her as he closed the door. The elevator rose slowly.

"I'm working very hard to impress you, Miss Patterson. Are you impressed?"

"Yes."

"Good. Miss Patterson," he began, "may I call you Dorothy?"

"No." Duffy shook her head. "No one calls me Dorothy."

"I see. Did your parents call you Miss Patterson?"

She smiled. "My father called me Duffy."

"Duffy?" he asked suspiciously.

"He once had a dog named Duffy that followed him wherever he went."

Charles nodded and then shrugged. "The dog could have been named Spot."

The elevator stopped. Charles held the door open. "Duffy," he said, trying it on for size. "Yes. It fits."

Viewing time was over in the third-floor exhibit rooms. Charles led her through a dimly lit corridor to an archway cordoned off by a red velvet rope. A large sign read DO NOT ENTER. Charles unhooked the rope.

"Where are we going?" she asked softly.

"Why are you whispering?" he whispered.

"I feel as though we're not supposed to be here."

"We're not."

"It's like sneaking into a store after it's closed."

"Shhh." Charles reached for her hand. "We are."

A simple gesture, offering a hand to lead her through a shadowy room. Natural enough, but the moment they touched, his fingers locked around hers. She realized she was afraid of Charles. He promised an excitement she had never known.

He led the way past display cases filled with T'ang Dynasty bronzes, Sung Dynasty carved figures, Han Dynasty pottery, celadon vases, blanc-de-chine, and Chinese Export porcelain. They stopped in front of a door that warned NO ADMITTANCE. Charles turned a key in the lock and opened it.

The room was dark, filled with Chinese furniture, illuminated only by the flickering light of ten giant candles. A circle of tall brass candle stands surrounded a carved red lacquer table. Ornate folding screens inlaid with ivory dragons lined the wall. Charles locked the door behind them.

"Where are we?" she asked.

Charles smiled. "You've been shanghaied."

"Then I should be afraid."

"Are you?"

Duffy took a deep breath. "Yes."

"Good. Tell me who you really are."

"And if I do?"

"Then you can have dinner with me."

"And if I don't?"

"Then you can have dinner with me."

Duffy smiled. "You win."

They walked across a K'ang-hsi rug with faded pink peonies. Large ceramic urns and rosewood couches had been moved to form a dining area. The red lacquer table was set for two. Blue-and-white Ch'ing dragon bowls sat atop octagonal famille rose plates. At each place were a pair of ivory chopsticks covered with silver filigree. An intricately colored Ming wine pitcher and two matching wine cups completed the service.

"Welcome to the most expensive chop suey joint in the world," he said. "We're having a rather important Chinese sale tomorrow."

"You're not serious about eating with these?"

"Well, I'm not selling them as new. Everyone expects they've been used. You do like Chinese food?"

Duffy laughed. "I love it."

"Splendid."

"What's the blue-plate special tonight?"

"That rice bowl of yours. It's been estimated at three to four thousand."

She took a step back from the table. "Dollars?"

Charles reached over and struck an enormous brass gong. The sound echoed ominously through the room. He pulled out her chair. "It wasn't until the eighth or ninth century that chairs were accepted in China. And, at that, only for men." Charles sat across from her. "A chair, like a suit of clothes, was regarded as a highly personal object. It was tailor-made to the proportions of the buyer."

"How much for the pair?" she asked.

Charles raised an eyebrow. "A set of Huang Huali armchairs? They should bring at least seven thousand."

Duffy looked around at the lit candles that encircled them. Charles asked, "A yüan for your thoughts."

"I feel as though I'm sitting on a birthday cake." She wished she hadn't said that. It made her think of Ben. "Do you entertain like this very often?"

"It's one of the fringe benefits. Last week it was Important French Furniture. You should have heard Scott Joplin being played on a Louis Quinze harpsichord."

"Are you married?" Duffy asked suddenly.

"No."

"Why not?"

"No one ever asked me," Charles said.

There were footsteps. Out of the darkness came an enormous Chinese man stuffed into a chef's uniform. He carried a heavy tray and puffed loudly with each step.

"Next time you get a fucking waiter!" the old man yelled. "These fucking dishes are breaking my fucking back."

Charles stood up. "I want you to meet Uncle Lou, one of the greatest treasures to come out of China."

Before Duffy could get a word in, Uncle Lou began setting

down plates of food. "I couldn't stand it there. Thought I would go out of my fucking mind until Goldberg found me."

Charles explained. "Mr. and Mrs. Goldberg gave one another intestinal bypass operations for their twenty-fifth anniversary and celebrated with an eating tour of China."

"Worse fucking day of my life when Goldberg died," Uncle Lou muttered. He sighed and then pointed to each plate. "Steamed buns with pork filling. Honeyed ham with dates. My specialty—General Goldberg's Chicken. You start with that." He frowned as he poured the wine into their cups. "I don't know why you don't have a decent Chablis instead of this fucking rice wine."

As soon as Uncle Lou had gone, they began to laugh. Charles picked up his wine cup and waited for Duffy to take hers. The wine was warm and incredibly fiery as she swallowed it. A moment later the fumes escaped through her nose. "Charles," she gasped, "why don't you have a decent Chablis instead of this fucking rice wine?"

He smiled and picked up his chopsticks. "The very rich in China used silver and ivory chopsticks not merely as a sign of wealth, but as protection. They believed that silver would blacken in the presence of poison and ivory would shatter."

"Are you trying to frighten me?"

"Yes." He paused and stared at her. "I want to make you talk."

She sat back in her chair and drank the rest of the wine. After admiring the cup for a moment, she asked, "How much?"

"Ming tou ts'ai? Should bring nearly ninety thousand. That is, if the Metropolitan bids."

Duffy stared at the cup. "Aren't you afraid I might break it?"

"Terrified."

She laughed and held out the cup as Charles poured more wine. "Do you always tell the truth?"

"I tell the truth the way other people tell lies. There are times when truth is more disarming."

Duffy raised her cup in a mock toast. "All right, you might as well know. I come from a family that's been in the diplomatic service for generations. My father, the Brazilian Consul General in Moscow, fell in love with a peasant on the eve of the Revolution." Charles stared at her for a long moment. Then he picked up his chopsticks and began to eat. Duffy drank her wine in a single gulp. "The peasant was, however, in reality the illegitimate daughter of Tchaikovsky and Mrs. Lenin." She covered her mouth as she laughed.

Charles didn't look up. "The chicken is particularly good. Mmm. Coriander, I believe."

Duffy reached out to him. "Charles . . ."

"You must try it. I hope the ham isn't too sweet for you."

"Charles . . ."

"You know why Chinese food is cut into small pieces prior to cooking?"

"To get to the other side?" Duffy giggled and poured some more wine.

"Lack of fuel. It shortens the cooking time to practically nothing."

"All right," she said. "I'm sorry." He stopped eating and sat back. Duffy took a deep breath. "The truth is I found them on Saturday night in a trunk that belonged to a poor old woman."

Charles leaned over and struck the gong. The sound was deep, as though he were growling. Yet Duffy felt wonderful. The wine had relaxed her. And, as Charles said, there were times the truth was disarming.

"I haven't had a bite," Duffy said, dropping her chopsticks.

"Not with the bait you're using."

She held up the chopsticks. "I don't really know how to."

Charles took her hand. His grip was cool, dispassionate. "Put one in the curve between your thumb and first finger. Let it rest on your third finger."

His face was close to hers. Duffy stared at him. She had told him the truth. That was important to her. "Charles . . ."

"Hold it tight. This one doesn't move. The other one is held between the tip of your thumb and the tips of your first and second fingers."

"But, Charles . . ."

"It's only the second one that moves. There. That's it." He turned as though he were going to kiss her.

"Yes?" She wanted him to kiss her.

"Duffy," he whispered, "do you mind if I call you Miss Patterson?"

All through dinner Charles told stories that Duffy devoured as eagerly as Uncle Lou's sea bass in hot spicy sauce. She heard about the dealer who overbid outrageously to establish a world record because he had an exclusive contract for the artist's work. He told stories about the "rings" dealers formed to keep prices down. They laughed at the rock star who thought he was collecting pieces made by a Frenchman named Art Nouveau. And then there was the senator who fell asleep after telling the auctioneer he was bidding as long as his eyes were closed.

Duffy wanted to tell Charles about the barn. She knew he would understand her struggle to keep it alive. But she had no right to discuss anything with him before telling Ben. She had no right to deceive Charles any further. Most of all, she had no right to deceive herself. It was time to go home.

They were alone, staring across the table at one another. Uncle Lou had brought dessert, a mountain of pureed chestnuts covered with whipped cream. Then he said good night and promised to check that the fucking door was locked. Exits were being sealed. Routes of escape were closing off when she needed them most. Duffy had to get out of there. Everything made her uncomfortable—the dazzling setting, the exquisite food, the amusing stories, the extraordinary company.

Charles took a jade spoon and scooped up some whipped cream. He leaned across the table and held it to Duffy's lips. She shook her head No. Charles kept the spoon there. Without taking her eyes from his, Duffy succumbed. She opened her mouth.

Charles reached for her hand and led her past the circle of lit candles. He pushed aside the lacquered screen. Without a word, he brought her to an enormous carved bed. It was enclosed on three sides and canopied by ornate rosewood filigree panels. Chales sat on the yellow silk mattress. He would not let go of her hand.

"How much?" she asked nervously.

"Should fetch forty thousand."

Duffy sat down. "What is it?"

"An opium bed. A place where dreams come true."

Duffy stood up. "Whose dreams?"

He took her hand and brought her close to him. She could feel his breath on her cheek. "We have the same dream, Duffy."

"Charles . . ."

"Shall I tell you the dream?" he whispered. "It begins here. Now. This moment."

"Stop," she said breathlessly.

"I can't." He kissed her. "It's your dream."

"You don't know my dreams. You don't even know me."

"Of course I do. You're Miss D. Patterson. You live in a Howard Johnson motel where your father and his dog brought you up. You collect missing million-dollar treasures."

"Do you kiss all your clients?"

"Actually, no. The rug dealers are too gamey."

Duffy turned away from him in a frantic search for reality. But all she could see was a flickering circle of candles and dancing ivory dragons. "Charles, I don't want this to be a dream."

"Then trust me. I can make it all come true."

Duffy wanted it to come true. She wanted to open her eyes and be on a Chinese opium bed with Charles Wyndham. There was a long kiss, mouths opening, a breathtaking exploration as tongues touched. She imagined it was the lingering scent of opium that clouded her mind, weakening her will so that she couldn't resist his pushing her down onto the yellow silk.

"We can break every existing record," he whispered.

"What?"

"I promise you the front page of the *Times*."

She opened her eyes. "Oh, my God."

"What is it?"

Duffy stood up. She didn't know what to say. For a moment she couldn't speak. The only thing to do was laugh. "Oh, Charles."

"What is it? Are you laughing at me?"

"No. It's me! I'm laughing at me." As Duffy walked toward the door, she turned back for a moment. "You can tell the senator he wasn't the only one who had his eyes closed during the sale."

The Czarina stared out the window. It was snowing and now that Nicholas had abdicated she feared there would be no more Romanovs to make fresh footprints. God had made the snow to cushion the boots of the Czar as he walked through the land. Each snowflake could survive the winter as part of those footprints, never by itself.

Poor Nicky. He did not have the seven-league boots of Peter nor the wind of passion that allowed Catherine to sweep across the country barely touching her feet to the ground. There would be no Nicholas the Great. Dear God, there was no longer a Nicholas at all.

Not only had Russia lost its Czar, but Alexandra Feodorovna had lost Russia. The shy German princess, a granddaughter of Queen Victoria, had embraced her adopted country as fervently as she had converted to the Russian Orthodox church. And now, her beloved Nicky had renounced himself as defender of the ruling faith, preserver of the dogmas, protector of the orthodoxy of belief in the holy church.

The woman known as Matushka, the Mother of the Russian people, had spent the night burning her letters in the palace at Tsarskoye Selo, some fifteen miles from the capital. She and the children were safer there, everyone thought, away from the strikes and cries of the revolutionaries. But their threats reached the palace gates. It was rumored the Czar would be put on trial. It was rumored the Czarina would be killed if she visited again the grave of her beloved Rasputin. Worse still, it was rumored the children would be kidnapped.

As she sat watching the morning snow, Alexandra Feodorovna clutched to her breast the ruby picture frame given to her by Nicholas II, former Emperor and Autocrat of all the Russias, Czar of Moscow, Kiev, Vladimir, Novgorod. . . .

Prince Alexander Vasilyevich bowed. "Sandro," she whispered, wondering if he would be the last to bow before her. "You will help me?"

He looked up with tears in his eyes. "The Empress has only to ask."

"I ask not as Empress, but as your cousin."

Sandro followed her to the window. "You have both loyalties forever."

Snow had always been such a comfort, Alexandra thought. A caress from God that covered mistakes. She motioned for Sandro to sit next to her on the window seat. When she turned to him, her blue-gray eyes were filled wih fear. "Tell the stablemaster something is wrong with your carriage. Tell him to repair it for you."

"Yes, Majesty."

She took hold of his hand with a viselike grip. Tears streamed down her cheeks. "I have gathered all of the jewels I brought with me, anything that is of value. The stablemaster will place the box inside the seat of your carriage." She turned from him and stared out the window, pausing to regain her composure. "You must use the jewels to save my children."

"Empress . . ."

She grabbed his arm, a drowning woman. "Sandro, save my children as though you were saving your own!" She put a handkerchief to her face. Her hand shook as she held out the frame with the pictures of Alexis and herself. "Three hundred rubies. A salute to the Czarevitch." Closing her eyes, she

handed him the double-heart frame. "Go, quickly, Sandro. You
now hold the lives of my children in your hands."

He stood up. "I pray that . . ."

The Czarina nodded. The snow was still falling. "I pray, too."

Emmett searched through *The Dealer's Price Guide to Collector Plates* while Rita fed Louis Comfort strained bananas for breakfast. They sat at one end of the long trestle table that Ezra Ryerson brought into the house over sixty years ago hoping to fill with his children and his children's children.

"Why the hell is a 1945 Christmas plate worth three hundred dollars and a 1946 worth only one hundred dollars?" Emmett asked.

Rita brushed aside her long black hair. Louis Comfort had just spit banana at her. "Which one you got?"

"What do you think? If there's one worth a hundred and one worth three hundred, which one do you think I have?"

Rita shook her head. She walked to the sink that was filled with last night's dinner dishes. She picked up a wet rag and cleaned the banana from her terrycloth robe. "Where the hell did Cissy Kennert even get a one-hundred-dollar plate?"

Emmett shrugged. "Well, it didn't cost a hundred in 1946. Maybe Raymond bought it for her."

"Where would he buy it? I don't see Raymond Kennert walking into the Stop 'n Shop and picking up a Royal Copenhagen Christmas Plate along with his six-pack."

"I'm telling you, Rita, there are things worth hundreds and hundreds of dollars that people don't know they have. It's all just sitting up there in the attic. They don't know what they're selling and the people buying don't know what they're buying."

Louis Comfort smiled, burped and spit up his entire breakfast. Rita began cleaning the highchair. "It's what she fed him last night. I told her, you don't give a baby Duck *à l'Orange.* Louis Comfort," she cooed, "tonight you're just going to have a plain American hot dog. Poor baby." Rita carried him out of the room. "I'm going to put him on the porch."

Without looking up from his book, Emmett said, "Don't put him near Duffy's room."

"But that's where the sun is," Rita complained.

"Don't."

Rita shook her head and groaned. "I can't feed my baby properly because one sister-in-law thinks she's Julia Child, and I can't let him have the morning sun because of the other. Why the hell don't we just auction him off on Saturday night and say good riddance?"

Emmett sighed as Rita slammed the door. Unbelievable. A 1945 plate listed at three hundred.

"Mornin'." Chip stood in the doorway. "Need anything in town?"

"Nope."

Chip paused, and then said accusingly, "You know, I could swear someone was using my Alka-Seltzer!"

"Maybe Lorraine's been cooking with it."

Chip scowled and then his face broke into a big smile. "Sure as hell would save time!"

"Morning." Rita nodded to Chip as she came back into the kitchen.

"Mornin', Rita. You need anything in town?"

"Yes. A dishwasher."

"I'll do them as soon as I get back."

Emmett took a cup and saucer from the carton at his feet. "What the hell is this? Looks like Occupied Japan."

Rita slumped down in her chair. "This whole place looks like Occupied Japan!" She pointed to Chip. "You're supposed to do the dishes after dinner. I have a right to wake up to a clean kitchen."

"I gotta go into town," Chip pleaded. He waited for her permission. "Rita?"

"I have a right to wake up to a clean kitchen," she repeated.

"Can't read the damn marking," Emmett mumbled.

"Morning, everybody." Lorraine, wearing a white T-shirt and white shorts, carried a cookbook. She looked at Chip. "Didn't you go yet? I can't make the *oeufs* without heavy cream."

Emmett looked up at Rita. "The what?"

Lorraine waved her book. "*Oeufs en Cocotte.* Baked eggs swimming in heavy cream."

From her end of the table, Rita pointed to the porch. "Louis Comfort was taken seriously ill this morning."

"My God," Lorraine squealed. "What happened to my darling?"

"He was poisoned," Rita said.

"Poisoned?"

"Rita!" Emmett shook his head. He held the cup to the light. "This has got to be worth B-I-G money."

"Louis Comfort is fine," Chip said. "It's their antique sense of humor."

"He threw up!" Rita said while making a cup of instant coffee. "There was Duck *à l'Orange* all over his highchair." She raised the kettle as she poured to simulate sound effects.

"B-I-G money. Got to be fifty bucks."

"I ate the same food," Lorraine snapped, "and I didn't throw up."

"It couldn't have been the food," Chip said.

Rita shrugged as she stirred her black coffee. "Then it must have been the company."

"You know what we're going to get for it?" Emmett asked,

holding the cup and saucer. "Nothing. That's what we're going to get because those turkeys out there don't know what they're buying. You need to put a price on things so people know what they're worth."

Lorraine slammed her book on the table. "I don't need a price tag to tell me what some people are worth."

Chip put an arm around Lorraine. "Honey, don't get upset. One of these days . . ."

Emmett looked up. "After you open your restaurant . . ."

"Or after you open your antique shop-pee," Chip snarled.

"Or after you do the dishes," Rita said.

Lorraine stamped her foot. "You didn't do the dishes?"

"I was going to," Chip said. "Soon as I got back from town."

"That's too late. You know I can't cook with a sink full of dirty dishes."

Emmett sighed and shook his head at Rita. "What the hell did you have to start them off for?"

"Me? Why is everything my fault? I didn't leave the dishes! I didn't cook the Duck à l'Orange! I didn't make Louis Comfort sick! All I want to do is be left alone. I'm tired of living in this three-ring circus. I'm tired of sharing a house and sharing a kitchen and sharing my baby!" Rita covered her face and began to cry.

Lorraine ran over and put her arms around Rita. She spoke softly. "I'm sorry. I know just how you feel. I hate living here with you, too. But there's nothing we can do about it. The boys are doing the best they can. Besides, it won't last forever." She waited for Rita to respond and then offered, "How about my just making us all some bacon and oeufs?"

Rita began to laugh. She patted Lorraine's hand. "I'm sorry."

"Well, you got to yell at someone. Might as well be me."

Chip's face beamed with pride. "Is that a woman or is that a woman?"

Lorraine pointed to the sink. "Are those dirty dishes or are those dirty dishes?"

"Honey, I got to go into town."

"Honey, you got to put your ass in a sling for the time being and get those dishes done." Lorraine threw him a dish towel and sat down. She gave her book to Rita. "How about my letting you choose the special for Saturday night?"

Rita sighed. "You just won't let me stay mad at you."

"If food be the music of love . . ." Lorraine sang. She watched as Rita opened the book. "You know, I was thinking. I have lots of duck left over. What do you think about duckburgers for lunch?"

Duffy stood in the doorway holding Louis Comfort. She wore blue jeans and a bright pink shirt with a strand of Victorian garnets. A tape measure was clipped to her belt. "Didn't anybody hear my poor nephew crying?"

Rita marched over and took him. "He couldn't have been crying for long."

"You know, I think we ought to get him a pet. Maybe a big dog," Duffy said. "Or a pony." She smiled. "Oh, I just bet he'd love a pony." Duffy glanced at the sink. "We ought to get a dishwasher, too."

"We already got a dishwasher," Lorraine said. "But he's broken."

"I mean a real one." Duffy poked around in the refrigerator. "You'd like that, Lorraine."

Lorraine looked at Rita and shrugged. Chip stood back and raised his eyebrows. Emmett took his feet off the table and said, "You're in a mood."

"I'm in a wonderful mood!" Duffy announced. "I've been up for hours and I'm just bursting with ideas. But first I'm dying for some breakfast."

"You never eat breakfast."

"I'm starving!" She took out a plate of cold spaghetti.

"You must have had some terrific tag sale," Emmett said.

"No. I didn't." Duffy ate the spaghetti as everyone watched suspiciously.

Chip leaned over from behind her chair. "You gonna tell us you're in love?"

Duffy laughed. "I'm going to tell you that I know just how to fix up the barn."

"What do you mean fix it up?" Emmett asked suspiciously. "Fix what up?"

She took a pad from her back pocket. They all moved close, looking over her shoulder. "I figured out how we can get in two more rows of seats if we move the kitchen and . . ."

"Move the kitchen?" Lorraine was horrified.

". . . and expand it," Duffy said, "so that you can really cook some of those fancy French things. Then, I want to redo the roof and put in those lights Papa used to talk about."

"Oh, is that all?" Emmett asked.

"No," she said, skipping over his sarcasm. "I want to paint the barn. Inside and out." Duffy hesitated. "Then I want to take Papa's name off and put my name on."

There was a stunned silence. One by one they sat down, taking battle stations: Chip and Lorraine at one end of the table, Rita, Emmett, and Louis Comfort at the other.

"Duffy, what's up?" Emmett asked.

"You know how I loved Papa. But we've been carrying on here as though we expected him to come back. We're not three little kids minding the store."

"What are you trying to say?"

"Emmett, I'm trying to say that I am a damn good auctioneer."

"Well, nobody's gonna argue that," Chip exclaimed. "That would be like arguing about Lorraine's fricassee."

Rita got the giggles again. "And God knows nobody would argue about her fricassee."

Lorraine stood up, laughing loudly as she performed bumps and grinds while chanting, "You can argue 'bout my quiche, you can argue 'bout my flan, you can . . ."

A car horn honked twice. Duffy put down her plate. "Gotta go." She ran out the kitchen door.

Ben was on the south porch outside her room. "I came as soon as I could. You in some kind of trouble?"

So much had happened between Saturday night and Tuesday. He looked like a stranger to her. "I have to talk to you, Ben."

"What is it?"

"Sit down," she said. Ben brushed off a space and sat on the porch steps. Duffy unbuttoned her pocket and took out the white envelope containing Miss Natalie's contract. "Ben, how many times has the bank been appointed administrator by the court?"

"That's not what you called me out here for?"

"Ben."

He loosened his tie. "Before or after we gave Judge Sutton his second mortgage?"

"How many times?" she repeated.

Ben shrugged. "All the time."

"And how many times have I sold the estates for you?"

"All the time," he said slowly.

Duffy paused. "What if I didn't want to handle one of them?"

He was becoming annoyed. "You would say, 'Ben, I don't want to handle it,' and I would find someone else."

She held up the envelope. "Ben, I don't want to handle it."

He smiled and shook his head. "Oh, no. You'd have to say it before you signed the contract." He pointed to the envelope. "That little thing."

"And if I said it afterward?"

"A contract is a contract."

Duffy took a deep breath. "Just like a rose is a rose."

"Is a signed and sealed rose." He was impatient. "I wouldn't break a contract with you, and I don't expect you to break one with me."

Duffy held her breath. "How do I know you wouldn't?"

"So that's it. Who's been talking to you? That guy from Hamilton County? You think I'm going to give him the estate sales?"

"I just want to be sure you won't ever break a contract with me."

Ben reached out to hold Duffy's hands. "I won't."

"Because?"

He sighed and then smiled as he said what he thought she wanted to hear. "Because I love you."

Duffy frowned. "Give me a better reason."

Ben let go of her hands. "A better reason than love?"

"Suppose you fall in love with the guy from Hamilton County?"

Ben stood up and began pacing. "Did it ever occur to you that I was not put on this earth just to make you feel good? You take every potshot you can at me but you expect me to keep telling you how great you are."

"Just acknowledge me, Ben."

"You're a damn good auctioneer," he said angrily. "That's why the bank gives you the contracts. It has nothing to do with the fact that I love you, or that I think about you all the time, or that I want you in my bed and in my life more than I have ever wanted anything or anyone."

Duffy breathed a sigh of relief. She put the envelope back in her pocket and buttoned it. She kissed Ben. "I'm sorry about Saturday night," she whispered.

"I didn't want to leave. I should have stayed. What about tonight?"

"Not tonight. Now."

He hesitated. "In the middle of the morning? What are you up to?"

Duffy turned to him, her eyes ablaze with excitement. "Ben, how many times have you been aware that your whole life was about to change? When was the last time you knew you were on the brink of something really big?"

He thought for a moment. "I guess when I started to get my last hard-on."

"Ben!" She leaned against the door. He pressed up against her. They kissed. "There's something else I want to ask you." She turned her head aside as he kissed her ear. "Ben, how much do you make for acting as administrator of Miss Natalie's estate?"

"Jesus!" He pulled back.

Duffy smiled and kissed his cheek. "How much?"

"The bank gets a percentage." Ben put his hands on her shoulders. "Listen, I don't know what the hell you're getting at, but I do know you didn't ask me to come here to discuss fiduciary obligations."

As he moved close to kiss her, Duffy asked, "How much?"

"Four percent." He kissed her again, his teeth pressed hard against hers.

Duffy took a breath. "Four percent can really add up on a large estate."

"You *are* kinky." He kept kissing her as he explained. "It's four percent up to twenty-five thousand dollars. Then it's three and a half percent of the next hundred and twenty-five thousand."

"Oh."

He bit her ear and whispered, "After that it's three percent of the next hundred and fifty thousand. Then it's two percent all the way home."

She opened her eyes as he held her in his arms. "What does that come to per million?"

Ben stopped kissing her. "You're sure going to a lot of trouble just to be sarcastic. We both knew the old woman had nothing."

"Why did you take it then?"

"I was appointed by the court. I took it for the same reason you did. If you turn down the small ones, you don't get the big ones. If I pay my dues, then I get something nice once in a while."

Duffy smiled. She took out her key and put it in the lock. "Ben . . ."

"What?"

She turned the key, then flung open the door. "Welcome to once in a while!"

The jewels covered everything—the desk, the table, the chairs, the bed, the dresser, even the floor. It was as though a great celestial prism had shattered and the pieces had come to rest in Duffy's room. Diamonds and rubies and emeralds, silver and jade and gold, enamels of purple, yellow, lime, and blue. A carved agate owl with sapphire eyes stared at a malachite frog eager to jump into the center of a ruby-and-diamond tiara. A lavender enamel picture frame set with diamonds held a photograph of the Czar, whose imperious gaze focused on the double-heart ruby frame from which the Czarina and Czarevitch stared out at their new surroundings.

"What is all this?" Ben whispered.

"This is what we have a contract on."

He picked up the strawberry enamel Rosebud Egg. "What is it?"

"It's a Fabergé egg."

Ben nodded slowly. He brought the egg to his ear and shook it. "Is there perfume in it?"

"Not *that* Fabergé! This was made for the Czarina of Russia, Ben." She enunciated clearly, "It's worth half a million dollars."

He stared at the jeweled egg resting in the palm of his hand. After a moment he looked at Duffy, then back at the egg. Ben's calculations collided with one another as he tried converting

Miss Natalie's estate into something of value, jewels into dollars, history into net worth. "How do you know?"

Duffy smiled. "Because, Comrade," she said, attempting a Russian accent, "I vent to Noo Yawk Zity. I vent to Vyndham's."

"And they told you it was worth half a million?"

"Da."

"Half a million *dollars?*"

"For one egg and no bacon!"

"That's impossible."

Duffy spread her arms in the air and whirled around. "Not bad for the junk man's daughter!"

"Miss Natalie had no money. All she had was Social Security and some money that barely got her by. You saw her house." Ben shook his head. "Where did you find all this?"

"In a trunk. Under some books. Strange books. Overthrow the government! Workers unite!"

"You think it was stolen?"

"You think Miss Natalie was a jewel thief?"

"Well, then how did it get there?"

"I don't know. All I know is I have a contract."

He walked around the room, touching each piece. "A little old lady," he muttered. "A goddamn little old lady."

"I figure five million plus."

Ben stood still, his eyes unable to take it all in. "Five million?"

"At least. Possibly ten."

"They told you that?"

"I figured it out."

"What do you mean you figured it out? What the hell do you know about this kind of stuff?" Ben felt suddenly hostile. "All you know is the junk you cart in and out on Saturday night." They stared at one another while he estimated twenty percent of ten million dollars.

"Two million," she said, knowing exactly what he was thinking.

"Duffy, don't be ridiculous. If it's not stolen, there must be someone with a claim on it. Someone was sending her money."

"Who?"

"I don't know who. I always figured it was from a relative. She'd come to the bank once a month to cash a four-hundred-dollar money order. But even after she died she got one. So it couldn't have been a close relative. The money order came in a blank envelope. No name, no address. Just the postmark. Shreveport, Louisiana."

Duffy sank into a chair. "You said there were no relatives. That's why it went to the state."

"We put ads in all the Shreveport papers. No one came forward. We waited three months. All we know is someone must have read the ad because the money orders stopped."

"That doesn't mean it's family."

"You'd be surprised how many relatives surface after they find out an estate is worth something. But even if there are no claims and even if it's not stolen property . . ."

Tensely, without any expression on her face, Duffy said, "A rose is a rose."

"Goddamn it, Duffy. Talk sense. You can't handle a sale like this. Who are you going to sell to? There isn't ten million dollars in the whole county, much less in Perry Falls."

"Charles Wyndham said they would come from all corners of the globe for this one. If they're coming that far, they'll make it to the Nickel Man Barn."

"The only person who'll make it to the Nickel Man Barn is Charles Wyndham himself. That guy must be laughing himself silly. You bet he's going to come. He's going to come to steal the stuff from you! He's the one who sells things for millions of dollars. Not you!"

"It's my sale, Ben."

He stared at Duffy. How many times had he been confronted with that same stubbornness? "Why the hell did you go to New York? Why didn't you tell me about it? You should have told me first."

Duffy spoke softly. "I had to find out if they were real. I thought it was my responsibility to find out."

"And it's my responsibility to protect the best interests of the estate, as well as the best interests of the bank." He sat on the edge of the desk. "I can't let you do it."

"It's my sale, Ben. I have a contract. You can't stop me."

Ben took a deep breath. "I can try."

"Don't."

"I have to. It's not me. It's the bank."

"You are the bank! You don't like to admit that, Ben. But it's always the bank."

"It's always the barn!"

Duffy turned away. She looked out the window, trying desperately to focus on something that would hold back the tears she felt welling up. "When I first met you, I was afraid to tell you who my father was. I thought you'd laugh at me."

"Duffy, this has nothing to do with us."

"One day, Papa came home with a table from your house. He didn't know I was in love with you. That night all he kept talking about was the rich banker's house. And all I could think about was you. I begged him not to sell the table. I felt like such a scavenger. A seagull, trying to stay afloat on debris from other people's lives."

Ben walked over and put his arms around her. "I'm sorry." Then he picked up the telephone and dialed.

Duffy leaned back against the door. "What are you going to do?"

"Barnett?" he said into the receiver. "I'm over at the Ryerson farm. Yes," he said, looking at Duffy, "the Nickel Man Barn. Get the security truck and two armed guards out here fast."

Duffy spoke nervously as Ben put down the phone. "I was going to suggest you keep them in the vault. They can stay there until . . ."

He reached out for her hand. "I'm going to try to stop you," he said softly.

She nodded as though acknowledging the inevitable. Then they both turned, hearing footsteps. It was Chip. "Hey, Duffy, you need anything in town?" Ben and Duffy held their breath as he stood in the doorway.

Chip's mouth dropped open. "What the hell is all this?" He looked at Duffy, then at Ben. "Holy shit!" he whispered, turning to Duffy. "This stuff looks real." He picked up the ruby-and-diamond tiara and held it out for them to see. He opened his mouth and bellowed, "Emmett! Emmett, you get your ass in here!"

Ben stood near the window, waiting for the truck. Duffy sat in Red's rocking chair, pushing herself back and forth. Chip groaned with disbelief as he picked up one piece after another.

"Emmett!" he cried out. "Emmett!"

Duffy looked at Ben. "What is this going to do to us?"

Ben shrugged. "I guess the same thing it's always done."

"Emmett!"

Duffy looked at him sadly, as though saying goodbye to someone she loved. "I guess."

"Emmmmmmeeeeeettttttt!"

The phone call from Ben came three days later. "Hi," he said.

"Hi."

"Can you be at the bank tomorrow morning?"

"Sure," Duffy said. "What time?"

"Ten?"

"Okay."

There was a long pause. "Duffy . . ."

"Yes?"

He paused again but changed his mind. "I'll see you tomorrow."

Duffy didn't want the call to end that way but Emmett and Chip were hovering over her. They hadn't left her alone since Ben and the security guards locked the pieces in the armored truck and drove away. She spent the rest of that day repeating the story over and over again, beginning with the discovery on Saturday night, her secret trip to Wyndham's, and a G-rated version of her meeting with Charles. If she skipped over a detail, no matter how slight, someone prompted her. Before going to bed, Emmett insisted on one more telling. For that last time, there was not a single interruption. They were children listening to their favorite fairy tale.

She had to retell the story again on Wednesday before the pickers came with their dishes and pictures and blanket chests. She had to tell it again after the truckers from Vermont left their reproduction oak furniture and newly electrified lanterns. By Thursday, the brothers were telling the story to themselves between pickups at local farms and stopping for consignments from dealers.

After the call from Ben on Friday, Duffy reassured them that he would honor the contract. But she was not as certain as she pretended to be. Duffy needed, most of all, to reassure herself. She found a can of red paint. Her heart pounding furiously with every stroke, she stood in the hot afternoon sun painting the side of the barn. She painted over the words that for a quarter of a century had proclaimed "Red Patterson, Auctioneer." Afterward, feeling every bit like Lady Macbeth, Duffy soaked in a hot tub still rubbing the red paint from her hands.

By dinnertime, not even Lorraine had the patience to cook. Uncharacteristically, the boys offered to drive into town and pick up some ribs. They compiled a shopping list amid such instructions as "lots of extra sauce" and "what the hell, see if they have chocolate cake" and "surprise me." There was a sense of abandon, a need for compensation, almost like holding a wake. Duffy convinced Emmett to stop for strawberry ice cream.

Someone suggested candles and Rita lit them as she heard the boys return. They waited in the kitchen for the party to begin. They were not prepared for empty hands or for faces filled with panic.

"On our way into town, we drove past Miss Natalie's house," Chip said. "Just to take a look."

Emmett spoke as in a state of shock. "Ben must have called the state police. They've surrounded the place."

The Perry Falls Savings and Loan was on the corner of Main and Schuyler, a site for which Ben's father had waited as patiently as the sun waits for the moon to go down. Jason Perry, acting as the architect for his dynasty, planned to bequeath to his adopted son a past, a present, and a future.

Duffy stood in the doorway to Ben's office. She was astonished to see Charles Wyndham sitting on the sofa. She felt betrayed. "I have a contract!" she shouted at Ben.

"I have a responsibility," he yelled.

"Hello," Charles said.

Ignoring him, Duffy demanded, "How could you do this to me?"

Charles carried on a conversation by himself. "Well, hello, Charles. How are you?" he asked.

"Why did you bring him here? Are you trying to make a fool of me?"

"No," Ben exploded. "I'm trying to stop you from making a fool of yourself!"

"Splendid, thank you. And you?"

Duffy turned to Charles. "I don't know what to say to you."

"Why not try 'Hello, Charles'?"

She took a deep breath. "Hello, Charles." There was a long pause. "Now what?"

"Now we go on to 'what's new'?"

Duffy turned away and collapsed into a chair. "Ben, how could you?"

He sat down behind his grandfather's desk. "You tried to trap me, Duffy. You knew you had more than junk. It was quite a scene you played out on the porch. 'Ben, take back the contract,'" he said, mocking her tone.

She spoke softly. "I had to be sure."

"You should have trusted me," Ben said angrily.

Duffy pointed to Charles. "And he's the proof of how much you trusted me!"

Charles shook his head. "If only people read their nickels. In *God* we trust."

"I have a right to know what the hell you're doing here," Duffy demanded.

"Ben called me on Tuesday," Charles said. "Needless to say we were up here faster than you can sell a rug to an Armenian."

"We?"

"Gregory and I."

"You and Gregory were in Perry Falls?"

"For the better part of Tuesday night." He leaned over toward her and whispered, "Not that I didn't want to call you . . ."

Duffy turned to Ben. "Why did you have to pick *him*?"

"The bank has the right to an outside appraisal."

"And so you called *him*?" She pointed to Charles. "He's probably the only person in the world who wants to stop me more than you do."

"I needed a professional!" Ben said angrily.

"And what the hell do you think I am?"

"I think you're a small-town Saturday-night auctioneer who doesn't know the first thing about selling anything but junk."

She leaned angrily across his desk. "There's nobody can sell better than I can. Ten cents, ten dollars, ten thousand. It doesn't matter what it costs. I can sell anything!"

"It's basically a matter of clientele," Charles clarified.

Duffy glared at him. "That's no problem. You told me they'd come from all corners of the globe."

"And they will," Charles said. "But they'll come to Wyndham's. Collecting is a disease. If you wanted the best treatment you'd go to the Mayo Clinic, not Perry Falls General."

"No one ever died of auction fever," she said.

"No one but the auctioneer." Charles reached for her hand. "I know precisely what this sale means to you. It *is* the sale of your lifetime. That's the fever, Duffy. The fever is wanting to say 'Sold!' and know it means millions."

She pulled her hand away. "How many millions?"

Charles reached into his inside pocket. "We took all the pieces back to New York. Gregory worked with people from the Gemological Institute as well as the curator of the Metropolitan's Russian Art Department. You should have seen their faces." He handed her a piece of paper.

Duffy skimmed the inventory to read the last line. Then she reread it.

TOTAL ESTIMATED VALUE: $20,000,000.

The figure raced through her head. Twenty percent. Four million dollars. It couldn't be! She looked up at Charles and saw from his face that it could. "I walked into this office expecting the bank to live up to its contract. I still do."

Ben glared at her. "I can go back to court and claim it was signed without foreknowledge of the true value of the estate."

"But you won't," she said. "No matter how much you hate the barn, no matter how much money is involved, Ben Perry honors his contracts." Duffy sat back in her chair.

Ben slammed his fist on the desk. "The bank is prepared to give you ten percent!"

"The bank knows I don't work on ten percent."

"Damn it! I'm giving you ten percent *not* to work!"

Charles took a deep breath. "He's trying to buy you out."

"And buy you in!" she snapped.

"Yes. Precisely." Charles got up and walked over to her chair. "But I wouldn't let him get away with that if I were you."

Ben's mouth dropped open. "What the hell are you saying?"

"It doesn't matter what I say. Or what you say. She's got the contract. You'll have a devil of a time getting it away from her."

"Whose side are you on?" Ben asked.

"The winning side." Charles smiled at Duffy. "There's an old saying in the jewelry business. You can't sell a diamond without a setting. I think the right setting for this sale is the Nickel Man Barn. That's where we should hold it."

Duffy asked, "We?"

Charles continued. "I want you right there to show everyone how you found the treasure. The media will eat it up. I want you on television. In the papers. On magazine covers."

"In other words," Duffy said, "you want me everywhere but on the rostrum."

"Not at all. I want you there right next to me."

"And which one of us is the dummy? No, Charles, I don't do that kind of act."

"Goddamn it, she can't handle a sale like this!" Ben argued.

"Not without coaching," Charles said, smiling.

"How much do lessons cost?" Duffy asked.

"Wyndham's will handle everything. We'll catalog, publicize and stage it. In your barn. I'll bring the buyers. I'll teach you my brand of auctioneering. I want the glory plus fifteen percent."

"Fifteen percent?" Duffy gasped. "Out of my twenty?"

Charles shook his head. "Lesson Number One in Uptown Auctioneering: We charge the buyer a ten-percent premium above the hammer price. You have a contract for twenty. Add on the ten-percent premium and that makes it thirty. Fifteen for you and fifteen for me."

"I won't charge my people ten percent for the privilege of spending their own money."

"You won't be selling to your people. You'll be selling to my people. And they're accustomed to it."

Duffy thought for a moment. "I have a contract for twenty and that's what I get. You can have your buyer's premium. The deal is twenty for me and ten for you."

"Done!"

Ben watched them shake hands. He was suddenly an outsider, feeling nothing but envy and anger as they shared a moment of triumph. He had sent for Charles to make things right. Instead, everything had gone wrong. It was two against one, the wrong two against the wrong one. Now he had to fight them both. Ben turned away and stared out the window. Perhaps there really was someone in Shreveport. If only he could find an heir.

"Where's the eighty?" Duffy looked at the young couple in the third row as they conferred. Then she turned to the crowd. "He says yes. She says no. Looks like the honeymoon is over. Okay! Got the eighty!"

"Yes," Emmett shouted.

"Yes," yelled Chip.

"Where's the ninety? Louise? Should be."

It was the next-to-last quilt, nearly the end of the sale. There was no use looking for Ben. If he were coming, he would have been there by now. "Got the ninety." She glanced back at the young couple. "Say a hundred? Give 'em a minute, folks. Don't want 'em mad at one another." Not the way she and Ben were mad at one another. That quiet, hopeless anger. Anger without rage, the emptiness that begins to diminish love. "Have the hundred. Sold!"

"Sold?" Emmett turned quickly to Duffy.

She realized that it had been knocked down too soon. "What's your number, kids?"

"I was bidding," Louise called out. "You didn't take my bid."

"Someone must have taken it because I didn't see it." Duffy turned to Mrs. M. "Number 46."

"But you didn't give me a chance," Louise complained.

Duffy winked at her. "Gonna give you a chance right now. Been saving this one for you. Emmett, hold up that last quilt. It's a beauty and it's for Louise."

Emmett nodded to Chip. "Hold it up. She says this one's for Louise."

"Now I'm telling you, I don't want anyone bidding on this but Louise." Duffy didn't want to admit, especially to herself, that she had let her mind wander during the sale. But she couldn't stop thinking about Ben. Worse, she couldn't stop missing him. "Gonna let you open it, Louise. Last one started at thirty."

Louise raised her hand. "Ten," she called angrily.

Duffy couldn't help smiling. "I got ten. Anybody?"

"Fifteen!"

"New bidder," Duffy called, turning to see who it was. She held her breath. It was Charles.

"Twenty!" Louise called out.

"Yes."

"Yes."

"Twenty-five." His accent electrified the air. Charles excused himself as he found a seat in the bleachers.

"Thirty," from Louise.

The bids were moving faster than Duffy could take them. She couldn't stop staring at him.

Charles was seated. He looked up at her and smiled. "Thirty-five."

"Yes."

"Yes."

Duffy turned to Louise. "I got thirty-five," she said with a trace of wonder. Thirty-five from Charles? Why? What was he doing there?

"Forty!"

Charles nodded. "Forty-five," he shouted briskly.

"Yes."

"Yes."

Louise went to fifty. Charles went to fifty-five. "Fifty-five," Duffy repeated, trying to regain control of both herself and the sale. "Looks like we're going over the speed limit," she said, her heart racing. "All right, where's the sixty? Give me sixty!" Duffy held tight to the sides of the pulpit. Charles was there to test her and she was settling in for the ride. "Louise? I said this one was yours. Don't make a liar out of me." Louise nodded. "Got the sixty. Where's the . . ."

"Sixty-five dollars," Charles enunciated as though it were a royal proclamation. Indeed, it might have been, for everyone turned to stare at him.

"Seventy? Louise? He's not going any higher. I know the type." She wanted Charles to understand her message, to refrain from bidding. "Give me the seventy and he's out!" Louise nodded and Duffy raised her gavel quickly. "Sold at . . ."

"One hundred dollars!"

Duffy's hand was in the air. People began to murmur. Louise tightened her lips and folded her arms. Charles beamed smugly.

"Got a hundred from a man with a tie on. He must know something I don't. Anyone? Hundred ten? No one?" Duffy slammed down the gavel. "Sold! You got a pie plate, mister?"

"I beg your pardon?" Charles asked.

"A number," Duffy repeated. "You got a pie plate with your number on it?"

"I'm dreadfully sorry, but I'm afraid I haven't a pie plate with a number on it."

"Miz M? We got a number for the gentleman?"

Mrs. M held up a plate. "Two-o-two."

"We got some more quilts coming in next week," Duffy said to Louise. "Come out of a house near Saratoga. Really nice stuff. I'm sure you're gonna find one you like." Emmett reached for the moosehead. "Looks like we got somebody's relative here. Hold him up. You can use him as a hat rack, girdle stretcher or back scratcher. Got its original glass eyes. Nicely mounted on seems to be mahogany. Should go for at least a couple of hundred. Who's going to open it at fifty?" She looked around the barn, careful to avoid eye contact with Charles. "Getting late, folks. You start it, I'll stop it. How about twenty-five? Nobody here got any respect for the dead? I won't open lower than twenty-five. Nobody interested, I'll pass it by."

Charles raised his hand and waved the pie plate. He smiled broadly. "Twenty-four!"

Duffy and Charles sat in the white Rolls-Royce, sharing the red leather seat with the moosehead and the quilt, six wooden soldiers, a round metal Coca-Cola sign, a porcelain shepherdess lamp base, a green depression glass tea set, a wicker doll carriage, and a dented, rusted copper watering can. The Rolls was parked in the "For Goombas Only" lot alongside Mario's Meatball.

"Madam."

Duffy opened the door and took two steaming meatball sandwiches from the chauffeur.

"Do be careful, madam. They're frightfully hot."

Charles lowered the burled walnut tray and spread linen napkins as Duffy put the sandwiches down. He set out two cut crystal goblets.

"The root beer is for madam?"

Duffy nodded as he poured the contents of the can into her glass.

As the chauffeur poured his cola, Charles said, "Thank you.

We'll be fine now." He closed the door, shutting out the warm July night. There was hardly a whisper from the air-conditioning. Charles bit into his sandwich and said, "You know, you're really very good."

Duffy nodded. "Are you talking to me or the sandwich?"

He smiled. "Very confident, too."

"Mmm. Aren't *you*?"

"I have to be," he said. "That's my business."

"Mine, too."

They continued to eat without speaking. Finally, Charles offered, "We have lots in common."

She smiled. "We have ninety-six lots in common."

"I don't mean just that."

"Well, we both like meatball sandwiches."

"I'm serious. Duffy, we're both children of auctioneers. It's in our blood."

"Now that really is one helluva line!"

He sat back and laughed. "That was awful, wasn't it?"

"Terrible." She began to giggle.

They stopped laughing and lapsed into awkward silence again. He stared out at Mario's blinking lights. "You were wonderful up there tonight."

She hesitated, afraid the compliment was a trap. "I'm supposed to be. That's the reason they come back week after week. They're comfortable with me. They know they're going to have a good time."

He looked at her and smiled. "I had a good time, too."

Duffy was embarrassed. She changed the subject. "What were you and Ben so busy about all day?"

"My contract. Your contract. Advertising. Reserves. Insurance. The catalog. Things I couldn't go back to the city without settling." He took her hand. "Duffy, I don't want to go back tonight." He leaned over to kiss her.

"No," she whispered. "Not in front of the moose."

"Give me a better reason." Their lips touched gently, parting for an intake of breath that unexpectedly became a sigh. "It's a long trip home," he pleaded.

Duffy moved back. "How much did you get for the Chinese bed?"

"I didn't sell it." He turned quickly and took Duffy in his arms. "I couldn't."

"I wish . . ."

"What?"

Duffy held tight to Charles. "I wish we had made love that night."

He caressed her hair. "It was near the end of the sale. The bidding had been brisk all morning. The more I tried putting you out of my mind, the more I kept thinking of you. The rice bowl. The Huang Huali armchairs. The cup. They weren't just lot numbers anymore. They were things that reminded me of you. I knocked down one lot after another. Suddenly I realized I was selling the bed. There was a fat dealer from Atlanta competing with a phone bid from Hong Kong. I kept looking at the fat dealer and then at the clerk who was calling out the phone bids and I found myself getting angry. I felt possessive about that damn bed. It was the one thing we hadn't shared. Yet."

"What did you do?"

"To the horror of the entire Oriental Arts Department, I bought it in. I thought to myself I must be crazy."

"Sometimes I think that." She smiled. "My selling those jewels is as crazy as being in a Chinese bed or sitting in a Rolls-Royce eating a meatball sandwich."

"But you're sitting in a Rolls-Royce."

"Yes."

"And you're eating a meatball sandwich." He held her hand

tight. "Trust me. You'll be on the rostrum for that sale."

Duffy leaned over. He put his arms around her. She held on to him for dear life. "Promise."

"I promise you'll be on the rostrum." As he held her close, he whispered very softly and very lovingly, "And in the Chinese bed."

Prince Alexander Vasilyevich had not touched his food. He sat in a private room at Pleskov's restaurant listening to the man across the table. At first, he despised merely the sounds that Trofim Osipovich made while he was eating. Then, he hated the words as well.

"Therefore, Your Highness, it will cost more." Trofim's mouth was filled with food. He did not hesitate to look directly into the Prince's eyes as he raised the price.

Sandro had met Trofim across a card table in Moscow. The man was a superb player and bragged of his connections with moujiks on all levels of society. Each time they gambled together, Trofim won.

"How much more?"

Trofim cut a thick slice of meat and shrugged. "Does it really matter?" He continued speaking as he forced meat into his mouth. "I tell you, Prince, the times are not only revolutionary, they are inflationary! Every day everything costs more." He looked up with a challenge in his eyes. "Double."

"You have the papers?"

"Mmmm," Trofim muttered. As he opened his mouth to speak, a piece of meat fell onto the table. "Right here," he said, patting his breast pocket. He picked up the meat from the cloth and put it back into his mouth. "Even the boat to Copenhagen will cost more. The captain had not expected to leave tomorrow morning."

"Tonight!" Sandro whispered. "I told you it must be tonight!"

He shook his head. "Oh, my. Then it will surely cost more."

"I told you I must get my family out quickly! With the Romanovs imprisoned at Tsarskoye Selo, it will not be long before the Bolsheviks turn their guns on the rest of us."

Trofim pointed a forkful of meat at Sandro. "The rest of you," he corrected. "Which is why a few diamonds more or less will not matter." He began to laugh.

Sandro rode quickly through the snowy streets, terrified he would be stopped by drunken soldiers. He ran into the house and locked the door. Yekaterina Lvovna was pacing nervously. She turned quickly to him. "It's done!" he gasped, trying to catch his breath. "I have the papers, the tickets, the money. Everything."

She began to cry. "I don't want to leave. I don't want to leave my children."

He put his arms around her. "Katya, darling Katya. God wants us to protect Sonya. Otherwise why was she alone spared from the sickness?"

"Even if the others are dead, they are still my children."

"And what of Sonya? She is all we have left. We must protect her." He looked directly into her eyes. "Our beloved cousin has given us the most precious gift of all—escape. When she handed me the jewels there were tears in her eyes. 'Take them, Sandro,' she said. 'Take them and leave Russia. Find a new home for little Sonya!' It is a gift only a Czarina can give. The gift of life."

Yekaterina Lvovna nodded reluctantly. "I have been thinking all day of those small graves. If only I knew there would be someone to bring flowers."

Sandro took a deep breath. He reached into his pocket. "We must think only of the future," he said, his voice quavering. "We can no longer even think of ourselves as Russians." His eyes filled with tears. He held out the papers. "Here are our new identities." She sat at the table and began to sob. He sat next to her. "I am no longer Prince Alexander Vasilyevich and you are no longer Princess Yekaterina Lvovna. We are Mr. and Mrs. Samuel Corbett. Samuel and Margaret Corbett," he said slowly.

Katya put a hand to her breast and shook her head. "Samuel and Margaret Corbett," she whispered. Then she turned to him. "And what is Sonya's name to be?"

He looked down at the papers. "Natalie."

Charles Wyndham's office was a baronial room with leaded glass windows, walnut paneling, and a huge white marble fireplace. The floor was covered with Oriental carpets. The walls were covered with photographs of record-breaking sales. And, at nine that morning, the mahogany desk was covered with Delphina's outstretched legs. They were prominently visible through the slit in her black beaded gown.

At fifty, Delphina's straight black hair was cut in blunt bangs that gave her the appearance of an ageless Egyptian priestess. She maintained a flawless, slender body with plump breasts that contradicted Newton. That was what pleased Delphina most about herself, everything was a contradiction.

Although her title was Executive Assistant, Delphina's real title was Princess Delphina Orestiana Marazarchios del Grasso. Her outstanding qualifications for both, as she often said, were that she neither typed nor wore underwear. But what Charles valued most was Delphina's record for having slept on every yacht registered in Monte Carlo since 1940.

She looked up as he entered. "My God, Zhukov was a lousy lay."

He closed the door quickly. "What else did you find out?"

"He told me I have a pimple on my ass. Darling, what am I to do?"

Charles kissed the tip of her nose. He was impatient. "Tell me what he said."

"He said, 'Your breasts are like . . .'"

"Delphina!"

She leaned forward. "Of course there was an inventory. When the Bolsheviks took over the workshop in St. Petersburg they also stole Fabergé's records." She raised an eyebrow. "Of course, it must have taken them a while to find someone who could read. But they know exactly what is missing."

"And?"

"And, my puppy chicken, we are indeed on the Most Wanted List."

"Then Gregory was right!" he said jubilantly.

Delphina reached into her bosom. She withdrew a piece of paper and unfolded it. "The emerald necklace was for her birthday. The black diamond bracelet was for their anniversary," she continued. "And, I presume, the ruby ring was for Tuesday."

"Do you know what this means?"

"Yes. Alexandra must have been fantastic in bed."

Charles put his arms around her. "It means, my darling Delphina, that I will have the sale of the decade!"

"You or your lady auctioneer?"

He stepped back. "It's my sale. Whatever comes out of her mouth I will have put there."

"I had no idea you were already that intimate."

"Don't you ever think of anything else?"

"Forgive me. I have something on my mind." She stood up, turned her back to him, and lifted her dress. "Look!" She pointed to an angry red spot on her white Meissen behind. He leaned over and kissed it.

Charles was sixteen and Delphina was the first princess he'd ever met. She was twenty-five, all Grecian mystery with her black tragic eyes and husky voice. Charles and his parents were down from London for the hunt at Lady Bannerman's.

He was seated next to her at dinner. Delphina was a devout vegetarian. She confided to Charles that she never ate anything with a face. The next morning, while the other guests had breakfast at the stables, Charles lost his virginity.

They remained the very best of friends, having decided never to be lovers again and risk the sweet memory of that morning. They were brother and sister, brother and brother, sister and sister. Delphina, after her fourth divorce, became Wyndham's goddess of grief: she circled the globe consoling widows and divorcées who were left major art collections.

"Is it still there?" she pouted, pointing to her buttock.

"Tell it you want to marry it. That's sure to make it go away."

Delphina lowered her dress. "Bastard."

He put his arms on her bare shoulders and spoke seriously. "I need you, Delphina. For the next few months, I need you here."

She pursed her lips petulantly. "What did the Romanovs ever do for me?"

Charles smiled. "Ask not what the Romanovs did for you, ask what you can do for the Romanovs."

"But, darling, you have no idea how wearing it is to indulge Zhukov's oral fantasies."

"Tell him you're a vegetarian." Charles sat down at his desk to compare Delphina's list with Gregory's inventory of the ninety-six lots.

The intercom buzzed. "It's Mr. Rosenko. He says it's urgent."

"Send him in."

Gregory was pale. "Charles, I have bad news." He glanced at Delphina.

"Go ahead," Charles said.

"He doesn't trust me," Delphina said. "Ever since the Revolution."

Gregory took a deep breath. "The Kremlin claims the pieces are forgeries."

"Like hell they are!"

"They say they have the originals. They've issued a formal statement."

Delphina was her own Greek chorus. "They want to frighten away the competition and pick them up cheap."

Charles yelled, "Well, goddamn it, I'm not going to let that happen!"

"Of course you're not, darling."

"You bet I'm not!" he repeated. "If they want those pieces, they're going to have to pay for them!"

"The problem is," Gregory said, "we can't offer a credible story as to where they came from. To say nothing of having to justify holding the sale in Whats-its-name Falls."

"You let me worry about that. I've already begun turning that to our advantage. But before I see the kids on Wall Street, I need some ammunition. I need figures."

Gregory handed Charles a printout. "I had the computer take all the basic data on Fabergé prices and track lots that came on the block more than once. Then, following the increase from sale to sale, I took into account inflationary levels at the time as well as the relative position of the dollar. I converted the increases into compatible percentages and can now project prices in terms of today's market."

Delphina groaned. "Tell me, tovarich, what percentage did you allocate for blood?"

"Princess," he said, rolling his eyes, "we are talking business."

"We are talking lost treasure. A dead queen. The last Czarina. The end of a dynasty."

"A little bit of everything to help push the prices up," Charles said. He took the printout and tossed it aside. "Here's what I really want to know." Charles began to pace the room. A runner stretching his muscles. "First, who owes us money? Aside from the dealers. I'm interested in the museums, the Metropolitan particularly. It's time to call in some chips. I want help in authenticating our little pot of gold. I want the names of those

collectors who've spent over twenty-five thousand dollars on
Russian Art over the past twelve months. Then, I want the dates
of every major auction to be held in the next six months, here
and abroad. God knows, we don't need a conflict in dates. I want
you to check with Cohen and Schroder and run a projection on
what's likely to happen to money markets after the next OPEC
meeting. Be sure to find out if there's anything in the Senate on
treaties with the Soviets, arms allocations, grain sales, whatever.
I want to know about anything that's likely to cause negative or
positive response to the Soviet Union. Are there any major
Russian Art exhibits, any publications, or cultural exchanges? I
want to know who's writing books on Russia and wants publicity.
Then figure out what the insurance will run us for, say, thirty
days. Match your costs against the projected sales. Check with
Publicity and get a budget from them. I want to be certain we
come out of this very deep in the black."

Delphina sighed. "Whatever happened to art for art's sake?"

"Inflation is what happened," Charles said. "As Cohen and
Schroder keep telling me, the only overhead Michelangelo had
to worry about was the ceiling."

Charles stood up. He pushed the padded brown leather swivel
chair away from the burled walnut conference table. He walked
across the royal-blue, triple-thick carpeting to the window on the
hundredth floor of the North Tower of New York's World Trade
Center.

Brian Hampshire was still reading the Gemological Institute's
report. "Mmm."

"Interesting." That was all Roger Danning would say. Interesting. The war whoop of the mutual fund investor.

Jacob Benson knocked his pipe on a crystal ashtray. "Very
interesting." The dynamic banker. The senior member of the
group, at fifty, he had most likely been fifty since his first day in
kindergarten.

"Are you really going to let her do it?" Roger asked. "Sounds like one helluva pushy broad."

Charles turned from the window. "You've missed the point, Roger." Typical of mutual funds. "I *need* her to do it. I fought her boyfriend the banker to make certain she's part of the deal. It's not that she needs us, we need her!"

"It's a pretty tall tale," Roger said. "Millions in jewels hidden by an old lady who wore them only on Sundays."

"Right! I wouldn't have the nerve to tell a story like that if I were drunk! Our only hope," Charles said, "is having it come from the horse's mouth. No one would ever believe me, that's for sure. But if we force them up to that quaint little town, pack them into that charming old barn, seduce them with a beautiful lady auctioneer who's got new-mown hay in her voice . . ." He opened his palms to the heavens. "Who would dare make all that up? It's too corny. It must be true!"

"There's still the problem of provenance," Jacob said, as he had many times about some of his closest friends.

Charles shook his head in exasperation. "Jacob, the way it's been set up, we don't need a provenance. We *are* the provenance!"

Brian Hampshire was the boy wonder who worked Wall Street into his art investment schemes. It was Brian's contact-lensed eye that guided the Simpson Soup collection of tureens, and toy banks for Hudson Savings. It was also Charles' credit that allowed him to do so. He finished reading the report, stood up to stretch. "I read about a pair of diamond earrings that sold for six point six million." Brian shook his head. "Can you imagine your wife losing one of those?"

"There's no comparison," Charles said. "I'm not talking Oklahoma crude. I'm talking history. Romance. Tragedy."

Roger raised an eyebrow. "What broker isn't?"

"I'm talking the coup of the century! This is the goddamnedest thing to hit the auction block in years! The lost treasure of the last of the Romanovs!"

"Hardly the last of them," Jacob said. "All you have to do is order Russian dressing on your salad and someone's bound to claim it belongs to dear Uncle Nicky."

"What bothers me," Roger said, "is that the Kremlin hasn't asked for the pieces to be returned."

"On what basis?" Charles asked. "How can they prove the old lady didn't get them fair and square? God knows, she could have bought them fifty years ago from any waiter on Delancey Street."

"I've got a couple of clients who should be interested," Brian said. "They've all seen how tangibles have outpaced paper. Today's art market is built on inflation. People panic and buy antiques. Even Roger's father isn't keeping profits in the mutual funds that bear his name."

"My father is of the old school. He's scared," Roger explained. "He's got a cellar filled with dried food and barrels of water. He's got gold coins and silver coins, currency from twenty countries. He's got a bag of diamonds and a bag of rubies." Roger shrugged. "Typical."

Jacob smiled. "He's right. You can't schlepp a big painting of icebergs across the border."

"I seem to remember a while back there was a lot of phony Fabergé coming out of Paraguay or Ecuador," Roger said. "One of those places without a decent Chinese restaurant."

"We guarantee they're real," Charles said.

Jacob smiled. "In what size type?" He turned to Roger. "The impression is that the house stands behind the authenticity of every piece. In fact, the house only stands behind that portion of the catalog description that's printed in boldface capital letters. CHAIR. FOUR LEGS."

"Jacob, you've been doing business with me for years," Charles said angrily. "Millions of dollars back and forth. No matter what size type. Even if it's printed on the men's room wall, we stand behind it."

"Assuming you're correct," Roger began, "and even if the pieces have been authenticated up the ass, there's still my father, sitting in his cellar with his dried banana flakes, rifle cocked, ready to shoot the first person who asks for something to eat. I don't see him recommending the purchase of Russian works of art."

"Damn it! The Romanovs weren't Communists!" Charles yelled. "It's probably the only thing they weren't guilty of. Surely your father knows about Malcolm Forbes and his Fabergé collection?"

Roger shrugged. "Malcolm rides in balloons. My father sits in cellars."

"You can count me in," Brian said.

Charles sat next to him. "I'm having lunch with Jonas today. We're planning a postsale exhibition to include pieces on loan from Forbes and Hillwood."

"Now that's the kind of PR I can sell my people. A nice boring retrospective to enhance the investment." Brian smiled. "You don't gather much moss, do you?"

"I can't afford to. You're only as good as your last world record."

"You really believe that 'world record' crap?" Roger asked. "Surely you realize something that sold for one hundred dollars in the twenties was worth far more than when it goes for a thousand dollars today."

Charles shrugged. "I know and you know, but who else is counting?"

Jacob banged his pipe on the ashtray. "I am. Charles, what is it you want?"

He stood up. "I'm pushing this sale through fast. I want it over and done with before the Russians, the Romanovs, or the rubes in Perry Falls know what hit them. That means my clients won't have the usual three to six months' lead time to put their money where their mouths are. I want to be able to extend credit so they can bid large and loud."

"How much?"

"However much," Charles said.

"When is the sale?"

"No later than the first week in October."

"That's too late for me," Brian said. "Both my clients end their fiscals on September thirtieth. They'll want to dump in September. Can you make it the twenty-ninth?"

Charles looked at his calendar. "Impossible. It's Rosh Hashanah. Can't hold a sale on a Jewish holiday. Not this one. We lose too many collectors." He smiled. "Besides, it has to be on a Saturday night."

Roger looked up. "Why Saturday night?"

He shrugged. "That's when the lady sells."

Jacob sat back. "You really think she can pull it off?"

Charles smiled. "Wait till you see her! She's a combination of Delilah and Barnum. She's got an irresistible down-home quality. But classy. Very classy. You'll love her. I guarantee it. She's going to have everyone eating right out of her hand!"

Jacob looked at Roger. Roger looked at Brian. Brian raised an eyebrow and said, "She must have been one helluva lay!"

Emmett and Chip were unloading the truck while Rita sat on a folding chair in the shade entering each item on her inventory. Desperately trying to keep herself occupied, Duffy stayed in the barn examining the andirons and cake plates as they were brought in. "Somebody say there was a four-quart bean pot?" Duffy called out.

"I dropped it," Chip admitted. "Now we got a five-piece four-quart bean pot."

Emmett grunted as he carried in a blanket chest. "Shit. I wanted that."

Chip shrugged as he walked outside to bring in another load. "Well, you still got the quilt."

"What quilt?" Duffy asked.

"Real beauty. Double wedding ring all in reds and blues."

"You can't have it," she said. "You may be leaving, but I'm not. I promised Louise and Ned I'd put one up on Saturday night."

Emmett sighed. "It's on the porch."

Rita came in out of the hot afternoon and handed the inventory to Duffy. "I'd be lying if I said I'd miss this part."

"Well, I'll still miss you." Duffy smiled. "Complaints and all."

"You do understand why we want to go?" Rita embraced her. "What are you going to do without us?"

Duffy pulled back. "I didn't mean to give you such a swelled head."

"You know what I mean. You can hire plenty of people for the barn. But you can't hire a family. You're going to be alone."

She shrugged. "It comes with the territory."

"Why the hell don't you marry Ben?"

"And make everything boy-girl, boy-girl?" Duffy shook her head. "No. I am who I want to be. I'm doing what I want to do. I don't know too many people who can say that. I am just coming into my prime." She fought to hold back the tears. "I'm on the brink. On the verge."

To keep calm, Lorraine made her favorite dish for lunch— Quiche Lorraine. She brought a tray into the barn and everyone sat down. Chip poured glasses of mulled cider. No one spoke. They sat like four strangers in an airport coffee shop. Lorraine was nervous as she smiled and said, "You know, I'm really going to miss good times like this." She kicked Chip.

He nodded and took a deep breath. "We've got something to tell you."

"We're gonna buy the Oak Tree Restaurant!" Lorraine announced.

"That dump?" Rita asked.

"It won't be a dump when we get through with it."

Duffy reached out and touched Chip's arm. "But you don't have the money yet."

"I'm not worried. Wyndham's will get us our money."

Duffy withdrew her hand. "Sure."

Lorraine shrugged. "It's just a matter of time."

"If it's what you want," Emmett said.

Chip smiled. "This'll knock your socks off. We're gonna rename it, the Nickel Man Café."

Duffy slammed her fist on the table. "Like hell!"

"You can't do that!" Emmett said angrily. "I'm calling my shop the Nickel Man."

"Oh, no you're not!" Duffy said.

"You know how much publicity Wyndham's is going to bring the barn?" Chip asked. "Why should we throw that away?"

"You two really take the cake," Duffy said. "You can't wait to get the hell away from here. You keep saying how much you hate it, but you sure don't mind cashing in on it."

"Listen, Duffy," Emmett said angrily, "we each own one-third of the barn and that contract is with the barn."

"That contract is with the Nickel Man Barn comma Duffy Patterson comma Auctioneer period. I don't think you want me to challenge in court that the contract calls for my personal services, which I just happen to be performing under the roof of the Nickel Man Barn this week but could certainly perform equally well under a tent in the drive-in next week."

There was a long silence. Emmett spoke softly. "We might not like the barn, but we worked as hard for it as you did."

Duffy nodded. "I know."

Emmett took a deep breath. "We all want out as soon as we

get our money. We had a meeting, the four of us. We decided, because you're alone, because you're not married, and because you have no one to take care of you, we decided to give you our share in the house and the barn."

Duffy had never felt so alone, so unmarried, so without anyone to take care of her. Was that the way everyone saw her? Was she so pitiful a figure they were giving her the house and barn as compensation?

"All we want is our share of the money from the sale," Chip said.

"I think it's the right thing for us to do," Lorraine added. "Considering."

Duffy's eyes filled with tears. "I can't accept."

"Of course you can," Lorraine argued. "We all want you to have it. Don't worry. It's not worth that much."

"It *is* worth that much," Duffy insisted. "It's worth a helluva lot!"

"The point is," Emmett said, "we want to go without feeling bad about leaving you."

Duffy smiled as the tears continued to fall. "Well, I'm afraid you're just going to have to feel bad. The barn is worth money. I'll buy out your shares."

"We don't want you to do that," Emmett said.

"Well, I want to. Otherwise, I'd be cheating you. I would be cheating you all because the Nickel Man is worth real big money." She paused. "But there is one thing you do have to promise me."

"What?"

Duffy sat straight back in her seat. "You find other names. I don't want the Nickel Man used on anything but the barn."

Emmett began to protest, but Rita nudged him. Chip nodded his agreement. For a long while there was nothing for anyone to say.

"Nobody's eaten a thing!" Lorraine said, pointing to the tray. "I got enough here to feed an army."

"Looks like you just got your army," Rita said ominously.

Duffy turned quickly to the door. It was Ben. And three state troopers. "You'll never take me alive," she called to them.

The troopers smiled at one another. "Same old Duffy," Ralph said. Ralph, Mark, and Matthew were high-school friends. How could they look that old? she thought. It must be the uniforms.

"Ben." She spoke his name as though it had been years since she'd seen him, too.

He nodded and reached into his jacket for an envelope. "I have the court order."

Duffy had been expecting it. She smiled. "I hope you're getting those wholesale by now. You could save a lot of money." Ben just stared at her. Why couldn't he say hello? She led the way and everyone followed. "I got it all set aside," Duffy said, unlocking the door. They entered the storeroom as though it were an ancient tomb. The furniture from Miss Natalie's house was piled in the corner.

Ralph took out a penknife. He smiled sheepishly as he put his hand on a chair. "I've never done anything like this before. It's like killing furniture." He slashed across the upholstered back. Everyone was silent as he reached in and grabbed at handfuls of yellow batting. "We got to be certain she didn't hide anything else."

"You know, I could have sold that chair," Duffy said. "It's worth money."

Ben spoke angrily. "You said it was junk."

"It is junk. But now it has a pedigree." She waved her arm as though making an announcement from the center ring. "The last of the mysterious Miss Natalie!" Mark and Matthew began hammering apart an oak table. "It has a history. That's why it's valuable."

"Is that the gospel according to St. Wyndham's?"

"What's that supposed to mean?"

"It means I can remember when you sold a chair just because it was a good place to sit down."

Duffy smiled. "Ah, callow youth!"

"I can even remember nights in Mario's parking lot."

"Oh, was that you I was with?"

"Yes. I was the one without the Rolls-Royce!"

She spoke defensively. "The only thing I've got going with Charles Wyndham is one helluva good business deal."

"Seems that's the only thing you've got going with me, too."

"I thought I had more." She spoke softly. "I was looking for you on Saturday, Ben." She reached out and touched his arm. "I missed you."

He looked at her lovingly for the first time. "I missed you, too."

Duffy sighed with relief. "What about this Saturday?"

"What about this Friday?"

"Friday?"

"Any night but Saturday. Or every night including Saturday."

She stepped back from him. "The whole world is changing so fast. Can't we at least stay as we were?"

The breaking apart and splitting of wood continued. "Nothing stays the way it was. People change. They need to change. I need a different kind of life with you."

"No more birthday cakes?"

"Only on real birthdays." They stared at one another. The hammering grew louder. They watched as the furniture was ripped and slashed and tossed aside. "Every time she came into the bank," Ben said, "I felt sorry for her. Nice day, Miss Natalie. Looks like rain, Miss Natalie. Can I give you a lift, Miss Natalie? Christ, she must have been laughing at me!"

Ralph called out, "What the hell is this?" He handed Ben a

newspaper clipping. It was over thirty years old. "I found it in back of a drawer."

The headline read BANKER'S SON OPENS NEW BANK. The picture showed five-year-old Ben cutting the tape as his mother and father looked on proudly.

Charles and Delphina walked quickly up the carpeted staircase that led to the Grill Room of the Four Seasons. The air was filled with ripe pronunciations of *option, advance, alternate selection,* and *reprint* that the literary lunch scene devoured far more voraciously than their pallid Perriers and grilled fish.

Oliver, the maître d', led them quickly away from the people who merely made money, through the long corridor with its enormous Picasso tapestry to the Pool Room where people actually had money. "Mr. Longley is waiting."

Jonas Longley was a slight man who looked as though he bought his clothes at the Harry Truman Memorial Haberdashery. Director of the prestigious Metropolitan, Jonas wore his white hair in a crew cut, his tie in a perennial bow, and looked askance at the world through his flesh-colored glasses. Everyone trusted Jonas: It was his image as Mr. Middle America. Even more, his refusal to alter his appearance despite radical changes in fashion endeared him to the Metropolitan's conservative board of trustees.

"They're real," he said, before kissing Delphina and shaking Charles' hand. "That's what you wanted to hear. Now you can enjoy your lunch. I had Oliver decant a Petrus '49."

"Darling," Delphina beamed, "however did you know the year I was born?"

Jonas waved a sheaf of papers. "My staff had tests made. Same as we do on a new mummy. Thermoluminescence dosimetry. Neutron activation autoradiography. X-ray fluorescence spectrometry." He realized no one was impressed. "Well, you're right. It's all a lot of crap." He looked at Delphina. "Pardon my French. But all those tests prove is how good the equipment salesmen are."

"Jonas, I need all the back-up I can get," Charles said, taking the papers.

"Used to be somebody sold you a typewriter. Now it's a word processing machine. Don't worry. They're not copies. I can see that with the eyes the good Lord gave me. That's all the equipment I need." He looked at Delphina. "No pun intended."

"I have no provenance," Charles continued, "and the Russians claim they're copies."

"So you want me to put my ass," he looked at Delphina, "excuse me, on the line?"

"No," Charles smiled. "I want you to put it up in lights."

Jonas reached for the wine. "Guess I needn't feel guilty for ordering the Petrus." Oliver raced to the decanter and began pouring. No one spoke. They raised their glasses in a silent toast. Everyone took a respectful sip.

Charles spoke quietly. "I need your help, Jonas."

"Used to be, in the days before art became big business, only people I had to worry about were the dealers. All they wanted me to do was buy a picture. Then they could double their prices and tell their clients how well hung the artist was." He looked at Delphina. "Nothing crude intended."

"You've got three Imperial Eggs gathering dust in a Russian Art Department that isn't going anywhere," Charles said.

Jonas continued as though he hadn't heard. "Museum business used to be a nice business. Take from the rich and give to the poor. Nobody cared so much what things cost. It was a millionaire's market. Then the IRS set up that Art Advisory Panel in '68. Now everybody knows the price of everything but the value of nothing."

"I want you to get the Forbes eggs on loan. And the ones from Hillwood. After the sale, we'll exhibit them with ours. All the

Imperial Eggs we can get our hands on. A tickets-only retrospective. It'll give the Kremlin collection a run for its money. My staff will organize it for you. All you have to do is act as advisor. We pick up the tab."

"You know," Jonas began with a smile, "these days everybody wants free advice. You wouldn't believe how many cab drivers call me up. They have some money put aside. Is there more growth in Manet or Monet?" He sighed. "Morgan. Whitney. Mellon. They never had to ask."

Charles knew Jonas was listening. "We're going to set record prices. The eggs you bought for next to nothing will go sky high."

"Naturally." Jonas looked at him for the first time. "That's what your business is all about. Inflating prices and making it impossible for people who bought cheap not to sell."

"How wicked you are," Delphina said.

"I expect you'll want to sell," Charles clarified.

Jonas smiled. "And I expect you want to sell them for me. That way I can pay off my bill, giving your accountants a black-letter day."

Charles shook his head. "No. We're happy to wait until your funding comes through." He smiled. "We're charging you very comfortable interest rates."

"Then, as the farmer's wife said to the Sears catalog, 'Whatever will I do with my egg money?'"

"Hold on to it. Until the Galloway sale."

"Galloway?" Jonas leaned forward. "Galloway is selling?"

"Shhh." Delphina put a finger to his lips. "They've separated quietly. He needs money for the settlement."

"What's he selling?" Jonas asked eagerly. "Not the Matisses?"

Charles smiled. "All four of them."

Jonas sat back. He swirled the purple wine in his glass and brought it to his nose. "In my experience most fakes arrive on the scene armed with an impeccable provenance." He tasted the wine and then licked his lips. He pointed to the crystal decanter. "But you don't need a label to know a '49 Petrus."

Charles raised his glass in a toast. "Not as long as you're there, Jonas, to tell us."

Jonas shook his head in amazement. "All four Matisses? That's one helluva settlement. Christ! He must have been caught fucking her mother!"

Within the hour Charles and Delphina were in front of Lutèce. They walked down the steps and entered the converted brownstone. Instead of a smile, Marcel greeted Charles with a helpless shrug.

"Monsieur, you put me in a very difficult position."

"Simply turn your back. I know where he sits."

"But he comes here to be alone," Marcel pleaded.

Charles followed Delphina through the small room that led to the "garden," a pink room with trellised walls and wicker chairs.

Serge Coussac sat alone at a table set for one. Five days a week he left his shop on Second Avenue and walked around the corner for the only civilized hour in his work day. From the moment he entered, he spoke only French, read great French literature, and ate the finest of French cuisine.

Coussac's father had worked in Fabergé's London shop from 1904 until it closed in 1915. The family moved to New York before World War II and opened Coussac et Fils, an international landmark for Fabergé works of art.

A man in his late seventies, over six feet tall, very thin, completely bald and with enormous features, Coussac wore a royal-blue velvet blazer, pale blue shirt and matching tie. As Charles and Delphina walked toward his table, he continued reading a leather-bound volume from A la Recherche du Temps Perdu. As though he had seen them approach with a third eye, Coussac looked up between bites of Foie Gras en Brioche and pronounced coolly, "They are fake."

"Because the Kremlin says so?" Charles asked.

"Because Coussac says so."

"You could be wrong, darling," Delphina said.

Without looking up, Coussac said, "No. I am never wrong." He put down his knife and fork, and snapped his fingers for the waiter. "How much less trying it would have been if you had merely forged a provenance. There's only one thing more boring than a dishonest auctioneer. And that's an honest one."

Charles and Delphina each grabbed a chair and sat down. The waiter asked, "Would the Princess and Monsieur like to order?"

"No," Coussac answered. "They would not."

"Jonas is mounting an Imperial Egg retrospective."

Coussac sipped his champagne without offering them any. "All the king's horses and all the king's men can't put the Romanovs together again."

Delphina leaned across the table. "These pieces are brand new to the market, Serge. They're not the same ones you've been selling over and over."

"So my clients tell me. I've had half a dozen frantic calls. Someone in your publicity pound has been working overtime."

Charles smiled. "Every piece has been documented very carefully. They check out. I'll have Gregory send you a copy of the report."

"Collectors buy from me because I am Coussac. They do not buy from me because I have a report to show them. I have only to show them my face."

"I'm trying to prove to you that the pieces are genuine!"

"So the Kremlin is wrong?" he asked wearily. "And Coussac is wrong? Only the lady auctioneer is right. We are all to pack picnics and drive to the village barn like village idiots."

"Serge, I'll be happy to send a car for you . . ."

"Do not dare to send a car for me. Coussac is not your puppet." He paused to make certain they understood. "I have my own car."

Charles glanced at Delphina. "Then you'll be there?"

"Of course, I will be there."

"But, darling," Delphina teased, "I thought you said they were fake."

Coussac nodded. "They are fake. But I have sold fakes before." He turned back to his book. "I am Coussac."

Father Kyril sat in a corner of the Russian Tea Room at a large round table covered with plates of food. His blue eyes reflected the glisten of brass samovars and golden tinsel. A black robe known as a *rysa* swathed his ample frame, and the puffy white beard that peeked out from under his veiled black hat gave him the appearance of Santa Claus on his way to a funeral. He smiled as Charles and Delphina approached the table. "I had begun to lose faith."

Charles smiled. "We're terribly sorry to keep you waiting. We were held up by the crosstown traffic."

Father Kyril nodded. "Come. Sit. I have taken the liberty of ordering the *zakuska* for us. Waiter! Bring another bottle!"

Delphina took a deep breath as she stared at the endless array of hors d'oeuvres. It was their third restaurant within an hour. "Father Kyril," she began, "we must discuss . . ."

"Not until you have tasted the *kholodetz*," he said, passing her a plate of jellied calves feet.

Charles rolled his eyes. "Father Kyril, I must ask you . . ."

Heaping pieces of herring onto a plate, he shook his head. "The answer is No! I will not do a commercial for Wyndham's." Father Kyril picked up the chilled bottle of vodka and filled their glasses. "I shall not tell a single soul about the treasure."

"But why?" Delphina asked.

"Because I want it!" he whispered. Without blinking his piercing eyes, he raised the glass and drank it dry in a single gulp. Then he sighed deeply and sat back. "It all belongs to the church anyway. Here," he said, passing a plate to Delphina, "the herring is superb."

She nodded and gave the plate to Charles. "Your congregation will find out about it sooner or later."

Father Kyril nodded sadly. "A problem in a country where the church is no longer the media. You know, I have always wondered why modern communications courses give so little credit to the clergy." He smiled. "After all, the six-o'clock news originated in church." He poured another glass of vodka. "We were the original anchor men, were we not?"

"I understand your wanting the icon," Delphina began.

"The icon of St. Princess Alexandra! How I have longed to hold it!" He paused for a moment. "The property of the church is not the property of the state!" He banged his fist on the table. "When Nicholas was head of the church, we were known as the 'eyes of the Czar.' That's why we must hold on to everything. To keep the vision alive." He pointed an accusing finger at Charles. "We are the second-largest body of organized Christians in the world. The Party claims some fourteen million members. But fifty million Russians attend church." Father Kyril poured another drink without interrupting his sermon. "Did you know the word for peasant is *krestyanin?* The word for Christian is *khristiyanin.* You may ask a peasant if he is Orthodox, but to him it means 'Are you Russian?'"

Charles spoke softly. "There is great interest in the pieces. You must be prepared for what they will cost. The Imperial Eggs alone should bring millions."

"The Romanov treasure belongs to us! Not to millionaire collectors or to museums. The church must guard these last relics of Holy Mother Russia!" Father Kyril took another sip. "Do you know what the church is like in Russia today? It is crowded. There are no seats. Old women are pressed together. They kneel and kiss the ground. The air is thick with incense, with the smell of old peasants, and with the scent of cologne from the young. Everyone stands close together as though sharing a single skin, clothed only by icons and frescoes and faith."

Delphina, for want of something to do, reached for the herring and pushed some onto Charles' plate. "But, Father," she asked, trying to rouse him from his dream, "where will you get the money?"

"In Russia, there is only one place for beggars. You will not find them on fashionable streets such as Kalinin Prospekt or Karl Marx Boulevard. There is only one place for the poor to get money. You must beg at the door of the church!"

It was nearly sunset and there were long shadows falling across Indian Creek Road. Duffy turned her car into the driveway. She sat staring at the dilapidated white frame house. It might have belonged to anyone. There were dozens of white frame houses throughout the county.

The door opened easily. No hostile hinges. No ominous squeaks. Whatever Duffy had expected to happen the moment she set foot inside did not happen. No sudden realizations. No clues from the past. Nothing but empty, unyielding silence.

The troopers had been there. Door frames, window seats and banisters had been removed in an effort to find more of the treasure. She stood in the dingy foyer, the paper peeling off the walls, water stains on the ceiling, torn linoleum on the floor. Amid the remnants of Miss Natalie's life, Duffy whispered, "I'm sorry."

The enamel on the refrigerator was chipped and yellowed. There were dark sullen stains in the sink. The empty cabinets were open. The empty drawers were open. Even the empty oven was open.

"I am very sorry," Duffy said.

She walked upstairs, through empty rooms, glancing into empty closets. At every window she stopped, hoping to find some lovely view, something that might have given Miss Natalie respite from the dreariness within. But it was useless.

Duffy sat at the top of the stairs, trying to console herself. She imagined the old woman alone, opening the velvet boxes and covering herself with necklaces and bracelets and rings. What if Miss Natalie hadn't known about the things in the trunk? Surely if she had, she would have sold them. She would have lived a better life. But if she had lived a better life, Duffy would not be sitting on the steps. On the brink. On the verge.

"My God, I am sorry. So very sorry," Duffy said. "I really am."

She walked down the stairs and toward the front door. She didn't want to look back or even look around. She was as desperate to leave as she had been to come. The doorknob. The lock. The key. The sound of the latch closing. The feel of the first evening breeze. The moon rising in a pink sky.

Duffy paused, and with her back to the house, took a deep breath. She said, "Thank you."

Behind the red brick walls of the sixty-five-acre fortress known as the Kremlin, the curator of the Kremlin Museum stood in front of Display Case No. 24: Works by the Fabergé Company. He stared at the Imperial Easter Egg given to Alexandra Feodorovna in 1904. His eyes fixed on the gold walls of the exquisitely crafted miniature Kremlin.

Gold walls within red brick walls was a meaningful image for Dmitri Leonidovich Kolmenkin. It was symbolic not only of the country he loved, but also of the life he lived. Walls within walls to keep the truth from escaping. Protection on one side, lies on the other.

Kolmenkin's outer walls revealed a man in his early fifties, tall, square-shouldered, muscular. His hair was graying, thick, cut short. He had deep creases in his face, originally from laughter but more recently from sorrow.

Staring into Display Case No. 24, he wondered whose lies had brought a Czar's treasure to a small town in the State of New York. How had ninety-six pieces traveled from Holy Mother Russia across borders of space and time? Why had they surfaced at this precise moment in his life? Of what master plan had Kolmenkin become part? Who was watching over him? Another fallen angel, no doubt. Ninety-six pieces. He would have to

[119]

move Nineteenth-Century Goldsmiths out of Display Case
No. 23.

"Dmitri!" The Minister of Culture smiled and came from
behind his desk. He embraced Kolmenkin. "You look splendid."
He patted him on the back. "I like your suit!"

Sergei was an old friend in addition to being his superior.
They had served in the army together, inseparable comrades
known as Minsk and Pinsk. Through the years, however, Pinsk
lost his hair, grew fat, and was forced to appear more satisfied
than he really was.

Kolmenkin opened his jacket to show the label. "Pierre
Cardin."

Sergei felt the fabric and nodded approvingly. "Did you hear
that *Pravda* has announced a contest for the best political joke?
The first prize is twenty years."

Kolmenkin laughed and sat down. He took out a package of
Dunhill cigarettes and offered one to Sergei. "How is Irina?"

"Since when do you smoke?" Sergei asked, taking a cigarette.
"In all the years I've known you . . ."

Kolmenkin shrugged. "Tell me, how is Irina?"

"Women! We have a *dacha* on the Baltic and she is unhappy
because it gets too cold. So, I get her a *dacha* on the Black Sea
and she complains it is too hot. Now she has decided we should
look for something in Zhukovski. She must think I am Lenin's
long-lost son!" He pointed a finger at Kolmenkin. "Why don't
you spend a weekend? You would give Irina something new to
be unhappy about."

Kolmenkin smiled. "Perhaps. To help an old friend." He
sighed. "I haven't even been back to Peredelkino. I've lost all
interest in being a *dachnik*."

"How are you really?" Sergei asked, with a directness that
startled Kolmenkin.

"I am very well." He smiled at the skepticism in his friend's eyes. "Really."

"It is . . . what? How long?"

"Nearly ten months."

"Is it any easier?"

Kolmenkin hesitated. Walls within walls. "The strange thing is, it gets more difficult. I tell myself I can't mourn Marya forever. But somehow it was easier in the very beginning. I find it difficult to accept this way of life as permanent."

"But it's not! You will remarry." Sergei continued over the objection of Kolmenkin's raised hand. "You cannot live without love. That is worse than being dead."

Kolmenkin exhaled a long puff of smoke. "Sergei," he began softly, "I am here to discuss something other than being the Merry Widower."

Sergei smiled. "I envy you."

"Shhh. Don't let Irina hear that."

"You can still make jokes. It is a sign of good character. That is the difference between us and the Germans."

"I thought the difference was we kept Poland."

"That is very clever. In the right circles. Sergei began to cough as he laughed. "You better stop smoking or you will sound like me."

"As long as I don't look like you."

Sergei shook his head and sighed. He opened a desk drawer and took out a box of Godiva chocolates. Kolmenkin refused politely as Sergei scooped up two at once. "Irina gave me these to help me stop smoking," he explained with his mouth full. "Now, every time I smoke I have a craving for chocolate and every time I have a piece of chocolate I need a cigarette."

It was the telephone call from Yelokhovskaya Cathedral that stopped their laughter. The call was from the Patriarch of the Russian Orthodox church.

"They can't be serious?" Kolmenkin asked as Sergei hung up the receiver.

"And why not? It is an old story with them. The state wants only your heart and your brain. The church wants designer jewelry as well."

"Those pieces belong in the museum."

"They belong anywhere but in the church. Or worse, with some stupid philanthropic capitalist who will exhibit them any time he can get an audience, like a pervert opening his raincoat." Sergei pounded the desk. "The blood of too many Russians has been spilled for some fool to make the Czar into King Tut!"

"Let me buy them."

"You *must* buy them! We have no choice." Sergei took another chocolate. His tone became businesslike. "You will go to New York immediately. Make arrangements to have Coussac bid for you. No one is to know the government is involved."

"But why? The pieces represent a national treasure."

Sergei slammed his fist on the desk. "They are a national disgrace!"

Kolmenkin sighed and offered him a cigarette. "They belong in the museum. They belong to the people. They are our history."

Sergei shook his head. "Dimochka," he said affectionately, "I am glad we are not dependent upon your political judgment for survival." He leaned forward. "The Supreme Soviet is in a phase of extreme conservatism. We have all been through enough. We are growing older and fear change. The only thing we have the strength to defend is the status quo. Unfortunately, our young people have been infected by the capitalist craze for nostalgia. For those who did not fight as we did, the Czarist regime has a certain romantic appeal. Bizarre, but true."

"And so you wish to bury the treasure again."

"No. I wish to break it up. Sell the stones. Invest the money in the future, not in the past."

Kolmenkin leaned forward. "You would destroy incomparable works of art?"

"Before they destroy us."

"Sergei, you are the Minister of Culture!"

"Yes. And I must decide what is culture and what is dangerous."

"And so you have invented fear of Fabergé?"

Sergei smiled. "No. The enemy is not Fabergé. As Tevye said, 'It's *tradition!*'"

As a member of the *nachalstvo*, the upper strata in Soviet society, Kolmenkin was entitled to a car and driver. But unless it was raining, he preferred to walk. That afternoon he felt like flying. Sergei had given him wings.

New York, he thought. The last time he had hated it. But this time, it would be perfect. Kolmenkin crossed onto Gorky Street, the wide boulevard known as "Broadvey." He passed the bright summer flowers being sold on the corner. He smiled. Give my regards to Broadvey!

Kolmenkin was stopped by two women shoveling hot asphalt as they repaired the street. A third, driving a steamroller, shouted at him to wait. "You cannot go!" she yelled. He felt a familiar gnawing at the pit of his stomach, the fear that something terrible was about to happen, something over which he had no control. It was the Russian way of life. The feeling was known as the "salt-mine factor."

In addition to receiving bank credit and *dachas* on the Black Sea, the Moscow elite never had to stand on line. They were exempt from the frustrations of waiting for hours at GUM to buy blue jeans from Poland, umbrellas from Japan, or oranges from Algeria. Although he usually shopped in one of the unmarked stores reserved exclusively for the *nachalstvo*, on Tuesdays Kolmenkin stopped at Gastronom No. 1. The food shop, still known by its pre-Revolutionary name of Yeliseyevsky's, had maintained throughout the years its unique Victorian splendor. There were huge mirrors, arches, columns, and patterned ceilings under which those with enough money lined up to buy caviar, smoked meats and other luxury items.

"Comrade Director!" The old woman behind the counter waved as soon as she saw him. "I have it ready." She reached down and picked up a paper bag tied with a piece of twine. He nodded and handed her six passes to the Kremlin Museum. She smiled and stuffed them quickly into her pocket. "Better to have a hundred friends than a hundred rubles," she reminded him. As he signed the bill, she leaned over and whispered, "I put in some fresh raspberries, Comrade Director. I remember how much your wife likes them."

Kolmenkin looked up, startled. He hesitated, nodded, and then left without saying a word. His heart was pounding as he walked along the street. He had not told her Marya was dead. There was no reason to. At least, there was no reason before the raspberries. He felt like a thief. He had taken something he had no right to have. The raspberries became the salt-mine factor. His pace quickened. Before he realized what he was doing, he found himself running. He was out of breath by the time he reached the Sudonovski Baths.

The old building was a block long and three stories high. But unlike Yeliseyevsky's, its turn-of-the-century elegance was barely visible. Going to the baths was a time-honored ritual. Russians of all classes shared the need to steam and cleanse themselves. Kolmenkin hurried up the marble staircase, passing vast corroded mirrors. It seemed as though the paint peeled from the gilded moldings almost as fast as he walked beneath them.

He bought a ticket and gave it to the attendant. The bearded man in the old blue cap nodded and then looked to be certain

Kolmenkin was carrying a paper bag. The man knew there would be a liter of vodka in there for him. He smiled as he tore the ticket. He gave Kolmenkin a sheet, a towel, and the key to the same private room he had used for years.

Kolmenkin unlocked the door. The room was spare. A large locker, a bench, a square table in the corner. A single bulb overhead. The floor had raised wooden slats, except around the tub where the decorative old tiles showed through. He breathed a sigh of relief. He was alone. He was inside the innermost of his walls.

Kolmenkin undressed quickly. He spread his sheet across the bench and sat down, cradling his head in his arms. There was a knock at the door. Without turning around, he called out, "*Zanyato!* Occupied!"

He heard the knob turn. The door opened behind him. Then he heard the door being locked from the inside. A familiar hand on his shoulder. "Dmitri, what's wrong?" Kolmenkin looked up. "Dmitri, you've been crying."

Mikhail put his arms around Kolmenkin and kissed him.

It was four o'clock in the morning. He was fully dressed. His bag was packed. He had been sitting for hours in a chair at Marya's side of the bed, just as he had those many months while she was dying.

"Poor Dima," she would whisper to him. "The sickness makes me thin and ugly. How painful it must be for a man whose life is art and beauty."

"Mashinka," he would say, looking into her terror-filled eyes. "I am an expert at finding beauty. I have not lost sight of yours. You are as radiant as the first day we met."

Marya worked in the Art History section of the Lenin Library. It was she who had told Kolmenkin he would someday be curator at the Kremlin. Together, they visited every museum, restaging every exhibit as they talked endlessly. They had many

"Russian lunches," staying up all night, arguing until dawn about art and life.

It wasn't a marriage of passion but one of affection and respect. Kolmenkin needed to make love, however infrequently, in order to maintain the "moral stability" he knew was vital for his career. Marya tolerated the arrangement because of her admiration for him.

Homosexuality was illegal and carried a sentence of up to five years. It was considered a crime against the state because such acts were unknown among workers or peasants. Homosexuality was seen as a vice of the decadent pre-Revolutionary upper classes and was, therefore, a crime to be punished harshly.

Whatever else he considered himself, Kolmenkin knew he was not a criminal. To be involved sexually with a man could end not only his career but also his life. He was no longer able to live under the diplomatic immunity of marriage. Suddenly, his papers had been revoked. He was no longer guaranteed safe passage.

One of the dangers of being a *zhopoyob* was the fallout from his own lies. He hadn't told the woman at Yeliseyevsky's about Marya's death because Marya never knew he stopped there. The packages were always for Mikhail. Every Tuesday afternoon for the past two years, he had met the mathematics professor from Moscow State University. If one or the other couldn't make it, there were no phone calls. There were no phone calls ever. No letters. No gifts other than perishables. It was a relationship without mementos. Without evidence.

Kolmenkin was still sitting in the chair as light began to stream through the windows. The sun was strong and shone on the empty bed as though to remind him that Marya was gone. He wanted to give up the apartment on Gorky Street. Impossible. It might look suspicious. Someone with his secret must never look suspicious. The system had passed judgment on his crime against the state. He was sentenced to a three-room apartment on Gorky Street.

He stared at her pillow, suddenly bitter. Even Marya, her body mutilated and wasted, had found a way out. Her brother administered an overdose when the pain became too great. But what of his pain? Marya had found a way to die with dignity. He still had to find a way to live with dignity.

It was time to go. He picked up his suitcase and stopped to look at the bed. Everything had died with Marya. There was no one left to love Dmitri Leonidovich in spite of himself.

Duffy stood in the doorway to the barn, arms folded tight across her chest to keep from fidgeting. She wondered what Papa would have said. Not about the day (a bright shiny penny just waiting to be spent), or about her brothers (they're like good luck: never there when you need them), or even about Miss Natalie (most books have a surprise on the last page). She wondered, as her stomach floated nervously, what in the world Papa would have said about the van marked WYNDHAM'S that kept circling the barn like a white steel vulture.

"They still there?" Lorraine asked. She was doubly annoyed because her iced mint tea was getting watery and the white bread on the finger sandwiches had begun to curl.

"Still there," Duffy said, without taking her eyes from the van. "Coming around for number eight."

"What the hell are they doing that for?" Emmett mumbled. He paced along the viewing tables, picking up and putting down vases and goblets and bowls without even looking at them.

"I think it's creepy," Lorraine said. "You just don't drive around and around without introducing yourself and saying hello."

The van stopped short, as it had many times before. It paused a moment, growled as it shifted gears, and continued to circle its prey. Duffy couldn't see in through the tinted windows at the people who drove around and around without introducing themselves and saying hello.

Chip sat in a front-row bleacher seat as stiffly as a runaway father forced to attend his daughter's wedding. "City people."

Rita looked up from playing "this little piggy" with Louis Comfort. "City people?" she repeated, smiling. "What about country people? Look at us. Sitting here like chickens on a Sunday morning."

"Top of the ninth," Duffy called out.

Everyone turned as they heard a piece of crystal drop to the floor. Emmett shook his head. "Sorry."

Rita sighed. "I don't know what the hell we're so nervous about. It's what we all wanted."

"A dream come true." Lorraine sat close to Chip and put her arm through his.

"Game's over!" Duffy shouted. Her heart began to pound as the van came to a stop in front of the barn. The door swung open to reveal a young woman in designer jeans, a signature scarf tied around her frosted hair. She leaned her head to one side and rapped her knuckles coyly on the barn door.

"Knock, knock." She had a smile that could cause cancer in laboratory animals.

"Come on in. I'm Duffy Patterson."

"Nedda Ryan. We've all been dying to meet you."

"You have?"

Nedda's plastic face changed expression. Deep concern. "I've just got to have more space for cars. That tree is making my life a misery."

"That tree?"

Dismay. "Just my luck. It's your favorite tree in the whole world."

The brothers and their wives gathered around Duffy. They listened in amazement. "She wants to cut down the tree," Chip whispered.

Nedda showed them her initialed acrylic clipboard, on which she had a sketch of the area around the barn. Business. All business. "It's got to go."

They stared at the tree. It had begun, Duffy thought. This time the snake wasn't satisfied with just an apple.

"Bang, bang. You're dead." Duffy turned around. The man behind her spoke in a clipped British accent. Although his thumb and forefinger were pointed at her head, Duffy couldn't stop staring at his eyes: one was blue and one was brown and they were looking in different directions.

"Hello."

"I just killed you," he said, smiling. "All of you, in fact." He sighed and shrugged. "To say nothing of stealing the entire treasure." He shook her hand. "Roland Mackin. Head of Security."

Duffy smiled. "And when did you do all that?"

"Before you put the coffee on at six-thirty."

"You've been watching us?"

"For days."

"You've been spying on us for days?"

"Spying *for* you," he corrected.

"I haven't seen you around here," Emmett said.

"You weren't supposed to."

"Does Charles Wyndham know what you've been doing?" she asked threateningly.

"Like the ghost of Christmas Past. Look, I'm only trying to protect you. Once all the publicity starts this is going to be convention headquarters for every international jewel thief."

"My agreement with Charles says you people begin today."

"We are beginning today. But in order to begin today, I had to begin last week."

"I don't like things going on that I don't know about."

"I know just how you feel," Nedda said. "I missed Liz Smith yesterday." Back to business. "Now what about the tree?"

Duffy turned back to Roland. "You know, we haven't seen an international jewel thief around here in months."

"Down at the liquor store," Chip offered, "Fred's got these decals on the window with a picture of a police dog on them."

Roland nodded. "No doubt they terrorize the neighborhood."

"Hell, no," Emmett said. "Everyone knows Fred's brother in Elmira prints them up."

"I didn't know that," Chip said.

"All due respect to Joyce Kilmer," Nedda began, lowering her voice, "either the tree goes, or else I'll have to gravel over that field across the road."

"But we don't own that field."

"I know that."

"How do you know that?" Duffy stepped back in amazement. "You've been up here, too. You went to the courthouse!"

"Sometimes I think I've been to more courthouses than F. Lee Bailey." Her smile darkened. "According to the estimates I got in town, it's cheaper to yell 'Timber!' than it is to rent the field, cover it with gravel, take up the gravel, and most likely reseed the field for dear Farmer Brody."

"You already spoke to Brody?" Emmett asked.

Before Nedda could answer there was a low moan from the doorway, followed by an exuberant, "Well, this sure beats the bejesus out of Norman Rockwell!" Everyone turned to stare at Ashanti Basil-Edwin, an elegant black woman with dozens of gold beads attached to the corn rows into which her hair was intricately braided. Her high-gloss lips parted in a broad smile as she saw Duffy. "You're the beautiful lady auctioneer who found the priceless lost treasure of the doomed Romanovs in her ruby-red country barn!"

Duffy extended her hand. "That's not exactly what they wrote in the yearbook."

Ashanti smiled and held Duffy's hand. "I'm the trendy

illegitimate daughter of a Third World diplomat who supports her local hairdresser by churning out brilliant publicity schtick."

Nedda cleared her throat. "Ms. Patterson. Back to business. To tree or not to tree? That is the question."

"This story is writing itself," Ashanti said. "It was like sighting Brigadoon, as I drove down the road and came upon this old barn rising out of the mist."

"Like sighting what?" Duffy asked.

"Brigadoon. You know, the funky little village that comes to life once every hundred years."

"We have an auction here every Saturday night!" Duffy said defensively.

"That's it!" Ashanti said. "My lead: SATURDAY NIGHT AUCTION FEVER!"

"Miss Patterson," Nedda pleaded. "What about Mr. Tree?"

"Mr. Who?" Duffy asked quickly. "Oh."

Nedda sighed. "Perhaps we'd better move on to portable toilets."

Roland slapped his open palm against the wooden slats of the barn wall. "I can just hear the bullets whizzing by."

Luther Selwyn, a distinguished-looking black man in a dark blue suit, walked into the barn and smiled at Chip. "How do you do? I'm Mr. Selwyn."

"Hi," Chip said, shaking his hand. "I'm Chip Patterson. You looking for . . ." He nodded in Ashanti's direction.

"No, I'm your more basic black. I'm the Head Porter."

"I bet you know the real inside story," Chip said. "Emmett, c'mere. I want you to meet the janitor."

Emmett smiled and shook hands. "Nice to know you."

"Head Porter," he corrected. "I'm in charge of the men who show the lots being sold."

"But that's what we do!" Chip whooped. "Emmett and me got the same job you do!"

Emmett nodded. "I'll bet he doesn't drop things."

Chip shook his head. "He never lets me forget that cake plate."

"Could have gone to twenty bucks."

Luther smiled. "I once dropped a Ming temple figure."

"One of those dynasty things?" Chip asked. He began to laugh. "You hear that, Emmett? How much?"

"Thirty thousand."

"Thirty thousand dollars?"

Luther spoke proudly. "The company record."

"And they didn't fire you?"

"Fire me?" He was horrified. "What for?"

Nedda pointed to the old movie seats. "Of course, these will have to go."

"Why?" Duffy recalled how proud Papa was the day he bought them.

"I've already ordered folding chairs. For security reasons we need at least three aisles."

Roland nodded his approval and smiled. "We don't want too many bidders caught in the crossfire."

"God help us," Nedda said, staring at the floor, "I wonder if these boards will hold everyone."

Carlos Baxter, head of computer services, walked in a circle behind Nedda. He stomped his feet as though doing a rain dance. "Never mind the people. I'm not even sure it will hold the terminals I need."

"What kind of terminals?" Duffy asked.

Carlos danced his way toward the door, mumbling, "And where the hell are we going to put the phone cables?"

"Hey, Duffy," Chip shouted, "did they tell you about the slides?"

"What slides?"

"It's customary at important jewelry sales to use slides," Luther explained.

"Well, it's customary in my barn to hold up what you're selling," Duffy said.

"A nice big color slide shows the client what he's bidding on."

"I thought we were going to show them," Chip complained. "Emmett and me were going to have these new T-shirts printed up."

Luther raised his eyebrows and looked at Nedda. "I assumed this was to be formal."

"You mean tuxedos?" Duffy asked.

Nedda rolled her eyes. "At all important evening sales, the porters wear black tie."

"Tuxedos in the barn?" Emmett began laughing. "Hey, Rita," he called out, "I'll bet you'll have to wear a gown while you make the hot dogs."

"What hot dogs?" Nedda prepared for war.

Duffy felt suddenly helpless. Vandals were rummaging through her most personal possessions and she had only herself to blame. In desperation, she walked slowly toward the pulpit, up the steps, and then sat down as though her very presence there might bring some order.

Emmett ran over. "You gonna okay this formal dress crap?"

Rita shook her head. "Now they're complaining about no air-conditioning."

"Duffy," Lorraine whined. "I have to talk to you this minute."

"Me, too," Chip said. "I thought I was going to be up front."

Everyone was looking at Duffy, waiting for a pronouncement. Even the Wyndham's people stopped talking. All eyes were on her, which was why no one was looking at the door.

"Oh, Charles, you're so right! She is beautiful!" Delphina, swathed in purple silk, stood in the doorway. Hardly missing a beat, she walked toward Duffy. "An absolute original. Darling, he hasn't stopped talking about you and now I know why." Delphina held her arms outstretched to Duffy.

The absolute original stood up. Her heart was pounding. She

wanted so to be rescued. But she hadn't expected the cavalry to be wearing purple. Duffy walked down the steps, staring at Charles while Delphina embraced her.

"I am Princess Delphina Orestiana Marazarchios del Grasso. But enough about me. You must call me Delphina."

Charles folded his arms and leaned against the barn door. "Hi," he called out.

Duffy smiled for the first time. "Hi."

"I made finger sandwiches," Lorraine offered.

Delphina smiled. "How lovely. But I fear I am a culinary Dracula. I never eat before the sun sets. Besides, there is so much to be done. I must see that house!" She pointed out the back door. "That is the one, isn't it? The wreck in which the old woman died?"

"No," Duffy said, smiling. "That's our house. We live there."

"All of you?"

"All of us. Like the five dwarfs."

Delphina laughed and glanced at Charles. "She's clever, Charles. Be careful."

"Would you like to come in the house and freshen up?" Lorraine asked. "We got three bathrooms," she said proudly.

Delphina put a jeweled hand on Lorraine's shoulder. "Darling, if you are to be my friend," she advised, "you must learn never to apologize."

Duffy walked toward Charles. Their eyes locked as she came closer. She started to speak. He motioned No and led her out of the barn so they might be alone. "I want to put my arms around you," he said.

Duffy caught her breath. It was what she wanted most in the world to hear.

"I want to kiss you," he said. "I can't stop thinking about you. No matter what I'm doing or where I am. No matter who I'm with, you're there."

Duffy lowered her eyes. "Even when you're with a princess?"

Charles laughed. "Once upon a time, long, long ago, I made love to a princess. Once. Over twenty years ago. She's my friend now. She works for Wyndham's."

Duffy smiled. "I could use a friend."

He took her hand. "That's not what I want to be. Can you use a lover?"

With a burst of exuberance, Duffy hugged Charles. "I've been waiting for you all morning."

He held her close, opening his mouth as they kissed. "I'm sorry we were late," he said softly. "We had to stop off at the bank. It took more time than I . . ."

"The bank?"

He kissed her nose. "Mmmmm."

Duffy wasn't sure whether she'd just stepped on or off the merry-go-round. "What for?"

Charles held her face in his hands. "Nothing. Details. Duffy . . ."

She pulled back. "What details?"

He sighed. "Credit arrangements. Things like that. All very boring. It has nothing to do with you."

"Like those people you sent up here without telling me?"

"It didn't seem important."

"This is my part of the world, Charles. My barn. My Wyndham's. It's all important."

He reached out and touched her hair. "There are other things for you to be thinking about." He took hold of her shoulders. "Duffy, I want you to come to New York."

"Charles . . ."

"I want you at Wyndham's. You're too special to be hidden away. There's nothing for you here."

"Nothing? Don't you believe in life after Romanov?"

"Duffy," he said intently, "you're too good to be stuck in the middle of nowhere."

"Knock, knock," Nedda shouted from the doorway. "I'm supposed to call Farmer Brody back."

Duffy looked straight at Charles. She took a deep breath. "The tree stays."

It was three o'clock and the bank had just closed its doors. It was the time of day Ben liked best. The bank became his again. The depositors and debtors were gone. There were no more applications, interviews, or inquiries. It was the banker's time for catching up on mathematics rather than dealing with emotions. But for Ben, two and two equaled three. One and one were zero. There was no way he could avoid dealing with emotions.

Damn Duffy, he thought, for dragging him into the whole Miss Natalie circus. She was the one who let in the outside world. The smart money. The beautiful people. Wyndham's.

All he could think about was Charles' making love to Duffy. It was a kind of love she wouldn't understand: New York City love, where you love your butcher, you love the guy who hails a cab for you. You even love your enemies. What would happen to Duffy after Wyndham's left? She would never be the same and that meant he'd never be the same. If only there were a way to stop the sale.

Ben picked up the phone and dialed extension seven. Albert Blair had been at the bank for thirty years and always picked up when you needed him. "Hi, Al. Can you get me the mortgage file for the old Morgan place?"

"Sure. But it's going to take a few weeks."

"A few weeks?"

"It's part of that batch still out being microfilmed. We had a helluva time getting it for the court after Miss Natalie died."

"Who went through that file?"

"I did. I was trying to find some next of kin."

"And?"

"Nothing. All very tidy."

"What about her mortgage application? Some relative must have been named on it."

"No. Matter of fact, she never filled one out. When the Morgans died, their estate paid off the house. Left it to her."

Ben reached into the drawer and took out the clipping. "My father handled that. He handled all of her business." He shook his head, thinking how lonely she must have been to cut out a picture of his father.

"That's what I thought. But he didn't. It was someone I never heard of. Out of state."

Ben paused. "Someone from Louisiana?"

"How the hell did you find that out?"

"You know his name?"

"No. But I remember it was Shreveport."

"Thanks." He was ready to hang up and then asked, "Al, do we still have the old ledger cards?"

"Jesus. You don't want me to find Miss Natalie's?"

"Right now."

The ledger cards were used prior to the bank's converting to a computerized system in the sixties. They were filed in the basement as back-up for data stored on tape. Within an hour Ben had her cards on his desk.

The account was opened on March 7, 1939, with a deposit of ten dollars. Each week for the first year there was an additional deposit of three dollars. The weekly deposits increased to five dollars and by 1944 were up to ten. During that entire period there hadn't been one withdrawal. There was a large deposit, five thousand dollars, at the end of 1944. It must have been some kind of inheritance when the Morgans died. And then twenty thousand in 1945. Perhaps that was the final settlement. After that, she began to make periodic withdrawals. But there were no deposits again for almost a year. Not until June twenty-fifth.

His fingers ran down the columns looking for deposit dates. There was only one deposit each year. Always around the same day. June twenty-fifth. His birthday.

•　　•　　•

The house was too quiet for six-thirty at night. Usually, Lorraine and Chip would be in the kitchen, shouting at one another as she cooked and he set the table. Louis Comfort would be crying because he didn't want to be put down. Rita would be complaining to Emmett that she didn't have time for a bath before dinner. Usually, Duffy would not be wearing a dress. She stared at herself uneasily in the mirror.

Although Ashanti said she was riding a comet that would lead her to the stars, Duffy felt more as if she were hanging on for dear life. And her dear life, as they had all told her, in no uncertain terms, wasn't nearly as good as it could be. It wasn't air-conditioned. Nedda found it stifling. Its foundation wasn't strong enough for Carlos. It was far too insecure for Roland. How had she survived, Duffy wondered, all those years. All that afternoon.

"You're beautiful." Ben smiled. "You left the door open."

"It's a bad habit of mine."

"I should have knocked."

Duffy walked over and put her arms around him. "Oh, God, I'm so glad to see you." She kissed him. Unlike Charles, he was gentle, needing to be loved rather than to conquer. His masculinity never threatened Duffy even though he demanded so much more. She looked at his face. "What's wrong?" she asked.

Ben shook his head. "Nothing. Everything's fine. Couldn't be better."

Duffy nodded. "Same here." They hugged one another, aching to tell the truth. "I want you to stay. Lorraine invited them all for dinner. I didn't even know if you were still talking to me."

"I'm still talking to you." He kissed her again. "But I'm not going to stay."

She turned away and began brushing her hair. "Are we really

hicks, Ben? Is it that we're country people and they're city people?"

"You're the one who invited them into your life. All Lorraine did was invite them into the kitchen."

"Ben, once the sale is over . . ."

"Things will never be the same."

She slammed her brush on the dresser. "You still think I should have walked away from it, don't you?"

"I don't like freak shows. What happens to you after the sale? What do you do the following Saturday night? What have you got left after those people go back to the city?"

"If nothing else, a couple of million dollars." She glared at him. "You expect me to give that up? You expect anybody to give up millions of dollars?"

Ben walked to the door. "You better be careful at dinner. They just might make you the main course."

"I can take care of myself."

He paused for a moment. "I wish to hell you couldn't."

Predictably, Delphina turned the old Ryerson dining room into a glittering salon. Wearing an embroidered red-and-black silk kimono, she held court by recounting tales of Romanovs she had known. "The truth is," she said, patting Emmett's hand, "Russia was the Texas of Europe. A vast region in which everything was more extravagant, more tragic, more passionate."

"Speaking of more, who's for seconds on the *gâteau?*" Lorraine asked.

Chip held up his plate. "Me! Terrific *gâteau.*"

Rita nodded. "It's really delicious, Lorraine."

Delphina had excused herself the first time around by explaining she never ate anything richer than she was. Charles held up his hand to signify No. Duffy pointed to the uneaten piece on her plate.

Delphina smiled and shook a finger at her. "My mother's second husband would always say, 'Think of the starving Romanovs.'"

"I have," Charles said quickly. "Hopefully, we'll have the sale over before they file suit."

"File suit?" Duffy asked.

"I've had at least ten calls so far," he said. "Nieces, nephews, cousins, lawyers."

"I thought they were all killed," Emmett said.

"*Christos* forbid!" Delphina implored. "Half the best help in Paris would be gone!"

Charles smiled. "There are legions of Romanovs, or would-be Romanovs. It's understandable. Before the Revolution, Nicholas was the single richest man in the world. There's still unclaimed money all over the place. But it's frozen. Either locked in by countersuits or by the courts, who've yet to recognize a legitimate heir."

"I once met that poor woman who claimed to be Anastasia," Delphina sighed. "Such tortured eyes. For her sake, I hope she was lying."

"You don't think they can stop the sale?" Emmett asked.

"The Romanovs? I don't think they could stop an empty taxi. By the time they get themselves together, they'll be fighting the State of New York for the proceeds."

"But what if they have a real claim?" Duffy asked.

"Not only do they have to prove who they are to the satisfaction of the court, but then they have to prove to the court that Miss Natalie had the items in her possession illegally. How can they do that?"

"I don't know," Chip said.

Charles smiled. "Not to worry. The only one who could stop the sale is a relative of Miss Natalie's, and there are none."

Rita sighed. "We're all going to make a lot of money off that poor old woman."

"I bet she didn't even know she had the stuff," Chip said.

"Of course she didn't," Emmett argued. "Else why would she live like that?"

Charles smiled. "You'd be surprised how many nuts hoard away squirrels."

"She wasn't a nut," Duffy said. "She wasn't crazy."

Delphina leaned over and asked, "Why do you think she never married?"

Duffy felt threatened again. "Do you have to be crazy not to get married?"

Delphina thought. "I suppose it depends upon whom you're not marrying."

"I'm not married," Charles said, coming to Duffy's rescue.

"Not married?" Delphina laughed. "You're married to Wyndham's. Charles, you're the most married man I know."

"And that's acceptable," Duffy said. "Everyone knows a man works hard to establish a business. There's nothing peculiar about his not being married. There are housekeepers to get the laundry done. Chinese restaurants that deliver. And lots of lovers. But poor Miss Natalie. She must have been crazy not to get married. Why else would anyone pass up the thrill of doing the laundry and the cooking and releasing the sexual tensions of someone with more important things to do?"

"Miss Natalie didn't have a job," Emmett said. "The normal thing would have been for her to get married. You have a job."

Duffy smiled. "I didn't think we were talking about me."

"I wasn't."

"Yes, you were. You were talking about old maids, Emmett. Spinsters. Lonely maiden aunts."

"I've had some wonderful marriages," Delphina began, "and they all included housekeepers and Chinese food and lots of lovers. What you must consider is not whether to marry or not, but the importance of marrying well."

Duffy drank the last of her wine. "The only thing I remember about her is thinking she must have been very beautiful. She looked to me like a young woman who had grown old too quickly."

"Darling, no one buries treasure in shallow water," Delphina advised. "My mother's third husband was Greek. He taught me lost ships are never found near the surface."

"Well, crazy or not, give me a little old lady any day," Charles said. "You can keep the heiresses and tycoons and, heaven help us, all the doctors' wives. There's nothing they don't know. Apparently, doctors' penises transmit great knowledge. No, I'll stick to crazy little old ladies. Preferably old maids. Ideally those on the verge of poverty or death."

"My God!" Duffy slammed down her glass. "You can't be that callous."

"It's a ghoulish business, darling." Delphina offered her loveliest smile. "We are all grave robbers."

"Culture vultures," Charles corrected. "It's a three-phase operation: desperation, divorce, and death. Most auctions are merely the second half of the funeral. The body's been disposed of, the tears are over, and now everyone has the fun of competing for the worldly remains."

"Maybe in New York," Duffy said angrily. "Not in Perry Falls."

"The Romans were the least hypocritical about it," he continued. "They auctioned the booty right on the battlefield. Someone speared a red cloth into the ground and a crowd gathered. The air was still thick with smoke. You could smell the village burning and hear the dying cry out. We've civilized it a bit more for the Saturday generation. But it's only a cosmetic difference. The Via Appia. The Nickel Man. Wyndham's. They're all the same."

To break an awkward silence, Delphina pointed to the cake. "Darling, your dessert should be on the cart at Maxim's."

Gratefully, everyone turned to look at the cake. "Maxim's?" Lorraine gasped.

"You've been there a lot, I bet," Chip said.

Delphina shrugged. "They're open in August."

"Is the food really that good?" Lorraine asked.

"The food?" Delphina paused as though having been asked the ultimate non sequitur. "I don't know."

"Well, I know," Charles said, eager to bring the evening to a close. "Lorraine, that was a magnificent dinner. You ought to be on a credit card."

"We will be," Chip exclaimed.

"That's right, you will," Charles said. He stood up and raised his glass. "To Lorraine and Chip. Best of luck in your new restaurant."

"Oh, that's just the most delicious thing I've ever heard," Lorraine squealed. "Our restaurant!" She jumped up. "To a new life!"

"Don't forget us," Emmett said, getting to his feet. "To our shop!"

Rita stood up. "To our new life!"

Charles looked at Duffy. She was the only one still seated. "To your new life."

"You bet!" she said with forced enthusiasm. "As soon as the sale is over, once I'm finally rid of the bunch of you, I'm going to have what I've always wanted." There was no way to stop the tear from falling down her cheek. "I'm going to have the Nickel Man all to myself."

Kolmenkin had the Manhattan telephone book open in his lap. His finger went down the center column on page one. He picked up the receiver and pressed the numbers for Dial-a-Joke. He glanced across the bed at the sleeping figure next to him. Suddenly, he began to laugh.

"Oh, shitskii," the sleepy voice muttered. "What are you doing?"

"Shh," Kolmenkin said. "Go back to sleep."

Gregory turned around. "How can I?" He lay his head on Kolmenkin's bare chest. "Who are you calling at this hour?"

Kolmenkin was still laughing. "A man walked into a hotel and asked the clerk for a room and bath. The clerk said, 'I can give you a room, but you have to take your own bath.'" Gregory sighed and nudged the phone book off the bed. Kolmenkin continued.

"I have also called the lottery. The winning number was 479. The Dow Jones average is down. The precipitation probability is twenty percent. Dr. Brothers talked to me about Lesbianism and said that homosexuality is the result of learned behavior. Then, to cheer me up, the Good Looks Line told me how to measure my breasts for the proper size brassiere. My horoscope says this is a good time to discuss a personal situation."

Gregory rubbed the palm of his hand across Kolmenkin's

chest. "Dmitri Leonidovich, do you know what the problem is with you Russians?"

"No, Gregory Konstantinovich, what is the problem with us Russians?"

He reached up and put his arms around Kolmenkin. "You are too fucking sexy."

Kolmenkin put the telephone back on the night table and held Gregory tightly. "Do you know what I want to do? I want to open the windows and shout into the street, 'I, Dmitri Leonidovich Kolmenkin, am a homosexual!'"

Gregory raised an eyebrow. "On the East Side? What else would you be?" He sighed. "I fear, Dima, that you are coming out of the closet through a revolving door."

"Grishulya," Kolmenkin began tentatively, "what is the Homosexual Help Line?"

"What?"

Kolmenkin reached for the phone book. "It is here, on page 646. The Homosexual Help Line."

Gregory pushed the book out of his hands. "Are you offering or seeking?"

Kolmenkin smiled. "What do you think?"

"I think you should be careful. We have a saying in the gay community: you should learn to walk before you fly."

He sighed deeply. "Do you think she is right? Are we the result of learned behavior?"

"You mean like Pavlov's fairies?" He sat up. "No. It is my theory that we are the result of a virus. There is simply no other way to explain it. I tell you, Dima, it must be an epidemic. Do you know, I actually went to bed with a man who'd never heard of Diaghilev or Nijinsky? Now there are even accountants among us!"

Kolmenkin wondered what it would be like to live as openly as Gregory. "Grishulya, do you miss Russia?"

"Desperately. I left when I was two. Good Godskii, you're not homesick already?"

Kolmenkin kissed him. He stared at the moonlight streaming in through the windows. He listened to the breathing of the man in his arms. "Grishulya," he whispered.

"Mmmm?"

"What is the number for Dial-a-Prayer?"

"You want to see them again?"

Kolmenkin nodded. "Da."

They sat on Gregory's terrace, wearing towels wrapped around their waists. The sun was still rising behind a Sutton Place view of the East River. Kolmenkin took a strawberry from the basket. He held it by the stem and bit into it.

Gregory put down his brioche and sighed. "But you know they're real. I've never led you astray. The Minister knows my information is to be trusted. Besides, you examined every lot yesterday. Why must you do it again?"

"Yesterday was for the Kremlin."

"And last night?" he smiled. "Was that for the Kremlin as well?"

Kolmenkin hesitated. "In a sense."

Gregory turned away. "Then I am truly sorry for you. Even I don't fuck for the Kremlin."

Kolmenkin laughed. He looked around the terrace. "What do you call this? The paintings? The furniture? The carpets?"

"I call it gratitude."

"I call it a whore's wages," Kolmenkin snapped. His anger surprised him. He had never thought of Gregory in those terms before sleeping with him. He sighed and then spoke in a more businesslike manner. "Gregory Konstantinovich . . ."

Gregory raised an eyebrow. "So now it's Gregory Konstan-tinovich, is it? When I suck your cock, it is Grishulya."

"Forgive me, Grishulya." Kolmenkin spoke softly. "I am not accustomed to waking up with a man."

Gregory nodded. "Poor Dima. You're not ready to come out after all, are you?"

Kolmenkin forced himself to remain seated, feeling more naked than before. It was a point of honor. To go inside and get dressed, which was precisely what he wanted to do, would prove Gregory right. How much easier it was to be a *zhopoyob* in the dark.

"Well, *tovarich*," Gregory began, changing the subject, "which lots do you want?"

"The eggs and the jewels."

"Good. Then there will be something left for the peasants. I suppose that bourgeois bastard Coussac will bid for you as always?"

"Yes."

Gregory took a sip of coffee. "Will you be back in September?"

Kolmenkin reached out for Gregory's hand. "If I am invited."

Gregory laughed. "Dmitri Leonidovich! If only you weren't such a Nervous Nellie."

"Of course I will bid for you," Coussac said.

"Good." Kolmenkin moved back from the railing. The wind carried a spray of water from the waves in the bay. He pointed to the New York skyline. "It's very beautiful."

"From a distance, perhaps. I have never been on the ferry before." Coussac looked around disapprovingly. "I have heard of it."

"We will dock in about twenty minutes." Without missing a beat, Kolmenkin added, "The Minister of Culture demands absolute secrecy. No one is to know you are bidding for us."

"No one ever does."

"It is especially important this time."

"It is always especially important for the Minister of Culture."
Coussac nodded his assurance. "There is too much interest in
this sale. This time it is Coussac who demands absolute secrecy.
My clients would be very unhappy to learn their bids had been
dumped in favor of the Soviet government."

"The Minister will be relieved to hear that."

"The Minister will not be relieved to hear what it will cost."

"I have authorization for you to buy at any price."

"I will need cash in advance to pay off the other dealers. If
they do not bid at all, we will get the pieces even cheaper. Their
percentages will cost you nothing. And they will be happy not to
have the market flooded with ninety-six new pieces."

Kolmenkin smiled. "I shall never understand capitalism."

"It is the art market you will never understand. The problem
is to maintain the very delicate balance between supply and
demand. Collectors must be fed in small portions. They must be
kept like hungry alligators who savor each bite. They must be
grateful to be fed at all." Coussac smiled. "I remember my father
explaining to me that the difference between a customer and a
collector is the collector thanks you for allowing him to spend his
money."

"I presume you have been thinking of how we might best
thank you."

"Krugerrands as usual." He paused. "Before the sale."

Kolmenkin nodded. "How many?"

Coussac stared out at New York harbor. "As you would
expect, I anticipate a large number of commission bids from my
clients. I should net one hundred thousand dollars. Con-
servatively."

"I am authorized to pay you one hundred fifty thousand plus
expenses."

"No. That will not be enough for a sale such as this. Two
hundred thousand plus expenses."

"That is very high."

"Indeed. It is outrageous," said Coussac.

"And for the others?"

"They will expect to be paid handsomely not to bid against me. I will need half a million to work with. In Swiss francs."

Kolmenkin nodded. He pointed. "That is the Verrazano Narrows Bridge. It is the world's largest suspension bridge and was completed in 1964. Three workers died during its construction."

Coussac stared and then shrugged. "When I admire a pearl, I do not think about the oyster's indigestion."

"What do you know of the old woman?"

"Only that she is dead." Coussac shrugged. "As for how it all came to be in her possession, it is perhaps better not to know."

Kolmenkin took a pad from his pocket. "I have information on who you will be bidding against."

"What does it matter?"

"I thought you might be interested."

"No."

"There is an art investment group . . ."

"Forget them," Coussac said. "It is street money. There is no passion behind it. Wall Street bids only for a safe price. They will fall out early."

"The exchange rates are extremely favorable for Japanese and German investment."

Coussac shrugged. "The Japanese spend money to reclaim their own plundered past, not yours. And I doubt even the West German economy will direct funds to preserving relics from a country at whose hands they suffered in two wars."

Kolmenkin continued. "The British crown."

"At last, you have struck blood. Yes. There is a worthy opponent. The Queen's collection is vast. Although the Czarina was a relative, they have more than a familial interest in preserving the memorabilia of monarchism."

"What can we do?"

"If we bid to buy, that means we win." Coussac waved his hand. "Put away that meaningless piece of paper. There is really only one man who shares your passion. That is Father Kyril. The church, as always, will fight you the hardest." He snatched the paper from Kolmenkin. "There is nothing of interest here for Coussac." He tore it into shreds and threw it into the wind. "Where did you get this list?"

"From Gregory Rosenko."

Coussac shook his head. "That fairy?"

Kolmenkin stopped breathing. There it was again. The viselike grip on his heart. The salt-mine factor. At any moment, a tap on his shoulder, the click of handcuffs, the echo of a steel door slamming shut forever. He raised his hand, steadying it as he pointed to the nearing shore. "Staten Island was named after a Dutch general. The population is some three hundred thousand."

Father Kyril smiled as the waiter put down a plate of meat-filled dumplings. "How wonderful! Italian *pelmeny!*"

Cardinal DiCrosti, a reed-slim man who always looked as though he needed a shave and a smile, peered annoyedly through his wire-framed glasses. "It is not Italian *pelmeny!* It is Italian ravioli!" Cars and motorbikes sped past as they circled the elegant Piazza del Popolo. The Cardinal and Father Kyril sat at an outdoor table at Dal Bolognese, where the Cardinal always lunched with VIP pilgrims to Rome. "The Chinese fathers tell me it is Italian won-ton. The Jewish clergy say it is Italian *kreplach.*"

"I say it is delicious!" offered Father Kyril.

"It is ravioli!" Cardinal DiCrosti snapped his fingers for the waiter to refill his glass. "Just as Chianti is Chianti. It is not Italian Chianti."

Father Kyril could not resist. He raised his glass. "Nor is it an Italian Pope."

A very practiced index finger pointed across the table. "The Pope is the Pope." The Cardinal nodded his head for punctuation. His eyebrows began a new sentence. "It just happens he is not Italian." He looked around to make certain no one was listening. "It is worth your life to pass the Vatican dining room in the morning. Those two Polish nuns he sent for are forever slicing *kielbasa* and frying bacon. Every morning that smell!" He leaned over, whispering, "Italian Popes have coffee and rolls."

Father Kyril leaned across the table. He whispered urgently, "I have been waiting for days with no word. I must have the money!"

The Cardinal rolled his eyes and sat back. He pushed his plate away and snapped his fingers again. The waiter was already bringing a steaming platter of *cotoletta al prosciutto*, with small bowls of every side dish in the kitchen—*polenta, risotto, gnocchi, risi e bisi,* and three kinds of salad. He nodded as the waiter heaped their plates full. When they were alone, he leaned over to his guest. "This is how it used to be when Sister Tobiana did the cooking. Now, an invitation to eat with His Holiness is an adventure in ethnic dining."

"Perhaps if I could see His Holiness about the money."

The Cardinal shrugged. "Why? Do you want it in zlotys?" The Cardinal laughed so hard that he began to cough. The waiters, unaccustomed to seeing him even smile, rushed to pat his back.

While the Cardinal sat catching his breath, Father Kyril spoke intently. "In the early 1600s, when the first Romanov became Czar, the church was in ruins. Education and morality had sunk to their lowest. The monasteries and churches had been plundered, priests taken captive. There was conflict between the Greek patriarchs and the Russian bishops . . ."

"In the early 1600s, we had just completed building Castel Gandolfo as a summer residence. The University of Rome opened its doors. Monteverdi was composing operas, and Caravaggio was still painting."

"Your Eminence . . ."

"*Basta!*" he commanded. "Eat your *polenta!* You will have the money!"

Father Kyril put down his knife and fork, crossed himself and then the Cardinal. "Bless you, Your Eminence. The peasants of Holy Mother Russia . . ."

"Thank you. Thank you."

". . . before the Revolution they had icons in every room, they crossed themselves on every occasion. It was the Bolsheviks who incited the peasants in order to destroy the church . . ."

"Thank you. Thank you."

". . . by destroying their belief in the Czar and in God."

The Cardinal stared at Father Kyril. "And was this Czar, this last Romanov of yours, was he a good Czar?"

Father Kyril never took his eyes from the Cardinal. "The Czar swore to keep Russia holy."

The Cardinal paused and then spoke in an almost perfunctory manner, considering he was talking about twenty million dollars. "I had a meeting with our financial advisors from Hambro's Bank in London, J. P. Morgan in New York, and Crédit Suisse in Geneva. They all concur with my opinion that the stones are a high-yield venture and as such would be a welcome addition to the Vatican's portfolio."

"Thank you," Father Kyril said.

The Cardinal shrugged. "The church is always open to new trends in investment. The Church of Rome," he clarified. "I doubt the Church of England would give you money to bid against the Queen."

"You are very generous."

"The papers are being drawn and will be sent to the Patriarch in Moscow for his signature. We shall extend credit for the purchase of the Czar's property. The jewels will belong officially to the Church of Rome, on loan to the Eastern Orthodox church for one hundred years." He smiled. "By then you will know whether the Revolution was a hit." He began laughing again but waved off the overly concerned waiters.

"We are grateful for your wisdom and generosity."

The Cardinal sat back. "Father," he began in his pontifical best, "*pelmeny* or ravioli. Won-ton or *kreplach*. What does it really matter? It is all the same recipe."

"Holy shitskii!" Gregory shouted, slamming down the phone. "He's bringing her here."

Gregory's assistant, Royce Whitley, of the Delaware Valley Whitleys, reached across the catalog proofs for her purse. "God, I must look like yesterday's caviar."

Gregory stood up and brushed eraser shreds from his Armani suit. "I thought we'd meet in *his* office."

Buried behind a pile of books in the corner of the office was Gregory's other assistant. Sondra Feinberg, of the Bronx Feinbergs, had hysterical brown hair and wore workman's denim overalls. "Relax, comrades. There is still time for a schpritz of feminine deodorant spray."

"Gross," mumbled Royce. "Haute Gross."

As he organized his desk frantically, Gregory called across the room to Sondra. "How about straightening out the Gulag?"

Sondra moaned loudly from behind the books. "This is definitely not a workers' paradise."

"Where the hell is the proof sheet for the double-heart frame?" Gregory rummaged through the papers on his desk.

A hand appeared over the pile of books. Sondra waved a piece of paper. "I haven't been able to date it."

Royce dabbed cologne behind her ears. "The story of her life."

Gregory stormed across the room. "Why the hell not?"

Sondra pointed to the photograph of the double-heart frame with the pictures of Alexandra and the Czarevitch. "It's this tiara that's the problem. You see, the kid was born in aught-four. Mrs. Czar didn't get her diamond beanie till aught-nine. And I know from babysitting with my little cousin Bernie that the kid in the picture is no five-year-old."

Gregory was furious. "That is why you've been holding up the catalog? That's why the dummy is late? Make it 1903!" he said, throwing the page at her.

"How do you know that?" she asked.

"I'm the expert, that's how! I am the head of this department and if I say it's 0–3, 0–3 it is!"

"But what if you're wrong?"

"Who the hell will know?" Gregory yelled.

Sondra shook a finger at him. "In your heart . . ."

"In my heart, you pitiful proletarian, I know this is the greatest sale of my life and it is being ruined by a hick who couldn't sell a chicken to a starving fox." The look in Sondra's eyes frightened him. He whirled around.

Duffy stood in the doorway. Charles, a hand to his forehead, was behind her. "Foxes never starve," Duffy said crisply. "Not in my neck of the woods. They always know how to get what they want."

Charles smiled. "I, for one, can attest to that."

Gregory nodded. He held up his palms in surrender. "Will you accept the apology of a very nervous New York chicken?"

Duffy took a deep breath. She extended her hand. "You can't be any more nervous than I am, Mr. Rosenko." She smiled. "It's the greatest sale of *my* life, too."

Charles was eager to resume business as usual. "How about making it the greatest sale of *my* life? Where's the dummy?"

Sondra offered her hand to Duffy. "I thought he'd never introduce me. Sondra Feinberg. Comrade at arms."

Duffy shook hands. "Hi." She turned to Royce. "Hello."

"Royce Whitley and absolutely mad as a hatter to meet you. As soon as we're through with the catalog I'm going through the attics in all our houses."

Gregory held out the catalog sheets. "The crowning achievement of my career," he said, proudly offering them to Charles, who indicated that they should be given instead to Duffy.

What she held in her hands was even more thrilling than that first velvet box. Duffy stared in wonderment at the title page.

Sale 1758

THE ROMANOV COLLECTION

**Highly Important Jeweled Works of Art
made for the
Court of Imperial Russia
by
Peter Carl Fabergé**

**The Property of a Lady
to be
Sold at Public Auction by Order of the
Administrator of the Estate
at
The Nickel Man Barn
Perry Falls, New York**

ADMISSION TO SALE BY TICKET ONLY

**EXHIBITION: September 11–17, Wyndham's New York
AUCTION: Saturday evening, September 19, at 7:00 P.M.
In sending bids or making inquiries, please refer to this sale
as
"CZARINA"**

**Exhibition and sale under the management of
WYNDHAM'S
Fine Art Auctioneers**

Duffy shook her head. "I don't know what to say."

Charles put his hand on her shoulder. "It's like playing New York for the first time. With your name up in lights."

Duffy stared at the page. She took a deep breath. "Where is my name up in lights?"

"What?" Charles asked.

"My name. Where is it?"

"We never actually print the auctioneer's name."

"You don't?"

"No."

Duffy nodded. "The Property of a Lady," she read aloud.

"Standard," Charles said.

"I see." She looked up at Charles. "Which lady?"

"Which lady?" he asked.

"The Property of a Lady," she repeated. "Which lady? The Czarina? Miss Natalie? Or me?"

Charles glanced at Sondra and Royce. "We'll be a while," he said. "Perhaps you two could round up the others and meet us in the auditorium."

Duffy knew she had said something wrong. Gregory sat down at Royce's desk. Charles closed the door and folded his arms as he leaned against it. "That bad?" she asked.

Charles smiled. "Of course not. We should have explained these things to you before. First, 'the property of' refers to the estate. Traditionally, the seller may elect to remain anonymous, or, as in this case, the seller's name may be meaningless. Therefore we use, 'The Property of a Lady.'"

Duffy began shuffling through the pages. Without looking up she said, "I don't see why you can't include my name. Anytime I take out an ad, it says pure and simple at the bottom, 'Duffy Patterson, Auctioneer.'"

"We don't do it that way. My name has never appeared as auctioneer, nor has anyone else's."

Duffy held up the title page. "It should say, Duffy Patterson, Auctioneer."

"Duffy . . ."

"Hit show. Lights," she reminded.

Charles looked at Gregory, who sighed and reached for his blue pencil. "At least, *Dorothy* Patterson?" Charles asked.

"No one would know it was me. Duffy! Duffy Patterson, Auctioneer. That's me. That's who I am."

Charles smiled. "Checkmate."

Duffy picked up the page with the double-heart frame. "Is this right?" she asked.

"I'm sorry," Gregory said. "It's out of sequence. We are verifying something on that page."

"That's not what I mean. I'm talking about what it says."

Gregory stiffened. "I say it is 1903 and I am the expert!"

Duffy didn't know what he was talking about. "Charles, listen to this." She began to read:

8. **FABERGÉ RUBY, DIAMOND, AND GOLD PHOTOGRAPH FRAME,** St. Petersburg, Workmaster Mikhail Perchin, circa 1903, of overlapping double-heart shape set with 300 cabochon rubies, the surround of 115 diamonds, an oval photograph of Alexandra Feodorovna on the left and an oval photograph of the infant Czarevitch Alexis on the right, the ovals bordered by 65 diamonds, mounted in gold, the back strut in the shape of the monogram and crown of Nicholas II.
Height: 10 inches (26 cm).
Est. value: $350,000.

Charles nodded. "An extraordinary piece."

Duffy waved the page in front of him. "You have to be a Philadelphia lawyer to understand that!"

Charles sat on the edge of the desk near Duffy. He spoke softly. "Our intent is to identify and describe, as accurately as possible, the physical characteristics of each lot."

"But you don't even say it's pretty!"

Gregory rolled his eyes. "It's not a Sears Roebuck catalog. We don't say snappy things like 'will look smart on your night table'!"

"Duffy, no one buys art because it's pretty. You buy wallpaper because it's pretty. You buy art for status and investment. The art we sell is too expensive to be pretty."

She stared at the page and shook her head. "But it reads like a parts catalog."

"It's a reference tool," Charles explained. "Something that will be used by art historians long after the sale is over. It's not a piece of junk mail addressed to 'Occupant.' You have to pay fifteen bucks just to get the goddamn catalog."

"You're sure not making it easy for them."

"We don't have to make it easy! People don't spend millions because it's easy. Or because it's pretty. They spend because rubies are a good investment and because it belonged to the Czarina. You're not selling pretty. You're selling heartbreak."

"In my barn, I sell pretty things." Duffy got up and began to pace. "Nice-looking chairs. A warm quilt. A solid oak sideboard. Things that make a home nicer to live in." She hesitated, and then whispered, as if uttering a curse, "Prettier!"

"But your clients are different," he explained. "Don't you see? Yours is a world in which ugly little girls buy brightly colored ribbons because they hope it will make them pretty. In mine, ugly little collectors buy ugly art and know they'll come out beautiful. Would you bid on *Guernica* because it's pretty? I wouldn't have it hanging in my bathroom! Duffy, your clients can afford to please themselves. My clients can't. They have to please their business managers or their trustees. You sell pleasure. I sell profit."

"Sounds as though you need a stockbroker to conduct the sale."

"I need an auctioneer who knows what he's doing."

"What *she's* doing," Duffy corrected.

Charles smiled. "Which is why we're here today." He gathered up the catalog pages. "Phase one. The offering is made by prospectus. We have ninety-six lots for immediate investment. Let's go down to the trading floor."

Duffy shook her head. "Whatever happened to just putting money in the bank?"

"I don't know," Charles said. "Whatever happened to money?"

Whatever happened to money was beginning to happen to Duffy. She felt herself floating, buoyant, hardly touching terra firma as she stood on the stairs with Charles. It wasn't real. She knew that. None of it was real. Like leaded glass lamps that once sold for twenty-five dollars and now sold for twenty-five thousand. Duffy Patterson, who was a moment ago arguing with Charles Wyndham, was now in his arms.

"Don't let me frighten you," he whispered. "No matter how hard I try."

"Why must you try?"

He kissed her. "Nature of the beast. Nature of the business. We're frightening people. Monsters, really. We deal in wealth the way morticians deal in death. Most people don't know how to handle either."

She pulled back slightly. "And what about handling lady auctioneers?"

He kissed her again. "I'm learning."

The Bids Department was located behind a locked glass door.

From the outside corridor, the four young girls looked like fashion models taking donations at a telethon. They wore headsets that left their perfectly manicured hands free to write down the caller's figures.

Charles pressed the buzzer. Across the room from her four busy signals, Jonesy (Grace Templeton Jones), who had once been married to a higher-up in the SEC and knew Absolutely Everyone, waved. She reached under her desk and pushed the button to unlock the door.

"Morning, Jonesy," Charles said. "Say hello to Sale Number 1758."

Tossing back her hundred-dollar hairdo, Jonesy smiled. "Miss Patterson. Welcome to the classiest bookie joint in town."

"Three thousand on Lot 56?" one of the girls asked her caller.

Charles smiled at Jonesy. "What's running?" he asked her.

"If I were Nick the Greek, or even Zorba the Greek, I'd put my money on 1702. What the hell is it?"

"Tempest in a teapot," Charles replied. "Porcelain. The collection of some aging film star. How about giving 1758 a quick tour?"

Duffy smiled at Jonesy. "My friends call me 17."

"Not around us they don't," Jonesy said good-naturedly. "We're a ruthless bunch of digit demons. To quote my first husband, 'The buck starts here.'" She took Duffy to a row of cabinets. "Each sale has a number. That's how our files are arranged. The moment a sale is booked and numbered, we set up a drawer." She pulled out one marked 1758.

"It's empty," Duffy said disappointedly.

"Nothing happens until the catalog is out. The girls take phone bids from people who can't attend. They make out a card: sale number, lot number, amount bid, name, address, and phone number. We do the same for bids received by mail."

Duffy looked at Charles and shrugged her shoulders. "I remember last year, I think it was, we had a big snowstorm and Ellen Coleman couldn't get her car out of the driveway. She called Emmett and asked him to bid for her on an old chocolate mold she wanted for her kitchen." Duffy smiled. "He forgot."

Charles continued. "The catalog we saw upstairs will be at the printer's this afternoon. It'll be in everyone's hands three to four weeks prior to sale date. That gives them time to get the moths out of their wallets."

"But they don't," Jonesy complained. "They always wait till the last minute. Every day is like Christmas Eve at Macy's."

One of the operators was on an overseas connection and had to shout. "Sixty-two thousand seven hundred and fifty dollars on Lot 73. Yes, *monsieur. Merci.*" She looked up and sighed. "They must think we're giving the stuff away."

No one but Duffy smiled.

Charles led her through two sets of locked doors that protected Wyndham's single largest investment, a computer center known as Art Central. It was here, behind the facade of Wyndham's Old World elegance, that an awesome NASA-inspired suite of electronic equipment followed the flight paths of world prices on everything from Italian Renaissance furniture to Chinese Export porcelain to Impressionist paintings.

Duffy followed Charles past the soundproof, temperature-controlled, dust-free environment. Six men seated amid the semicircle of terminals known as the Mother Ship turned and watched them go by.

Charles led her to the bookshelves on which the auctioneer's catalogs were stored. "It's all recorded here, where our follies begin and end." He took down one of the catalogs and broke the red band that kept it sealed.

A polite voice from an overhead speaker. "Good morning, Mr. Wyndham. May I have the number of the catalog you've opened?"

Duffy looked up, startled. Charles pointed first to the speaker and then to the hidden camera. "1409," he said. "Thank you."

"Thank you, Mr. Wyndham."

Sale No. 1409 was *Fine English Furniture.* The auctioneer's catalog contained the highly confidential reserves. Lot numbers circled in red had a reserve price below which Wyndham's and the consignor had agreed the lot couldn't be sold. The amount was entered in red pencil. Order bids were written in black pencil. Secrecy was assured by coding the dollar figures.

Duffy pointed to the red notation next to Lot 251. "GID?"

Charles smiled playfully. "Ridiculous! The reserve should have been at least FUID."

"I give up. Why the code?"

"Suppose you were a double-dealing dealer and you wangled a peek at the catalog prior to the sale. You look up Lot 251 and find that this Regency inlaid mahogany writing cabinet was the property of . . ." He feigned surprise as he read the consignor's name printed in red beneath the lot description. ". . . the Metropolitan! As a dealer in Regency flotsam, you might be aware the piece was donated for tax purposes at an appraised value of forty-five hundred dollars. But," he said with a great flourish, "a mere glance at the auctioneer's catalog tells you the Met's willing to part with it for a mere GID. Can you imagine? Only GID? Theoretically, then, all you have to do is bid a buck more than GID and it's yours. What a steal!"

"But I'm not the only bidder. There are other dealers in the room."

Charles nodded. "With whom you've made a deal not to bid on Lots 34, 58, 107, and 223 in return for their sitting on their hands when 251 comes on the block. You get the piece for GID plus one. The Met and I get zilch."

Duffy was counting. One finger for each letter. "W-Y-N-D-H-A-M-S. That's only eight. You need a ten-letter word."

"Or a combination of words."

"The code, Charles," she pleaded.

He smiled. "It's dreadfully difficult to learn. Worse than Pig Latin."

"Try me."

"All right. How much is Y plus Y?"

"Charles, I have to know the code, don't I?"

"Of course. It's impossible for a Wyndham's auctioneer to conduct a sale without knowing the code."

"But Charles, when will you show me how a Wyndham's auctioneer does it?"

He smiled. "I'll show you tonight."

Charles unhooked a red velvet rope in front of the closed door. A sign read, SALE ROOM CLOSED TODAY. He opened the door. Duffy still believed in signs and was unprepared for the crowd inside the room. She was even less prepared for the burst of applause as she entered.

Gregory. Jonesy. Ashanti. Roland. Nedda. Luther. Among others. They stood smiling as though welcoming her to a surrealist nightmare. "I thought we were going to practice," she said.

"We are."

"In front of all these people?"

"They're part of the cast."

Duffy smiled as she spoke through gritted teeth. "Why did you do this to me? Why did you make it sink or swim?"

"It's not sink or swim. It's swim. It's swim all the way!" With a firm hand on Duffy's arm, he led her down the side aisle toward stage right.

Ashanti reached out. "Don't be nervous. It's only your life at stake. I tell you, this is the hottest ticket in town."

Duffy pressed Ashanti's hand. "Maybe, but I'm beginning to feel I was cast against type."

"You think you've got problems! I'm supposed to sit here and bid like a White Russian!"

Charles pointed to the stage. "The porters will hand each piece to Luther as you announce the lot. There'll be a security man and two guards for the release and check-in of lots. Luther, get the screen down!" Charles turned to Duffy. All business. "As you announce the lot number, Luther will hold up the actual piece while we flash on the appropriate slide."

"Oh."

"Arthur, are you there?"

A voice from backstage. "Yes, Mr. Wyndham."

Charles smiled. "Arthur's working the video console. He'll intercut the slides with the live pickup." He pointed to cameramen on each side of the room.

Duffy nodded. "Live pickup?"

"For the satellite transmission."

"Oh."

He stopped reluctantly to explain. "Eight P.M. in Perry Falls, five P.M. on the Coast. We've got a room set up with a large screen to allow for simultaneous long-distance bidding from San Francisco. It'll be one A.M. in London, and we've arranged for full video coverage at a private club. Fortunately, it will be ten in the morning in Tokyo."

"Oh."

"The department head and his people are usually right next to the auctioneer." Royce, Sondra, and Gregory nodded. "Reason for that is the DH knows both ends of the sale best. It's his baby. He's cataloged it, and he knows most of the bidders from past sales."

"Oh."

Charles pointed casually to the auctioneer's rostrum. "That's you. But I'll be close by, don't worry."

"Worry?" Duffy felt herself make the transition from worry to panic almost as she spoke.

A tall white-haired man who looked like a UN delegate nodded politely. "Mr. Carmody," Charles announced, shaking his hand ceremoniously, "is your third eye. He stands right next to you and watches the dealers for secret bid signals. He prepares his own catalog with notations to look at Mr. X for a twitch of the nose on Lot 10, and at Mr. Y for a blink on Lot 25."

"Oh."

"Roland likes to position himself up here to keep an eye on the security people."

Winking at Duffy, Roland made a gun with his forefinger and thumb. "Don't want anyone pointing a thirty-eight at you."

"No," Duffy agreed, as though someone were.

"And over here at this table, we have Lucille, queen of the computer printout. She records the hammer price and bidder's name. Mr. Carmody's nephew, Leonard, runs a carbon copy over to accounting for instant credit check and billing."

"Oh."

"Jonesy holds the fort next door with her long-distance hotline. We take phone bids from those who can't be on the scene. We're planning at least three operators plus Jonesy for this baby."

"Oh."

Charles kissed Laura Clayton, the last in the receiving line. An avalanche of white, she was an oversized woman in a white suit with curly white hair as shiny as her triple-strand pearl necklace. "Laura handles special clients who wouldn't make a move without her. She keeps their identities and bids to herself. Nothing goes through the Bids Department or ever gets into the auctioneer's catalog. We never know who or what she's got up her sleeve."

Laura reached out to Duffy. "Charles thinks all I have to do is wave my hand and the borscht will part."

"That will tell us just how far it parts." Charles pointed to the currency conversion board above the rostrum. "As you call the bids, our Mrs. LaBarbara in the back operates the console that converts dollars into pounds sterling, French francs, Swiss francs, lira, yen, German marks, and for a touch of schmaltz, into rubles."

Duffy nodded. She kept on nodding, not to signify understanding, but to keep herself from shaking as she looked around the room. Luther. The porters. The security men. The Russian

Art Department. Mr. Carmody, head of Secret Signals. Roland to make her feel insecure. Lucille and the Big Bid book. Mr. Carmody's nephew. Jonesy plus her three. Laura the White Queen. And above them all, the whoosh of the slides and the pulse-quickening clickety-clickety-clack of the conversion board.

"What about Chip and Emmett?" she asked softly. Almost plaintively. "I've never done a sale without my brothers."

Charles was suddenly more frightened than Duffy. He had expected resistance. Sparks flying. Perhaps even a fire. But Duffy seemed lost. He wasn't prepared to deal with that. Especially not in front of everyone. "Come, let's get you settled where you belong." He led her to the rostrum, a very serious piece of mahogany behind which generations of stern British schoolmasters had stood. A step led up to the high-backed architect's chair with its thick red velvet cushioned seat.

It reminded Duffy of trying on one of Mama's dresses when she was a little girl. That burst of exhilaration followed by a searching smile that asks "Don't I look all grown up?"

"Brava! Brava! Bravissima!" Delphina stood in the doorway applauding. "You are a picture, darling," she exclaimed, walking down the aisle. "Your hair is wonderful. That color! The lips are gorgeous. Perhaps the eyes need to be accented. Charles, what do you think? More blue shadow on the upper lids?"

Charles spoke directly to Duffy. "I think she's perfect just as she is."

Delphina stepped up to the rostrum and embraced Duffy. "Don't lose your nerve," she whispered.

"I'm terrified."

"Darling, everyone will be more frightened than you. They will be desperate. Competing to buy a piece of the Romanov tragedy. They will be a mob consumed with passion and greed. They will need to be ruled." She took hold of Duffy's hand and spoke slowly. "You cannot train lions if you are afraid of them."

Duffy stared for a moment in disbelief. Delphina challenged her as a woman, the same way Charles did as an auctioneer. Yet neither of them seemed to be competing with her. Each time they brought her dangerously close to the edge, they provided a net. Each time they shuffled the cards, they dealt her an extraordinary hand, raising the stakes higher than she could ever have imagined.

Duffy looked around the room. Everyone was waiting. She leaned back against the chair. Surprisingly, it was comfortable. The world looked better from a rostrum. It always did. "I'll need some hot tea," she announced. After taking a very deep breath, she tapped the microphones. "Why do I need three of these?"

Charles breathed a sigh of relief. There were signs of life. "This one is for amplification and this is for the satellite transmission. The end one is for our files."

"And what is this?" She pointed to a small piece of paper taped to the inside of the rostrum.

"Jonesy gives us three new dummy names for each sale," he explained. "In the event a lot doesn't reach its reserve, we simply knock it down using one of her names."

Duffy nodded as she read the list of dummies. Snyder. Green. Evans. Then she opened the cardboard pages of the auctioneer's catalog. Lot One. FABERGÉ CARVED JADE RABBIT. She glanced at the reserve figure marked in red. "Twenty-nine thousand dollars?" she exclaimed.

"Duffy!"

She held her hand up in mock apology. "I know. I'm not supposed to announce the reserve."

Charles shook his head. "They're confidential figures. That's why we code them."

Duffy pointed to the page. "You didn't code this one."

"Because you don't know the code. We made up dollar figures for today."

"Sure hope someday somebody's going to teach me the code."

Charles nodded. "Let's get started. First thing is to practice looking at all of us while keeping one eye on the catalog."

"The catalog with the coded figures." She took a deep breath and, as Red taught her, filled her lungs with air. She smiled brightly as though it were an actual sale. "Good evening, folks. I want to welcome you to the most exciting sale we've ever held."

Charles put a hand to his forehead. "Duffy . . ."

"I see we've got lots of new faces out there tonight. Most of you probably have never been to a country barn before . . ."

"Duffy!" he shouted.

She turned quickly. "Too loud? Am I talking into the wrong microphone?" She began tapping each one. "Testing."

Charles came over and put his hand over the live microphone. "Duffy, you can't open that way."

"I'm sorry, Charles. I know I was a little too stiff. I need to relax more and . . ."

He took a sheet from the catalog. "You open the sale by reading this. Do not utter one word other than what appears on this sheet."

Duffy raised her eyebrows. She began to read aloud in her deepest, most affected Alfred Hitchcock voice. "Good evening, ladies and gentlemen."

Charles shook his head. "Duffy!"

She waved the piece of paper and spoke in her most outraged Duffy Patterson. "What does this mean? 'Welcome to Wyndham's'? It should say 'Welcome to the Nickel Man Barn'!"

"All right!"

"Good evening, ladies and gentlemen. Welcome to the Nickel Man Barn. We have for your competition this evening highly important jeweled works of art made for the Court of Imperial Russia by Peter Carl Fabergé. I'd like to bring to your attention the conditions of sale as printed in the forepart of your catalog, especially the condition which states that everything is sold on an 'as is' basis, and that which refers to state sales tax where it applies. There is a ten-percent commission added to the hammer price of the lots sold and for those of you who are unfamiliar with our procedures, I would like to say that when the auctioneer says 'to the absent bidder' or 'to the order bid' it indicates the auctioneer is executing a bid on behalf of someone who cannot be here tonight. We start this evening's session with the Fabergé carved jade rabbit, Lot One." She put down the paper, took a deep breath, and leaned forward on the rostrum. "Folks, this is one of the cutest things I've ever seen. It's got two big genuine diamond eyes . . ."

"Duffy!"

She sat back and folded her arms. Gregory shook his head. Royce put a hand over her mouth to stifle the giggles. There were eyes being rolled, throats being cleared, feet being shuffled.

Charles stood over Duffy trying to appear stern. But the affection in his eyes betrayed him. "You can't do that."

"It's my sale!"

"But it's my style!" He helped her down the steps. They walked behind the rostrum. "It's your sale. It's your barn. You're the auctioneer. But the buyers are mine. And they're just not ready for a Duffy Patterson. They're serious. Tense. Hyper. The sale must proceed with precision and control. The buyers are about to make life-and-death decisions. They didn't just get into the car and say, 'Why don't we see what's doin' down at the old barn?' These people have planned and schemed. They've sold short and borrowed big and mortgaged God-knows-what. They've agonized for days to determine the biggest possible bid they can afford. And then they've sweated out how to go even higher because they can't stand the thought of not winning. They don't need you to tell them the rabbit has diamond eyes. They can tell *you* how many facets there are on every stone. And what mine the diamonds are from. There's nothing about that damn rabbit they haven't researched and had verified."

"I'm an auctioneer. My job is to work the crowd."

"No," he said, putting his hands on her shoulders. "Your job is to make sure the crowd doesn't work you. Your job is to sight the target and fire the first shell. Then you stand back and call the rest of the shots as you see them. Fair and square."

"And boring."

"No one comes to be entertained. They come for blood. They come to win."

"You're not running an auction, you're running a war!"

"Exactly." He smiled for the first time. "Now you're beginning to understand the auction business." He put his arm around her. "You've got to be Joan of Arc. Believe in what you're doing. Make them believe it. Then lead them into battle." His voice filled with genuine excitement as he announced, "Good evening, ladies and gentlemen. We have for your competition . . ."

Instinctively, Duffy reached out and put the palm of her hand on his chest. She felt his heart beating. Except for Papa she'd never met a man who talked about auctions the way other men talked about women. She imagined her hand against his bare chest. Did one passion always lead so inevitably to another? She sighed. "You know what happened to Joan of Arc."

He held both her hands. "Listen to the voice of Blessed St. Charles."

"And what will happen to me?"

"Anything you want!" He led her back to the rostrum and waited until she was seated. Charles spoke softly, with a fervor that shattered realities of time and space. "Hold on tight," he whispered, as if making love to her. "No matter how much you want to get off, no matter how dizzy you get. Trust me."

It took all her strength to turn away from him. Duffy reached for the catalog. "Lot One," she said into the microphone. "The Fabergé carved jade rabbit."

The catalog showed a reserve of twenty-nine thousand dollars. It also showed order bids of thirty, forty, and fifty thousand dollars. She looked up at Charles. He nodded, anticipating her question. "We've booked in bids higher than the reserve. Therefore, you know the piece will sell. The question is how high. Assuming there's not even a single bid from the floor. You know the hammer price will be forty-two thousand dollars."

"How do I know that?"

"Simple. Mr. X bid fifty and we know he's going to win. We also know the underbidder at forty will exceed his limit by one. Order bids are usually accepted on a 'plus one' basis. No one wants to lose for not going the extra step. Therefore, if you bring in the forty bid on an odd number, he'll have to bid thirty-nine. Mr. X bids the forty. Then you use the underbidder's 'plus one.' That brings you to forty-one. Mr. X has to go to forty-two."

"That's not fair!"

"First rule: all's fair in love and auction. Our duty is to the consignor, to get the best possible price for *him*. That's what our contract says. Besides, Mr. X was prepared to hit fifty. We saved him eight thousand bucks."

"You know, you're right," Duffy said. "They're not here for a good time."

Charles smiled. "That's why we try to get them out fast. No one likes sitting around for hours and hours. We do our damnedest to get them in and then we do our damnedest to get them out. Normally we try to move a hundred lots an hour. A sale like this, however, you probably won't do more than forty."

"When do I breathe? That's only a minute and a half per."

He shrugged. "You don't breathe. And you don't talk. All you have to do is count out loud."

"Doesn't sound too hard."

"Good. Let's hear you."

She narrowed her eyes. "One, two, three . . ."

"One *thousand*," he corrected. "Two *thousand* . . ."

"Three thousand, four thousand . . ."

"Five *hundred* thousand!" he called out.

"Six hundred thousand, seven hundred thousand . . ."

"By halves," he shouted.

"Seven hundred and fifty thousand, eight hundred thousand, eight and a half hundred thousand . . ."

"Eight and *a half hundred* thousand?" He shrugged. "Is that an upstate number?"

Duffy gritted her teeth. "Eight hundred and fifty thousand, nine hundred thousand, nine hundred and fifty thousand . . ." She hesitated.

"Don't be afraid. Say it."

She put a hand to her forehead. "I can't!"

"Say it!"

Duffy leaned over toward the microphone and spoke softly. "A million."

"*Uh* million!" Charles exclaimed. "What the hell is *uh* million? There's no such figure. *One million dollars!* Loud and clear!"

She took a deep breath, allowing anger to propel the words from her mouth. "One million dollars!"

Charles smiled. "Needs work." He snapped his fingers and looked around at the staff. "All right, let's do some serious bidding." He sat in the center of the room. "Luther, I want those slides operating. And the conversion board."

Duffy looked down at her prepared opening. "We start this evening's session with the Fabergé carved jade rabbit, Lot One." She was stunned as a slide of the rabbit flashed on screen. Her heart began to race. She realized she didn't know how to start the bidding. She had thirty, forty, and fifty marked in the catalog.

"You've got thirty, forty, and fifty marked in the catalog," Charles called out, as though reading her mind. "Where do you want to start?"

"Well, we know it's got to go for at least forty-two," she said nervously.

"Who knows that?"

"I do," she said.

"Who else?"

"No one else."

Charles smiled. "Then it's your deal."

"I'll start it low."

"That'll waste a lot of time," he warned.

"But it's only the first lot. I have the time. I'd rather build it up."

"You're absolutely right," he said. "That's exactly what I would have done."

Duffy hadn't expected praise. Now she was even more frightened. "I'm not going to ask for an opening bid," she said.

"You damn well better not."

"I announce the figure at which I'm going to open?"

"Absolutely! The opening figure is determined by the auctioneer. It's your sale. Your rules."

"Okay." She nodded that she was ready. "Ladies and gentlemen, we have a great deal of interest in this rabbit. I'm going to open the bidding at twenty-five thousand dollars."

Charles called out, "That is very good!" Delphina raised her hand and the conversion board overhead began to clickety-clack its way up to twenty-five thousand dollars before bursting into half a dozen currencies.

Duffy accepted Delphina's bid. "Twenty-six." Clickety-clack. She looked down at the book. "Twenty-seven." Clickety-clack. Delphina nodded and Duffy acknowledged, "Twenty-eight." Not so difficult. Clickety-clack. Down at the book again to pick up, "Twenty-nine."

"What the hell are you staring at the book for?"

Duffy looked up, startled, first at the angry figure of Charles standing with his hand raised, and then at Jonesy, Ashanti, and Laura. They all had hands raised.

"I didn't come here to watch you read," Charles yelled as he stood up. "I came here to bid. I want you to take my bid."

"Twenty-eight!" Duffy called angrily.

"You're going backwards," he yelled. "You were already at twenty-nine!"

"You're confusing me," she said defensively.

"Start over. Reopen the bidding. Forget that goddamn book so long as you've got action on the floor. Don't use the order bids until you need them. And then use them as a cattle prod."

Duffy began again. "Ladies and gentlemen, we have a great deal of interest in the rabbit . . ."

"By the way," Charles said. "This isn't a pet shop. It's not a rabbit you're selling. It's Lot One."

"Thank you for telling me," she snapped angrily.

He shrugged. "Just want to help."

"We have a great deal of interest in Lot One. I'm going to open the bidding at twenty-five dollars."

"Good God!" Charles stood up. "May I hear you count, please?"

Almost speechless with rage, Duffy began, "One, two, three . . ."

"One *thousand*," he yelled. "Two *thousand*. Twenty-five *thousand!*"

Duffy took a sip of tea. By this time she didn't know who was more frightened—she or Charles. "We start this evening's session with the Fabergé carved jade rabbit, Lot One. We have a great deal of interest in this lot. The bidding will open at twenty-five thousand dollars." Clickety-clack. She looked at Delphina and nodded. "Twenty-six thousand."

"Where?" Charles asked.

"Twenty-six thousand on my left."

Kevin called out to her, "Twenty-seven," as he pointed to Ashanti.

Duffy looked at Delphina, who nodded. "Twenty-eight." Then she added quickly, "On my left."

"Twenty-nine," Jonesy called out, holding an imaginary phone.

"You're not confirming the bids!" Charles called out. "You didn't confirm Kevin's twenty-seven. I want your voice on the tape, not his. Same thing with Jonesy. The audience has to hear the bids being accepted by the auctioneer. They must never question that you are in complete control."

Duffy was in complete control by the time they reached forty thousand.

"Forty-one thousand," Mr. Carmody called, pointing to an empty chair.

"Forty-one thousand on the aisle." She expected a bid from Jonesy, but instead got a blank stare. Careful not to miss a beat, she picked up a bid from the catalog. "Forty-two thousand to the absent bidder."

"Terrific," Charles said. "Now you've got them worried. Who the hell is this absent bidder? How high is he going to go?"

Jonesy nodded and Duffy called, "Forty-three thousand on the phone." Laura raised her hand. "Forty-four to the order bid."

"Fifty-five thousand dollars," Charles shouted.

Even the staff was surprised. They turned, smiling, to watch. Without batting an eye, Duffy said, "Thank you. I have fifty-five thousand dollars in the center. Fifty-five thousand." She looked at Jonesy, who mimed hanging up the phone. Laura shook her head No. "In the center at fifty-five thousand." Ashanti waved her hands in disgust. "I have fifty-five thousand." Delphina merely lowered her eyes. "Fifty-five." No one moved. No one even whispered. Everyone waited for Duffy to knock it down. "Fifty-five thousand dollars in the center." Again, she checked all her prior points of contact. Nothing. "The bid is fifty-five thousand dollars in the center of the room." Charles was beaming. He winked at Delphina, proud of his pupil's progress.

He waited for her to knock it down. Instead, she leaned forward and smiled. "You people aren't really going to let this cute little bunny go for only fifty-five thousand?"

The Chinese bed was surrounded by blue-and-white Ming vases bursting with brilliantly colored peonies. The sterling silver wine cooler was crowded with bottles of champagne. One crystal bowl was heaped with pearl-gray caviar, another with fresh raspberries. There were Meissen platters layered with peaches and pears. Soft white French cheeses sat upon a pink marble tray.

Charles lifted the scented yellow silk sheet. He leaned over to kiss Duffy's breast. She opened her mouth to moan. He fit his lips gently upon hers. They lay motionless breathing in and out of one another.

Charles nuzzled his face in the curve of her shoulder. "You were extraordinary," he whispered.

She smiled, tracing the outline of his lips with her finger. "I felt as though it were the very first time."

Charles raised an eyebrow. "Tell me about it." He bit her gently on the chin.

She laughed. "You don't really want to hear that."

"I do." He inhaled the scent of her hair. "I want to know everything about you. Every detail."

"Now?"

He put his arms around her tightly. "Right now." He kissed her hard. "And don't leave anything out."

"You're serious." She looked up at him and took a deep breath. "All right. It was Saturday night . . ."

"How old were you?"

"Fifteen."

"Fifteen?" He pulled back for a moment. "That young?"

Duffy shrugged. "The country."

"Fifteen," he repeated, pushing her hair from the nape of her neck, kissing her. "Go on."

"Well, Papa had a terrible cold. He'd been selling for two hours and his voice was gone. I was sitting next to him as usual. He handed me a note that read, 'Your Sale.' Emmett held up a little white wicker table. I got three dollars for it and I thought I was going to die of excitement. Then I turned to Papa . . ." She stopped and reached out for Charles. "Wait a minute! I can't believe I'm lying in a Chinese opium bed with a terrific man, and all I'm doing is talking."

"Don't people talk in the country?"

"You talk at the supermarket," she said. "You talk forever at the gas station or the post office. But you don't talk in bed. Not unless you're married."

"What do you mean by terrific?" he asked.

"What?"

"You said I was a terrific man."

She began to laugh. "Do you really want me to sweet-talk you?"

"Of course I do. Haven't you heard of equality of the sexes? Men's liberation? I want you to tell me about the color of my eyes. The hair on my chest. My gorgeous legs."

Duffy smiled and pulled back the silk sheet that covered him. "The next lot, ladies and gentlemen, is entitled, *Charles' Thing*, a work of art of dubious provenance, either by the hand of God or the process of evolution. Circa . . . 1940."

He leaned over to kiss her. "No, 1941."

She cleared her throat to signify she meant business. As clinically as possible, she reached out and touched him. "Of cylindrical shape, the top being rather bulbous and somewhat softer than the very hard elongated stem, the surround of which is a dense patch of curled black hair. Circumcised by . . ." She turned to him for help.

He shrugged. "Attributed to the Old Master school."

Her fingers traced gently all around the top. She looked closely at it. "Mmmm. Unsigned. The colorations varying from deep pink to rose red." She grasped it tight. "Very, very hard. Width . . . very wide." She raised her hand to measure it. "Length . . ."

"In inches *and* in centimeters," he reminded her.

Duffy groaned and sprawled across his chest. "In your hat," she whispered.

Charles put his arms around her. "You were doing so well. And you were almost finished."

"Finish it for me," she pleaded.

He turned around and lay on top of her, gently easing her legs apart. "With objects of extreme value we sometimes insert a comment." As Charles spoke he began to penetrate, stretching the tightness around him. "Despite innumerable public view-ings, the work has remained the property of the present owner." The words came slowly, measured to his languorous entry. "It has never before been offered to a private collector."

Duffy whispered, "I'm not a collector."

Once he was fully inside, they held their breath, as though the fit of muscle around muscle was the sole life support they required. Then, after a moment, he kissed her breasts, sucking hard on the nipples. "It's a proper fit, Duffy." He cradled her in his arms. "It's perfect."

They held tight to one another. As he drew back, Duffy gasped. "How do you know it's perfect?"

Charles thrust deep inside her. "Because I'm an expert."

She opened her eyes and looked at him. "Oh, yes, Charles. You are. Was it hard to become one?"

"You can't become one unless it is hard."

Duffy turned her head from side to side as he began to rock. "Charles," she whispered.

"Yes?"

"You truly are an expert." She gasped. "In the Department of Magnificent Sex."

He pulled back abruptly. "I've been promoted from that department," he whispered.

Duffy opened her eyes to stare at him. "Where are you now?"

Charles smiled. "The Department of True Love."

FUCKING MAD

Duffy looked at Charles in amazement. "You're kidding!"

"Scout's honor."

"That's really it."

"That's it."

"Not very elegant."

"But descriptive."

"Of?"

"Of this whole fucking business." Under each letter, he put a number.

FUCKING MAD
1 2 3 4 5 6 7 8 9 0

Duffy took the clipboard from him and stared at the code. She began to laugh. "You're serious? This is really truly it?"

They were sitting alone in the sale room. He put his arm around her. "Yes. This is really truly it. Duffy . . ."

She moved away from him. "Charles, please. I've got to learn this thing."

"I want to ask you something."

"Charles," she pleaded.

He put his lips to her ear. "Three hundred and fifty?"

She smiled. "C-I-D."

"Mmmm," he said, biting her ear lobe. "Six hundred and twenty-five thousand?"

Duffy stared at the clipboard and smiled. "N-U-I-D-D-D."

"Get ready for the big time," he whispered, before kissing her gently. "One million four hundred and twenty thousand."

Duffy laughed and put her arms around his neck. "I love you," she said.

"Then it's settled. We're officially in love."

"No, we're officially in the sale room. That's all we can be. Right now, I feel like Frankenstein's auctioneer. A part of you, a part of me. I don't know where you end and where I begin."

"That's how it should be."

"In bed, Charles." She smiled and put her hand to his face. "It was wonderful in bed but it won't work on the rostrum."

"Why not?"

"Because I am a very defined person," she said, picking up the clipboard. "I'm headstrong, independent . . ."

He sighed. "They just don't make monsters the way they used to."

"Give me some time. Give *us* some time." She shrugged helplessly. "We don't know how we'll feel after the sale."

"After the sale? What the hell has the sale to do with us?"

"Oh, Charles. It has everything to do with us."

"Why?"

Duffy held up the clipboard. She waved it at him. "What happens if I 1–2–3–4 it all up?"

"You won't. We'll work on it together." Charles smiled. "Even if I have to stay with you all night." He kissed her. "But before we go back to the laboratory . . ."

"What now?" she asked apprehensively.

"You'll like this. It's backstage." Charles sat down while Duffy went into the wings. He sighed deeply, wishing it were all over. She just might be able to pull it off, but he couldn't be objective about her any longer. Not after making love to her. And certainly not after seeing her walk on stage.

Duffy's bright red hair cascaded onto her pale pink shoulders. She wore the strapless black velvet gown he'd selected. Her lips were half-smiling in naive wonderment. She held out her arms and turned in a circle. "Oh, Charles. I feel beautiful and ridiculous and wonderful and silly."

He walked on stage without once taking his eyes from her. "There's still one more thing."

"Please, Doctor," she begged. "Don't make me wear little electrodes coming out of my head."

He reached into his shirt pocket and took out a diamond necklace. A shiny new nickel, surrounded by diamonds, hung from the center. "This," he said, fastening it around her neck, "this is the property of a lady I love."

Duffy threw her arms around him. She whispered, "Charles, I'm scared to death."

"I told you. There's nothing to worry about."

"I don't want to disappoint you."

He kissed her. "You're going to be superb. You're going to waltz right through it. Trust me."

"Charles . . ."

"I told you to trust me."

"But, Charles . . ."

"What?"

Duffy began to laugh. "I can't imagine myself holding on to Papa's old gavel in this get-up."

Charles looked up suddenly. "Papa's old what?" he asked.

"Gavel," she said nervously.

"Come here," he said. "Bring your wrist with you."

He sat her inside the rostrum and opened the drawer. He took out an hourglass-shaped cylindrical piece of ivory. He put his palm flat on top of it, then curled his thumb around the indented middle. He waved his hand in the air. "You see? No handle. No long stick to prevent the wrist from moving." He gestured as though conducting a sale. "Your bid, madam! To my left!" He banged it down hard. "Sold!" He opened her palm and put the piece into it.

Duffy nodded, fitting it in place as he had done. She gestured, bending her wrist, pointing with her index finger while holding it, and rapping it down sharply on the rostrum. She shook her head No. "I've never done a sale without Papa's gavel."

"You're not selling mooseheads anymore. You're selling for

Wyndham's!" He picked up the ivory gavel and put it back in her hand. "Do it!"

Duffy took a deep breath. "Sold." She rapped the gavel.

"What?" he asked. "I can't hear a thing."

"Sold," she repeated angrily.

"Bang it down harder!"

"Sold!" she said, rapping the gavel sharply.

"That's better. Now do it again."

"Sold!" Duffy shouted. "Sold! Sold! Sold!"

In 1932, the Great Depression was at its worst. People all over the world were frightened and angry. But none more so than the man who stood on a bench in the rain and shouted, "How many Bolsheviks do you think it took?" He raised his fist and the rain poured down his sleeve. "A handful!" he yelled. "How, you ask, could a handful of ignorant peasants overthrow the Czar? How? Because they were not alone! The army, the police, even the so-called landed gentry were united against the tyranny of the bloodthirsty Romanovs!"

"What's the use?" asked his friend, Boris. "Get under the umbrella."

It was Sunday in Union Square Park on Fourteenth Street. An open-air Carnegie Hall for New York's radical elite. But it was raining and no one was there. No one but Sam Corbett.

"Come on," Boris said. "We can still catch the movie. Garbo plays Grusinskaya. My sister will get us in. Sam!"

Sam stared at the empty park through his red-rimmed eyes. So what if it rained? There was so much to explain. He began to shiver. His clothes were soaked. "Maybe I ought to go home," he said.

Boris shook his head. "What are you going to do there? Sit and stare at the walls? Listen to the Applebaums fight again? Or Zimov's baby cry? Come with me, Sam. We'll see a movie. We'll go to the Automat after. My cousin works there. He never lets me leave hungry."

Sam shook his head. "No. I should go home."

"Life goes on, you know. Because someone dies, it doesn't mean . . ."

"It wasn't someone!" Sam shouted.

"I'm sorry. But . . ."

Sam rubbed his eyes. He looked around the empty park. "You know what's wrong with this country?" he shouted. "Bread doesn't taste like bread! Beets don't taste like beets! Nothing tastes the way it should!"

"Papa, go to sleep." Natalie was seventeen and had been taking care of her father since her mother, Margaret, died. The girl also worked as a maid for a couple in Gramercy Park. They were fond of Natalie and would give her food to take home. When Margaret was sick, they paid for medicine and even sent their own doctor down to the Lower East Side. But it was already too late. "You'll ruin your eyes, Papa."

"Soon."

The chicken leg and tomato she had brought for dinner lay uneaten on his plate. "It was Alexandra who wanted to dissolve the Duma," Sam explained, looking up from his book. "She was afraid of what they were saying about her. That German whore! Sleeping with Rasputin! She deserved everything she got!"

"Papa. Put your books away."

"It was all her fault. She brought the monarchy to its feet. She encouraged Nicholas to go to Mogilev so that . . ."

Natalie reached for the book and slammed it shut. "I'm tired of hearing about the Romanovs! I'm tired of hearing about Lenin and Marx! Papa, this is our home. It is not Union Square!" Natalie kneeled at his chair. She sighed and then spoke softly. "You didn't eat again. How can I leave you for the summer?"

Sam caressed her long blond hair. "You must not disappoint the Morgans. They have been very kind to you. To us. Besides," he said, forcing a smile, "it will be cooler upstate. When do you go? Next week?"

"Tomorrow, Papa."
"Tomorrow? Is it already tomorrow?"

After Natalie was asleep, he unlocked the trunk as he had done every night since his wife died. One by one, he took out the books and piled them on the floor. Then, as he did every night, he counted the boxes. There were only ninety-six left. The Czarina had given him nearly two hundred, but most of the valuable ones had long since gone. That thief Trofim Osipovich! The captain of the boat to Copenhagen! The steward on the Kungsholm who got them through customs!

They had lived well that first year in America. They had lived well until July of 1918 when it was reported all the Romanovs had been murdered. How could he have known it would come to that? Even the children! He had ninety-six pieces left on the day he read the headline.

Everyone understood. It was not Sam's fault. Everyone knew he was poverty-stricken and could not afford a doctor when Margaret got sick. He had ninety-six pieces left on the day she died.

Chip kicked open the screen door. He walked onto the porch, a bottle of beer in each hand, and called, "Hey, when you gonna get your head screwed on right?"

Emmett was tying a mattress over the cartons and suitcases piled on the truck. He had been loading for hours, as though afraid to stop for a break. "What the hell is it?"

"Nothing much." Chip shook the sweat from his forehead. "You forgot Louis Comfort's highchair. That's all."

"Shit."

Emmett jumped down from the truck. He paused for a moment, annoyed that all he owned in the world fit on the pickup. He became angry. It was hot. He looked up accusingly at the sun. It was the end of August and the midday sun was angry, too.

Emmett stepped onto the porch and took a bottle of beer from Chip's outstretched hand. He hesitated before bringing the bottle to his parched lips. He should have said something, Emmett thought. But there was no place to begin and worse, no place to end. He held up the bottle. They toasted in silence.

Inside, Duffy sat feeding Louis Comfort while Rita and Lorraine packed a carton of canned goods. "The first thing to do when you meet the governor," Duffy said, spooning mashed carrots into the baby's mouth, "is to shake his hand, look him straight in the eye, and offer him some of your zwieback."

"Zwieback!" Rita groaned. "That's what I forgot."

"You two aren't gonna win the Parents-of-the-Year award," Chip said. "I wouldn't be surprised if you drove off without the baby."

"They got stores in Albany," Emmett said. "We'll pick up zwieback later." He slumped into a chair and looked around at the room he'd known all his life. "You ought to get this kitchen air-conditioned, Duffy."

It was a simple enough remark. Casual. But deadly. The orderly transfer of power had taken place in a single suggestion. Emmett was moving out and now it was Duffy's kitchen.

"Those aren't my canned peas," Rita said. "I hate peas."

"Well, I do not buy canned vegetables," Lorraine defended, putting the peas into the carton. "They must be yours."

Emmett shook his head. "They got stores in Albany."

Rita nodded and took the peas out of the carton. She slammed them on the table. "Leave them here. Duffy'll eat them."

Duffy smiled as she continued feeding the baby. "Let them eat peas!" she proclaimed. The baby laughed. "Oh, God, I'm going to miss you."

"It's only an hour away," Rita said. She put a hand on Duffy's shoulder. "We don't expect Aunt Duffy to be a stranger in our house," she said, picking up the baby. "Do we, sweetie pie?"

The final blow: Aunt Duffy. My, how you've grown! Do you remember . . .

"Throw the goddamn peas out!" Chip said. "How much do they cost?"

Lorraine looked at the bottom of the can. "Forty-four cents."

Chip took the peas and tossed them into the garbage. "After the auction, you can deduct one can of peas from my one million three hundred and thirty-three thousand three hundred and thirty-three dollars and thirty-three cents."

Emmett began to laugh. He banged his bottle on the table. One by one they started to giggle. Everyone except Aunt Duffy.

She looked at Emmett. His face was beaming the same way it was the day he told them that Zach Baines and his wife were desperate to sell their shop and get out fast. Emmett was desperate to buy it and get in fast.

Ben cosigned the loan for Emmett and arranged all the transfers. He cosigned another loan for Duffy that allowed her to pay Emmett his share of the barn. Within forty-eight hours, the pickup truck was packed and ready to go.

Rita took the half-used ketchup bottle out of the carton. "I'm buying everything new!" she announced. "New ketchup for my new life!" She began unpacking with a vengeance. "New peanut butter for my new life! Even new Oreos!"

Duffy turned from the leftovers that were filling up the table in the kitchen that she ought to have air-conditioned. She walked to the door and stared out at the truck.

"Champagne!" Rita shouted. "Duffy, look! We're having champagne!"

Chip waved the bottle as Rita and Lorraine hugged one another. "Oh, I am going to miss you," Lorraine confessed.

"We're only going to be an hour away," Rita said.

"It'll never be the same!" Lorraine began to cry.

Emmett and Chip stared at one another. They'd never lived apart, except when they were in the army. "When did you buy champagne?" Emmett asked, getting up for glasses.

"Other day." Chip turned away and added defensively, "It wasn't my idea." He looked back at Emmett. Simultaneously, they threw their arms around one another.

Rita and Lorraine were on one side of the kitchen, Emmett and Chip on the other. Louis Comfort sat on the floor banging a wooden spoon on an old pot. Duffy leaned against the screen door, tears streaming down her cheeks.

"Mailman!"

Oscar was carrying a square brown envelope. Duffy opened the door. "It's Oscar!" she shouted.

The brothers and sisters-in-law stopped hugging one another

and suddenly began to sob as they said, "It's Oscar!" Rita ran to Emmett, and Lorraine hugged Chip.

Oscar shook his head. "Guess you folks don't get much mail."

"We're having champagne, Oscar." Duffy pointed to the bottle.

"Hate to be around when you get a phone call," he said. "Will you sign here?" he asked, handing Duffy his pencil. He leaned over and whispered, "Better not tell them it's special delivery registered till after I leave."

She kissed Oscar on the cheek. He left, mumbling that he sure could get five dollars from the *Reader's Digest* for that one. The envelope was from Wyndham's. Duffy's fingers ripped anxiously at the brown paper. She stared at the catalog. Against a glossy black background the deep red letters of the word CZARINA filled the cover. "Look," she whispered, holding it up.

As though signaling ship to shore, Duffy showed the cover to Emmett and Rita, and then turned to show it to Chip and Lorraine. Louis Comfort beat militantly on the pot. Duffy sat down at the table, the two couples gathering behind to look over her shoulders. She rubbed the cover gently with the palm of her hand, smiled self-consciously, and opened the catalog.

The last line of the title page was circled in red. The bold black type said

DUFFY PATTERSON, Auctioneer

But what made everyone gasp was the message written next to it.

I love you,
Charles

Chip let out a war whoop. Rita and Lorraine hugged Duffy. Emmett sat down next to her and said, "You be careful. I didn't know you were fooling around with him."

Duffy began to laugh. Her fingers wanted desperately to touch the message. She needed an "I love you" to hold on to. The cavalry had arrived in time again. "Did someone say champagne?" she asked.

Chip opened the bottle as Duffy leafed through a twenty-page introduction by Jonas Longley, a mini-catalog of Imperial Easter Eggs, the story of how the treasure was found (signed by Charles Wyndham), and finally the section in which each lot was described on the left-hand page and illustrated by a full-page color photograph on the right.

They stood in a circle, toasting as they drank the champagne. Emmett spoke. "We may all be millionaires. But let's never forget that we're still a family." He looked at Duffy. "We're still going to take care of one another."

Duffy leaned over and kissed him on the cheek. "Thank you." They clinked glasses and drank.

"I have something else to say," Emmett began. "I don't know how to say it except that . . ." He faltered as his eyes filled with tears. Again, he stared at Duffy. "I am very proud of you."

"Emmett . . ." Duffy covered her eyes with her hand.

"You've given us all much more than a million dollars . . ."

"Yeah!" Chip said. "Closer to one million three hundred and thirty-three thousand three hundred . . ."

"You've given us new lives," Emmett continued. "I thank you for getting me out of here and giving me that new life."

"Thank you for getting me out of here," Rita said.

"Duffy, I don't know how to thank you for getting us out of here, too," Lorraine sobbed.

"There's something else," Chip said. He put his arm around Lorraine as she cried. "I don't know how to tell you this, but . . ." He shrugged his shoulders as the tears streamed down his cheeks. He looked at Emmett. "Don't sell the highchair."

Rita gasped and reached out for Lorraine. "You're gonna have a baby!"

Lorraine laughed as the tears fell. She put one hand to her stomach. "I got a new life, too. Right in here."

"You hear that, Duffy?" Chip cried out. "You're gonna be an aunt again!"

Duffy thanked God everyone was crying. They couldn't tell her tears were not of joy. She held on to Emmett and Chip. The five of them pressed against one another, crying and kissing. Without anyone noticing, Duffy reached for the catalog. She held on to it with all her might.

It was all there in the file on Ben's desk. Everything and nothing. All the questions and all the answers. The problem was knowing which were which.

The file headed MORGAN/INDIAN CREEK ROAD had been returned from the company that was microfilming the bank's old mortgage records. Although he'd waited impatiently for it, when the file finally arrived he let it sit unopened on his desk, wishing he had never sent for it. All day long Ben kept reaffirming his identity. He signed letters and sent memos. He authorized loans. He even went to the basement to discuss the oil bills with the janitor.

Ben waited until everyone left the bank. Even then he locked his door. But he was never alone from the first moment he opened the file. His office was filled with ghosts.

The Morgans were killed in 1944 in a head-on collision. The date and circumstances of their deaths were noted in pen and initialed JP. Jason Perry. His father. Written in that same unmistakable scrawl was a notation that the Morgans were two payments ahead at the time of their deaths. A letter from Deene, Bailey and Rodgers, dated a month later, notified the bank it was, on behalf of the Morgan estate, assuming responsibility for all future mortgage payments. The law firm of Deene, Bailey and Rodgers was in Shreveport, Louisiana.

The letter was signed by Edgar Deene. Within a few minutes Ben was on the phone. "Mr. Deene, please."

"May I ask who's calling?"

"Mr. Perry of the . . ."

"Just a moment, Mr. Perry. He's expecting your call."

Ben held his breath as the call was transferred. A man began to speak. "Jason, you've got to stop worrying!" The man paused. "Hello?"

"Hello," Ben said. "Is this Edgar Deene?"

Another pause. "Edgar was my father. He died some years ago. This is Bob Deene. Who is this?"

"Ben Perry."

Deene cleared his throat. "I'm sorry. There appears to have been a mistake. I thought you were another client . . . someone else. May I help you?"

"You thought I was Jason Perry!" There was silence. "Mr. Deene?"

"I'm sorry. I'm not at liberty . . ."

"You thought I was my father. Why would my father be calling you? What was he worried about?"

"Mr. Perry, perhaps if you told me the nature of your business. Who suggested you call us?"

"I'm calling in reference to Miss Natalie Corbett."

Hesitation. "I'm afraid we have no such client."

"I have a money order made out in her name. The postmark is Shreveport."

"Mr. Perry, I really don't know what this has to do with us. I'm not even certain what this has to do with you."

Ben drew a deep breath. "I'm her son."

"St. Petersburg used to be a wonderful place." The old man laughed. "Before they changed the name. It used to mean something to belong to the St. Petersburg Yacht Club. Now it's the St. Pete This and the St. Pete That." Jason Perry glanced uneasily at Ben. For a few moments they walked in silence along the beach. It was sunset. The sky was red. "First Walt Disney. Then the Cubans. Florida will never be the same." He paused briefly. "I know why you're here."

Ben stopped walking. "Was she my mother?"

Jason was in his early seventies. The laugh lines around his eyes were accented by a deep tan. But there was no humor as he pointed back to the shorefront building. "Your mother is on the twenty-third floor back there! Don't you ever forget that!"

"Was Natalie Corbett my mother?"

"You knew from the beginning you were adopted. It never made a difference. Not to any of us." Jason reached out and held Ben's arm. "Edgar's son told me you called. I never liked that kid."

"It must have been torture for her." Ben's head pounded with BANKER'S SON OPENS NEW BANK. He agonized over the image of her sitting alone and clipping the article so neatly. Keeping it hidden at the bottom of a drawer. "She came in every week like clockwork. The more I think about her, the more I remember. No matter what the weather. Two o'clock on Thursday you could count on seeing Miss Natalie. She walked all the way from Indian Creek Road into town. And then back. Always seemed pleasant. Very polite. She always stopped to say hello. I always said hello. Banker's Son Says Hello."

Jason hesitated. "All your mother knew was a woman in Shreveport gave birth to an illegitimate child. Edgar took care of it for us."

"Where did Natalie Corbett come from?"

"I don't know. She never wanted to talk about her family."

"And you didn't try to find out?"

"I didn't care!"

"Who was my father?"

"What's the difference? It's not going to change anything. You're too old for it to make any difference."

"I want to know, goddamn it! Who was he?"

Jason stared out at the water. He spoke with a sudden urgency. "I don't know what it was exactly, but when I was young, I just couldn't seem to get laid often enough. Clerks, tellers, secretaries, waitresses. Anybody! I was the town banker when that still meant something. There was hardly a woman in Perry Falls wouldn't be happy to entertain the town banker. I had everything! I had power. I had money. I had a beautiful wife. But she couldn't give me a child. I had to find someone who could!" He reached over and touched Ben as though it were for the first time. "I wanted a son who was my own flesh and blood."

Ben sat down on the sand. He drew his knees up close and hunched over. His voice wavered. "If you only knew how much I wanted to be your real son. I tried so hard to be just like you. To compensate. I tried to talk the way you did. I practiced your walk. I even combed my hair the way you did."

Jason's lips trembled. For a while he couldn't speak. He pointed back to the oceanfront condominium and shook his finger. "What about her?" he asked as his voice cracked. "I couldn't hurt her! I couldn't tell her the truth!"

"My God," Ben said. "I might have lived my life a hundred other ways. If only I hadn't needed to prove how much like you I was." His voice had a bitter edge. "To be as fine and decent a man as you."

"I made a good home. I was a good husband and a good father. No one could say a word against me."

"Not even Natalie Corbett?"

"No. I took care of her."

"What was she like?" Ben asked.

"I don't know. She never meant anything to me. I loved your mother. I never loved anyone else. I just needed to get someone pregnant. I didn't love Natalie. How the hell could I? She was a maid. Uneducated. A foreigner. Goddamn it, I was president of the bank! The town was named after my grandfather!"

"Did she know what was in the trunk?"

"How could she? Do you think she would have lived the way she did?"

"After you read about it, why didn't you tell me? You just stopped the checks and hoped I'd never find out."

"Ben Perry did not inherit twenty million dollars. You're my son. Not hers. That was the deal."

"The contract," Ben muttered.

"Had it been up to me, I'd never have told you. I didn't feel I was denying you anything. I felt I was protecting you."

"But it's twenty million dollars!"

"Which can only be claimed by the son of Natalie Corbett!" Jason turned to Ben with tears in his eyes. "All those years I was the only one who knew who you really were. Now you've got to decide for yourself."

The sign outside the barn read

CLOSED FOR RENOVATION
REOPENS SAT SEPT 19
BIG SALE!

but to Duffy, from the inside of the barn, all signs pointed to disaster. The rows of theater seats had been ripped out. The kitchen was stripped bare to make room for the computer equipment. The pulpit was moved back to accommodate extra seating. Even the floor had been torn up, despite complaints from the mice. Miles of cable for phone lines, for satellite transmission, for computers, snaked across the barn and up to the rafters. Metal scaffolding hugged the roof to support the lights and closed-circuit cameras. The black conversion board was suspended on chains from the rafter that once held old Mrs. Jackson's quilts.

It was Saturday night, the first Saturday night the barn had been closed since Red died. Duffy sat in the top row of the bleachers amid the ruins of her old life. Her new life could be found in the catalog she clutched. CZARINA. But how would she get through the next month until she was reborn? And then how would she get through the months after that?

She heard a car come to an abrupt stop. Someone else who didn't know the barn was closed. She listened for the motor to start up again. Instead, the door opened. It was Ben. Duffy leaned against the back wall, never so glad to see anyone in her life.

Ben looked around at the barn. He shook his head. His face was expressionless. Without a word, he stepped over the cables and climbed up the bleachers.

He sat down next to her. Duffy reached out and put her arms around him. They embraced for a long time, Duffy pulling back only because she suddenly felt he needed to be held more than she. "Ben?"

He shrugged. "Saturday night. Where else would I go? Guess it's true about a bad ruble always turning up."

"Ben, what's wrong?"

"What's wrong," he said with a deep sigh, "is this." He took a bottle from his pocket. "I can't get drunk."

Duffy looked at the bottle. "Vodka."

"It seemed appropriate." He opened the bottle and offered her some. She shook her head and watched as he drank.

"What is it, Ben?"

"What it is is I want my money back. This stuff doesn't work." Duffy put her arms around him. He sat staring ahead. "Maybe it does. This place looks like hell."

"I know. And I haven't even been drinking."

Ben held up the bottle. "We who are about to cry salute you."

"Let's go inside for some coffee."

"No." He took another drink. "You sound like my mother." She smoothed his hair. "I mean, I think you do. Can't be sure. Banker's Son Can't Be Sure."

Duffy took the bottle from him. "I need to talk to you, Ben."

"I need to talk to you, Duffy."

"Ben, I feel as though my whole world is coming apart."

"Duffy, I feel as though my whole world is coming apart."

"What's wrong? Tell me."

"We need to make a new world," he said. "Our own kingdom. The dawn of creation will be our wedding. Nothing before that day ever existed. We are who we are at the moment we say 'We do.'"

She put a hand to his cheek. He leaned over to kiss her. As their lips touched, he felt himself gasp and only then realized he was crying. Duffy was terrified. Even as a child Ben had never cried. She held him in her arms and rubbed his back as he sobbed. Finally, he took a deep breath, nodded that he was all right, and sat back.

"You know what I've been doing all day?" he asked. "I've been straightening out drawers and closets. I put all my blue ties on one side of the tie rack, then the brown, then the others. I did the same thing with my socks and shirts. I went into the kitchen to make myself a cup of coffee and while I was waiting for the water to boil I worked on the refrigerator. All the cold cuts over here. All the green vegetables over there. Milk. Soda. Beer. Then I went back inside and did my desk. Black pencils, red pencils. Small clips, big clips. Rubber bands north to south. Staples east to west. By then I had a headache. I went into the bathroom and did the medicine chest." He smiled for the first time and began to laugh, "Then I did all my books. Alphabetically by author!" He held up his hand as they both laughed. "Wait! That was just for fiction. I did the nonfiction by subject." They were doubled over. Duffy held her sides. Ben stood up, waving his hands. "I'm still not finished," he blurted out between giggles. His voice went up an octave as he tried to outshout his laughter. "Then I stamped my goddamn name in every book!"

Their joyless laughter echoed through the barn. Duffy's arms were folded around her waist. Ben lay face down on the bleachers. They became quiet. They breathed deeply. Recovering. He reached out a hand. She took hold. He pulled her toward him. They lay in one another's arms stretched along the top platform.

"You're crying," Ben said.

"It's my turn."

He kissed her tears. "You should be happy."

"I am happy." She reached for the vodka.

"Everything is going just the way you wanted it to."

Duffy nodded. "Going is right. Emmett. Papa's movie seats. Even the stupid kitchen." She drank from the bottle. "Why did you say your whole life was coming apart?"

"Did I say that?"

"You said it right after I said it."

"First, you tell me why your life is falling apart. In twenty-five words or more."

She took another drink. "Why My Life Is Falling Apart, by Duffy Patterson."

"Catchy title."

"My life is falling apart because . . ."

"I know!" Ben shouted. "Because they've come and ruined your barn."

"No."

"Because Emmett moved out?"

"No. I expected that."

"Aha! But I bet you didn't think Chip would leave!" From the expression on her face, he realized she hadn't. He winced and reached for the vodka. She stared at him while he drank. Then he offered her the bottle. "I'm sorry," he said.

"It's all right. I expected that, too. I was thinking about the baby. They're going to have a baby. Everything all at once." She smiled without pleasure. "I'm going to be an aunt again."

Ben took hold of her. "Have my baby," he pleaded. "Let's make a baby now. I know how to do it."

There was a long silence. Duffy began, "My life is falling apart because . . ."

"Because you don't have any babies," he yelled. "Because you're not married to me. That's why!"

Duffy put a hand to her forehead. "I thought this was my story."

"It is. I'm sorry." He took another drink. "I won't say a word." He held up his hand as though taking an oath. "Czar's honor."

"My life," she said, her voice quavering, "is falling apart . . . because."

Ben waited, then held up his fingers and counted. "That's only six words."

"Things must be worse than I thought," Duffy said softly. Then, suddenly angry, she stood up. "It's twenty-five words or *less*, not twenty-five words or *more*."

He shook a finger at her. "Listen, if your life was really falling apart you could certainly come up with more than twenty-five words. God knows, I could." He spoke slowly, his voice rising with each word. "My life is falling apart . . ." Ben hesitated and then, without stopping for breath, unleashed all the things he wanted to say. ". . . because of you and your goddamn sale, because you won't marry me and I need you so, because I'm afraid that once you get all that money something will happen to you, because I'm pretty sure you've already slept with Charles Wyndham and I can't stand the idea of that, because I'm the kind of person who needs to know exactly who he is and what he is and what he's going to be, and because I hate Miss Natalie Corbett. I hate her for what she's done to my life!" Ben stood on the top bleacher, gasping almost convulsively.

Duffy stared at him, breathing nearly as hard. She nodded with approval. "That's more than twenty-five."

"I told you I could do it."

"Then damn it, I don't see why I can't." Duffy sat down.

Ben walked toward her. He sat and thought. "Let me help you."

"Would you?"

He nodded Yes and took a deep breath. "Your life is falling apart because . . ."

"Yes?" Duffy waited eagerly.

"Because you're not getting any younger and you're not married."

"That's right!" she said excitedly.

"Also, everybody's leaving you."

"They are!"

"You're going to be all alone in this big old house."

"I am! I am!"

"You don't know what the hell those people are going to do to your barn. You don't know that you'll ever be able to get things back the way they were."

"I *don't*. You're so right!"

"And that son of a bitch in New York thinks he's going to marry you!"

She reached for his arm. "Ben, you're making it all so clear."

He smiled. "Furthermore, you don't want to marry me. I'm too straight. I'm boring. Not bad in bed but no one you'd want to go to bed with every night."

"Ben?"

"Yeah?"

"Is that more than twenty-five words?"

"Yeah."

"Thanks, Ben."

"Welcome."

"Ben?"

"Yeah?"

"I really don't want to go to bed with you tonight."

"Oh, sure. Absolutely."

"It has nothing to do with you. I just don't feel like making love."

"I don't either."

"Thanks." She leaned back in his arms. "That feels good."

"You didn't have to say that."

She sat up and sighed. "I didn't say it to make you feel good. Goddamn it, I wasn't even thinking about you. I was thinking about me. I need to feel good."

"That's okay."

"Okay." She nuzzled against him, moving until she found a comfortable position. "Mmmm. That's a good spot. For *me*."

He smiled. "For me, too. It's okay that you like it. I like it, too. And *that's* what counts. I don't care if you like it. I like it." He put a hand to her breast. "I like doing this. Me. I am getting my pleasure now."

"Well, it just so happens, Mr. Perry Falls Savings and Loan, that I am getting pleasure from it, too."

"Who cares?"

Duffy sat up. "I want you to take your pants off."

"Sure." He stood up, took them off and folded them neatly.

"Underwear, too."

He nodded and slipped off his shorts over his shoes. "Now what?"

"Stand in front of me." She leaned her head against his stomach and began to touch his genitals. "I want to feel where the baby stuff is."

He took her hand. "It's right in here. Don't press them too hard."

"I won't."

He guided her fingers as he spoke. "It comes out of there inside a tube that leads right up along here. Then it goes all along there until it comes out right at the tip." She began tracing the route.

"That's right." He smiled. "That feels good. I like that. Keep doing it. I like the way that feels."

"Ben, I wanted it to stay soft!"

"It doesn't matter what you want. That's what happens."

"You should have had some consideration for me. You ruined it. I was just beginning to enjoy myself."

"Okay. Okay. I know what to do. Take off your pants and lie down."

"This better be good."

"I guarantee it."

She took off her pants.

Ben put his hand on Duffy's knee, then slowly around her thigh. He moved her legs apart and began to massage slowly, his fingers reaching inside her. "You're right," she said. "I like it." Duffy moaned softly. "Ben, you know what I want you to do now?"

"Of course I do. But there's a problem. I have to be honest with you, Duffy. If I do what you want me to do, it's going to make me feel good, too."

"Why do you always have to spoil everything?"

Ben kissed Duffy to keep her quiet. While their tongues pressed against one another, he entered quickly, thrusting forward so rapidly that she gasped. "Surprise!" he whispered. "This fuck is for me, too, goddamn it!" He rocked desperately back and forth. And then, suddenly, he stopped. Ben withdrew and sat up. "I was wrong. It didn't make me feel good at all!"

"Me neither."

They both dressed and sat next to one another without speaking. Finally, Ben said, "Guess I better go."

Duffy looked at him. "What's wrong?"

He turned away. "I don't know. I just don't feel like myself."

"Save my books," he whispered. "Keep them. They are for you." His message delivered, Samuel closed his eyes forever.

It was the summer of 1938 and Natalie had been upstate with the Morgans. She hurried home after Boris called to tell her Samuel had collapsed in the park. Despite double pneumonia, he refused to die until she came home. It was when she stepped inside the door that he opened his eyes for the first time. He looked up anxiously, as though late for a very pressing appointment, and whispered his final words.

If only he had said, "I love you." Even on his deathbed, Papa was thinking about his books. The Morgans paid for the funeral and Natalie went to live with them, winters in Gramercy Park, summers in Perry Falls. It was perfectly natural for her to move upstate with them when Mr. Morgan retired. She had no ties in the city. No one had ever said "I love you."

On March 7, 1939, Natalie went to the Perry Falls Savings and Loan to open her first bank account. That day she met the young banker, Jason Perry, who personally welcomed each new depositor. He was eager to hear her stories about the city and they spoke briefly whenever they met. One very rainy Thursday, just before closing, she came in soaked to the skin. Hearing that she had walked the three miles from Indian Creek Road, Jason insisted upon driving her home.

Natalie was twenty-four and a virgin. Jason was twenty-nine and insatiable. He took her down to the boat house, and undressed her with more tenderness and appreciation than she had ever known from a man. She hardly knew what he was doing to her and thought it couldn't possibly be over by the time he began to gasp, almost as Sam had when he died. Except Jason Perry did whisper, "I love you."

He whispered "I love you" to Natalie at least once a week for the next five years. Although it was merely his way of saying thank you, those half hours with him were the closest she ever had, or ever would, come to romance. Despite himself, Jason began to mean it. He stopped sleeping with everyone but Natalie and his wife.

When the Morgans were killed in a car accident in 1944, Jason called Edgar Deene in Shreveport. He knew Natalie wouldn't take money from him so they invented a trust fund. He planned it so that she had just enough money to stay but not enough to go. The Morgans had left everything to Natalie, but everything was little more than the house and a mortgage, which Jason paid off. After Ben was born, he began making deposits in her account. They never once spoke of money. Confessing to cash would have been embarrassing for the banker who used "I love you" as the currency of gratitude. And it would have been humiliating for the woman who had given him a son.

Natalie had spent the whole day cooking, even though he told her he couldn't stay for dinner. She planned and prepared all of his favorite dishes, the things she heard him mention but had never seen him eat. It was wrong, she knew, to use a month's worth of ration coupons for a dinner no one would have, but she preferred rejection to oblivion.

By four-thirty, she sat waiting. She wore her best dress and some cologne he had brought her nearly five years earlier at Sisters of Mercy Hospital. She pretended that her husband was late again at the office. And after she'd slaved over a hot stove all day! She'd give him a piece of her mind when he came home!

When he came home, Jason asked, "Why are you all dressed up?" He looked at the table. "I told you. I can't stay for supper." He handed her a newspaper. "Here."

There was a picture on the front page, captioned BANKER'S SON OPENS NEW BANK.

"Perry Falls? Why are they having the sale there?" the old woman asked.

James, the doorman at Wyndham's, took her arm. "I guess because that's where the treasure was found."

"Ridiculous! I didn't have to go to Cairo to see King Tut." Myra Delaney held on to James' arm to be certain she didn't trip on the metal threshold. She was in her early seventies, and with her friend, Sophie, had attended the opening day of each new exhibit for nearly ten years. "Sophie," she warned, as she always did, "be careful of the threshold. You'll fall."

"They'll take you up there by bus," James said. "For free."

"Will they give us lunch?" Sophie asked, taking James' arm.

"No, ma'am."

"Well, then I'm not going! I get my lunch at the center five days a week. Lunch is the least they could do for an old lady. Here." Sophie handed James a small brown bag. "Your favorites. Tollhouse. In case you get hungry."

"Bus leaves at two on Saturday afternoon," James said.

Myra looked pleadingly at Sophie. "The center's closed on Saturday."

"I can get you two tickets for the sale," James whispered.

Myra raised her eyebrows. "Good seats?" He nodded. "Sophie?"

"Well, if the center's closed we have to make our own lunch anyway." Sophie turned to James. "But it better be a good sale!"

"We'll do our best, ma'am."

The lobby was more crowded than usual. They couldn't even see what the girls at the desk were wearing. "So many people," Myra said with excitement. She smiled and held tight to Sophie's arm. "This is going to be fun."

Fun was only one of the reasons they came to Wyndham's. Most important was they could touch things that museums would never let them near. Once or twice a week, Myra and Sophie became acquainted with beauty such as they had never dreamed. And then, as the frosting on the cake, they would attend the auctions to see who bought what. They even made penny bets on the hammer price for their favorite lots.

Sophie, who was an undisclosed number of years older than Myra, greatly appreciated that Wyndham's was properly heated in winter and air-conditioned in summer. Also, there were clean toilets, ice water, and frequent celebrities. It was their favorite place: educational, entertaining, and free.

"Remember him?" Myra whispered, nodding toward the short fat man who walked quickly past them. "From the last Russian sale."

"I certainly do!" Sophie said. "He bought my little pink picture frame with the portrait of Princess Olga."

"Yes," Myra said angrily, "and that lovely enamel bowl of mine."

The man who kept his finger not only on the elevator button but also on sugar and cocoa prices was Gustav Nemec, a prominent Swiss chocolatier. Having arrived that morning by private jet from Geneva, Nemec was impatient to examine the seventeen lots he was determined to take back with him. He pushed ahead as the elevator doors opened. Edgar, the operator, helped Sophie over the threshold. "Morning, ladies."

"Thank you," Myra said. "Nice to know some people still have manners."

"Two!" Nemec announced.

"Missed you yesterday," Edgar whispered to Sophie.

"Please! I am in a hurry!" Nemec said.

"Yes, sir!" Edgar rolled his eyes and closed the doors.

The exhibition room had been filled to capacity within ten minutes of opening. A line of people waited in the hallway.

"Never saw anything like this," Myra said.

A sign posted near the entrance explained that lots would be taken out of the display cases upon request but could be handled only by the staff. Those who wished to examine the pieces had to make an appointment with a member of the Russian Art Department. Armed guards were posted at all the exits.

"They won't let us touch anything!" Myra complained. "That's not fair!"

"Old ladies shouldn't have to stand on line," Sophie said. "That's not fair either."

Nemec walked directly to the entrance. He was stopped by the guard. "I have an appointment. I am expected by Mr. Rosenko."

"May I have your name, please?"

Nemec's nostrils flared with anger. He shouted into the exhibition room, "Rosenko!"

He might as well have yelled "Fire." Everyone in the room stopped talking and turned toward the source of the outraged cry. Gregory, already besieged by an army of collectors, nearly had a heart attack. He whirled in the direction of his accuser. He breathed a sigh of relief. "Herr Nemec," he said, putting a hand to his chest. "*Guten Morgen. Wie geht es Ihnen?* Did you have a pleasant trip?"

"*Ja, ja, ja.* I want to see the lots at once."

"Of course. Let him through!" Gregory ordered the guards.

The walls of the exhibition room were covered in purple velvet. Four enormous photographs hung from the ceiling: the Czar, the Czarina, Fabergé, and Miss Natalie. Each of the lots was displayed within its own glass case atop a purple velvet pedestal. People moved slowly. They clustered in twos and threes, whispering while exchanging coded glances, studiously making notes in their catalogs.

Two armed guards stood at the tables where clients examined the lots. Plainclothes detectives mingled with the crowd to insure further security. But the most dramatic deterrent to crime was the imposing figure of Father Kyril. He watched the eggs as protectively as a mother hen.

"Which lot would you like to see first?" Gregory asked, seating Nemec at one of the inspection tables.

"Before you show me anything else, I must see fourteen."

Father Kyril nodded. "An extraordinary piece." His voice reverberated through the room. "It was called the Alexandra Diamond because Nicholas gave it to the Czarina on the twenty-fifth anniversary of their meeting."

14. **"THE ALEXANDRA DIAMOND,"** of fine lilac color, mounted in diamonds as a pendant by Fabergé, the central cushion-shaped stone weighing approximately 25 carats.
Est. value: $1,250,000.

"Look at the color on that stone!" Solomon Davidoff shook his head. "Adele?"

She shrugged. "I'm looking."

"In all my years on 47th Street, I've never seen such a color."

"Sol, the estimate says over a million dollars!"

"It says! So it says! That doesn't mean it goes!" He whispered. "Your brothers and my brothers, we'll form a syndicate."

"Your brothers and my brothers couldn't form a matzo ball."

"Adele, it belonged to the Czar's wife."

"So what? We're related?"

"Practically! Adele," he explained with great pride, "it was the same Czar who killed off all Tanta Zilpa's family!"

2. **FABERGE JADE CIGARETTE CASE,** St. Petersburg, Workmaster Henrik Wigstrom, circa 1910, of Siberian jade (nephrite), a curved

rectangular shape, the borders alternately set
with cabochon rubies and cabochon emeralds,
the cover applied with a diamond set Imperial
Eagle with two ruby eyes.
Est. value: $25,000.

Peter Harms turned to Eliot Sampson. "Well?"

"I'm thinking."

Peter, who thought he did all the thinking for his clients, asked, "What's there to think about? Eliot, I'm not letting you walk away from this one."

"What should it go for?" Eliot asked.

"It doesn't matter. I don't care how much it *should* go for."

Eliot's collection of cigarette cases was on permanent display at company headquarters in Winston-Salem. That it belonged to Sampson Industries was a technicality—it was Peter's, his knowledge, his passion, his victories. Peter had all the qualifications necessary to become a brilliant collector except one—money. The obvious solution was to spend other people's money, which he did very well. He had spent a minor fortune to develop Eliot's whim into a blue-chip corporate investment.

Peter often paid more than Eliot authorized and sometimes even refused to bid for lots he personally found of marginal interest. The ten percent of the hammer price he received as commission was well earned. But he would have done it for nothing. Eliot knew that and trusted Peter implicitly.

"Peter, just give me a ballpark figure."

"Do you know what it takes to slice jade that thin? In that shape?"

"All right." It was useless arguing. "But for the record, Peter, this is one piece I really don't like."

"Eliot! What the hell do *you* know?"

8. **FABERGÉ RUBY, DIAMOND, AND GOLD
PHOTOGRAPH FRAME,** St. Petersburg, Workmaster Mikhail Perchin, circa 1903, of overlapping double-heart shape set with 300
cabochon rubies, the surround of 115 dia-

monds, an oval photograph of Alexandra
Feodorovna on the left and an oval photograph
of the infant Czarevitch Alexis on the right, the
ovals bordered by 65 diamonds, mounted in
gold, the back strut in the shape of the monogram and crown of Nicholas II.
Height: 10 inches (26 cm).
Est. value: $350,000.

Frederic Bascombe had flown in from Toronto solely for the exhibition. "Laura, I must have it!"

Laura Clayton, Wyndham's very special consultant for very special clients, hadn't a doubt in the world the Maestro would want the double-heart frame. The problem was how much he would spend.

"Five hundred thousand?" he whispered.

"Maestro! For cabochon rubies?"

"Five fifty?"

Laura took his arm and led him to a corner. They were all such children, she thought. This one especially. Bascombe was one of the world's leading orchestra conductors. His vast collection of *objets de coeur* was internationally recognized. "Maestro," she began gently, "in all honesty, I'd advise you not to go that high. It's not worth it."

"To whom? Were you born on St. Valentine's Day or was I?" He smiled broadly. "Laura, I've spent years saving more hearts than Christiaan Barnard."

"And I've spent years helping you to spend your money. Not throw it away."

"Laura, my darling, the rubies burn with the fire of Old Russia. I have only to look at it and I hear Rimski-Korsakov! Tchaikovsky! Rachmaninoff!"

"Well, then I must be tone deaf. When I look at it, I hear uncut stones. A little voice inside me says cabochons are simply not worth that much. Maestro, they're not even Burmese rubies! They're pretty enough, but . . ."

He held up his hand. "Laura, put away your gemological

report and take out your crystal ball. Tell me, when will we see one like this again?"

"Maestro . . ."

"Tell me, when? Tomorrow? Next week? Next year? Laura, when will you have another double-heart frame that belonged to the Czarina?"

68. **FABERGÉ GOLD, ENAMEL, RUBY AND DIA-MOND TIARA,** made for Alexandra Feodorovna on the occasion of the Tercentenary Ball, designed as two sprays of laurel leaves, the gold stems enameled a rich emerald green, each spray comprising thirty ruby and diamond set leaves.
Est. value: $625,000.

"Is anyone looking?"

"No. Go ahead."

Sophie pretended to be studying the tiara as she took a small scissors from her purse. Smiling nervously at Myra, she cut the string that held a display copy of the catalog. "Did anyone see? Are they looking?"

"Certainly," she snapped. "They hired all these extra detectives just to catch Sophie the catalog thief."

"I'm not stealing it!" Sophie said. "It's just on permanent loan." She held the catalog up and pretended to read.

"The string!" Myra whispered in horror. "Take off the string!"

Sophie gasped. She dropped the catalog to the floor. "Now look what happened."

"Pick it up!"

"I can't bend. I'm wearing my brace!"

Myra held on to Sophie's arm and slowly bent down. "I'm too old for a life of crime."

Before she had gone halfway, a man's hand reached out. "May I?" he asked.

Myra froze, her foot hiding the tell-tale string as he picked up the catalog. "Thank you so much," she said, as grandly as her nerves would allow.

The young man, in his fifties, with nicely combed hair, smiled. Myra nodded and began leafing through the pages. "Now, what was that lot number?" she asked Sophie.

"Sixty-eight," the man said, staring at the tiara.

"Thank you," Sophie nodded, turning quickly back to busy herself in the catalog with Myra.

But he wouldn't leave them alone. "What do you think it is?"

Myra and Sophie looked at one another, then at the page, then at the tiara. "There's something about it," Sophie said, not knowing what she meant.

"I can't quite put my finger on it," Myra mused.

"That's it exactly! I know just what you mean!" He moved closer and whispered. "There's definitely something wrong with the stones."

"There is?" Sophie said, trying to make her question sound like a statement.

"Well, not that *they're* going to tell you," he said, waving his catalog. "In and out. Turnover. That's the name of their game. Everything is fast, except paying people like me."

"Like you?" Myra asked.

He shrugged his shoulders. "I have an aunt who once had lots of money. But she's been sick." He leaned close and whispered. "Hospital bills. They eat up everything. I brought in her four best pieces of Fabergé. Original boxes, too. She's desperate for cash. But they want her to wait three months before they pay. Well, she just can't wait."

"Oh, my," Sophie said.

"So, she's got to sell cheap. She needs money." He sighed and shook his head. "Someone's going to pick up quite a bargain."

Myra smiled at Sophie. It never failed. Someone always had quite a bargain.

91. **FABERGÉ FANCY-COLORED DIAMOND NECKLACE AND MATCHING EARRINGS,** the necklace set with twelve different fancy-colored diamonds of unusual quality and intensity, each weighing approximately 9.5 carats, within white diamond collets, the earrings each set with three different fancy-colored diamonds each weighing approximately 3 carats.
Est. value: $3,600,000.

Linda Norton and Jennifer Bayer were dentists' wives who came in from the Island once a week for lunch. While in college, they had eaten well-done burgers and browsed in bookstores. During their first marriages, they switched to omelettes and rummaging through wine shops. These days, they had sushi and made the auction scene.

"It's perfect in every way, Linda."

"I'm afraid I don't agree, Jennifer. The true artist makes use of his past experience, consciously or unconsciously, to express himself in an emotionally recognizable form using color, sound, texture, or even words. There's nothing here that expresses love, hate, fear . . ."

"Linda, you're being obtuse. Fabergé was a modern-day Cellini."

"Ridiculous. He was merely the Gucci of St. Petersburg."

"The eggs, Linda. Are they Gucci?"

"Borderline, darling."

"The carved animal figures."

"Technically passable, perhaps, but cold. Brrr!"

"Excuse me, but are you dealers?" The middle-aged man with an exfoliative malocclusion smiled politely. "I couldn't help noticing how carefully you were scrutinizing the necklace."

"Dealers? No, we're not."

"Ah, then you must be collectors?"

"In a way. We send out the bills every month."

"Are you a dealer?" Linda asked.

He laughed. Lower right molars in very bad shape. Acute gingivitis. "I wish I were. I'm trying to find one." He came closer and whispered. "You see, it's my aunt. She's been terribly ill and has four pieces of Fabergé she's forced to sell. Someone's going to pick up quite a bargain."

CONDITIONS OF SALE
4. The highest bidder, as acknowledged in the sale room by the auctioneer, will be the purchaser.

Coussac walked through the crowd to the Men's Room. Neville Greene, of San Francisco's Arts of Old Russia gallery, followed him. They checked to be certain no one was in the booths. Neville walked to the urinal.

Coussac frowned. "It's impossible to do business while you urinate."

"Why? *You* expect me to do business while you shit all over me!" They waited in hostile silence until Neville pressed the flusher. He walked to the sink and turned on the faucet. "Now, let's begin again."

"The offer is the same," Coussac said. "Take it or leave it."

"I thought we'd pool as we did at Fleming's."

"Not this time."

"Why not?"

"Because this time I want everything."

"Don't be absurd," Neville said. "This is likely to be the most important Fabergé sale of our lives. You can't expect the ring to walk away empty-handed just to help you out with a difficult client."

"I've made this offer because you're part of the ring. Otherwise I'd gladly let you walk away empty-handed. My authorization is bid to buy. Naturally, I wish to secure the lots as reasonably as possible for my client. It's cheaper to buy you out than to bid you out. Either take what I'm offering or you won't even cover your expenses."

"How do I know you're not bluffing?"

Coussac opened his briefcase. It was filled with Swiss francs. "This is how."

"I still don't trust you."

"Assume you won every lot you bid on, which is unlikely. Also assume you had to go to your top bid, which is even more unlikely. I will give you twenty-five percent above your commission on those bids to sit on your hands."

"No! You're asking me to freeze out my best clients. I have integrity as a dealer." Neville took a deep breath. "It will cost you one hundred thousand."

Coussac handed Neville two fresh packets of thousand-franc notes. Neville stepped into a booth, took off his jacket and unzipped the wallet he carried in a shoulder holster. Neville smiled. "So the Russians are that eager, are they?"

73. **FABERGÉ CHAMPAGNE DIAMOND RING,** set with an octagonal step-cut champagne diamond weighing 12.45 carats, set in a circular mount of alternating matched golden pearls and champagne diamonds.
Est. value: $275,000.

Henrietta Carr was a very blond, very heavy woman of sixty who described herself as looking like two Ginger Rogerses. The handbag she had carried through U.S. Customs the day before had a false bottom and contained nearly seventy thousand dollars in little Victorian rings. Victorian rings were her business and she was known at her stall on London's Portobello Road as "Little Vicky." She stared through her harlequin-shaped glasses with a highly practiced eye. Bloody beautiful, she thought. It was time for a little champagne in her life.

45. **FABERGÉ GOLD, JEWELED AND TRANS-LUCENT ENAMEL PRESENTATION BOX,** St. Petersburg, Workmaster Mikhail Perchin, 1901, of rectangular shape, the cover mounted with a signed oval miniature of Nicholas II within a border of diamonds and surmounted by a diamond-set Imperial crown, the body enameled translucent mauve over a gold sunburst field.
Length: 7½ inches (19 cm).
Est. value: $80,000.

"What in the world would you keep in a box like that?" Myra asked Sophie.

Gregory reached in front of them to open the case. "Pardon me, madam."

"Young man," Sophie asked, "can you tell us something about this box?"

Gregory was in a hurry. Nemec was waiting at the table for him. The last thing he needed was two old biddies who wanted a bedtime story. "It was a gift from the Czar to the Czarina. He had Fabergé make it in her favorite color, mauve. It was a big surprise and she loved it." He nodded and said, "Now, if you'll excuse me."

"I have always loved history," Myra said. "I didn't know her favorite color was mauve."

"Neither did I. Well, it's always been a favorite of mine, too," Sophie said. "You remember that coat I had?"

"It was never warm enough for you."

"If only I could think of something to do with the box," sighed Sophie.

"Oh, oh," Myra whispered. "He took it over to you-know-who." They both watched Gregory hand it to you-know-who, who had bought Sophie's little pink picture frame.

"Why does he always want the same things I do?" Sophie wished she could overhear what Nemec was saying.

"It is perfect," Nemec whispered as he took out a loupe to

examine the diamonds. He smiled for the first time. "It is perfect for my chocolate cherries!"

18. **FABERGÉ DIAMOND AND EMERALD RING,**
the center old-mine diamond cushion shape, weighing 35.65 carats, surrounded by 25 cabochon emeralds set in yellow gold.
Est. value: $60,000

And what have we here, Little Vicky asked herself. Very nice, very nice indeed. A definite possibility. Three-five point six-five carats. My dear! She looked hurriedly through her catalog. Mmm. The champagne diamond was only twelve point four-five. Much more reasonable, this one. She held her bag close and sighed. Trade in all her little dearies for that, she would. After all those years of little Vicky rings, to stroll down Portobello with a flash like that on her finger! Like the ruddy Queen of Russia herself. And why not? Wasn't that the whole idea?

Well, it was Bert's idea. Saddest day of her life that was, packing up his spoons knowing they weren't going to Portobello anymore. After all that time, too. Sitting in the cold, she behind her trays of rings and Bert behind his trays of spoons, the two of them warming their hands on little paper cups of tea. In the rain, eating soggy cheese and cress sandwiches. In the sun, drinking warm lemon squash. She preferred the orange, always had, but Bert liked the lemon. More tart, he'd say, giving her a pinch. Imagine, someone giving a pinch to a sixty-year-old woman. Who else but Bert? No one.

She still bought the lemon out of loyalty. But it tasted more bitter than ever. That was why she had to get out. Get off the Road. First thing was to sell Bert's spoons. All except the Russian enamels. She'd never sell them. He displayed them in the case just for the pleasure of turning down offers. He loved them, he did. Made him feel like the ruddy Czar.

CONDITIONS OF SALE

7. All lots sold "AS IS." The statements appearing in this catalog are opinion and are not to be construed as fact. Notwithstanding any other terms of these conditions, Wyndham's will refund the original purchase price of any lot in this catalog proved within a two-year period to be a deliberate forgery.

Aldo Frinelli, of the Frinelli Galleries in Rome, patted his bulging jacket pocket and smiled. He looked around the Men's Room. "To tell the truth, I have done business in worse places."

"I have no doubt," Coussac said.

"Whoever your client is, I hope the Soviet government enjoys the pieces."

"I have nothing to do with the Soviet government."

"And I do not belong to the ring," Aldo said, shrugging his shoulders and smiling. "Ring? What ring?"

By forming a ring and agreeing not to bid against one another, a group of dealers were able to obtain lots at auction for an artificially low price. Immediately after the public sale, the ring held a private auction among members. The difference between the sale room price and the higher "knockout" price was then shared equally. Rings weren't formed out of camaraderie or to limit competition among dealers, but simply to put the profit from that competition into the dealers' pockets rather than leave it at the auction house.

"I made a fortune from the knock money after the Fleming sale. Now, even if I don't bid on anything at that God-forsaken barn I still make a handsome profit! Perhaps I should close the gallery, cut my overhead, and simply work the ring." Aldo began laughing.

"I believe we have concluded our business."

"Yes." But to Coussac's annoyance, Aldo walked to the urinal instead of to the door. "So. Now you will control the sale. It is no longer a question of how much you will spend, it is how much the others think you will spend."

"Is that why you bid so heavily against me for the Virgin of Smolensk at the Fleming's knockout?"

"Oh, no, no! No. It is because I had overpaid for another Smolensk icon a few weeks earlier. I needed you to pay more than I paid. Then, after you sold yours I could sell mine cheaper than 'that thief Coussac'!" He began laughing again.

40. **FABERGÉ SILVER-GILT AND SHADED RUSSIAN ENAMEL KOVSH,** St. Petersburg, Workmaster Victor Aarne, circa 1900, the traditional form of drinking vessel enameled in the Pan-Slavic manner with multicolored exotic flowers alternately set with cabochon carnelians and chalcedonies as the center of the blossoms, applied with silver beads and filigree scrolls.
Length: 10¾ inches (27.4 cm).
Est. value: $35,000.

"Goddamn, that's one helluva *kovsh!*" Oscar Sorensen, president of Ivanov Vodka, Ltd., looked up at Father Kyril, who sat at the next table. "Excuse me."

Father Kyril held up his hand. He had just bitten into a piece of honey cake and his mouth was full. Raising a finger, he signaled Oscar to wait a moment while he took a sip of tea. Someone had brought not only Father Kyril's chair but also a basket filled with *pirozhki* and honey cake to have with the fresh tea delivered hot every hour.

The Czar's sentinel grabbed the enameled cup. "Do you know the origin of the *kovsh?*"

"Yes, Father."

"I will tell you. We have traced the ladle shape back to the Scythians. Originally, the *kovsh* was in the shape of a duck . . ."

"I know."

". . . the neck of which was the handle. But through the years, as everything else, it has become more abstract."

"Father, with all due respect, I have been collecting Fabergé for over thirty years. I intend to have this for my collection."

"And I intend to have it for God."

"Father, the Sorensen collection is very well known."

"So is God."

"When I die, Father, the collection will go to the Sorensen Wing of the Metropolitan. On permanent display."

Gregory leaned over and asked discreetly, "Mr. Sorensen, if you're through, I have another client waiting to see this lot."

"Who?" they asked in simultaneous outrage. Oscar turned, and upon seeing Nemec whispered his name as though uttering a curse. Then, as quickly as Nero had lit the first match, Oscar pointed to Nemec and said aloud, "That's the man we should ask!" Both Father Kyril and Nemec looked up in surprise. "Perhaps you would help the good Father and me?" Oscar asked. "Is it your opinion the *kovsh* is by Semenova or Saltykov?"

Gregory snapped, "Neither! It is Fabergé!"

Oscar shook his head, clearly humoring him. "Of course, of course." Nemec walked quickly to Oscar and handed him the *kovsh*.

Gregory was furious. "This piece was not made by Semenova or Saltykov!"

Oscar held up his hands. "Of course it wasn't." He leaned toward Nemec and asked confidentially, "Which one was it?" Nemec stared at Oscar while rubbing his thumb and forefinger together. Then he looked at the bottom of the *kovsh* and rubbed his fingertip over the Fabergé signature stamped in the metal. Before he could form an opinion, Oscar whispered, "See what I mean?"

"Herr Nemec," Gregory began, "I assure you . . ."

Nemec's eyes narrowed as he pushed the *kovsh* away in disgust. He stood up, bowed curtly, and without ever having uttered a single word, walked back to the other table. Gregory followed, begging him to reconsider.

Oscar winked at Father Kyril. "So much for the competition," he said triumphantly.

Father Kyril reached for the *kovsh*. He looked at Oscar, winked back and shook his head. "There is no competition."

92. **FABERGÉ RUBY RING,** set with a faceted cushion-shaped pigeon blood Burmese ruby weighing 9.06 carats, surrounded by two rows containing a total of 32 old-mine diamonds. Est. value: $900,000.

Little Vicky stared at the picture in the catalog but couldn't see anything. All of her senses were focused on Waneta Ballard, who was appraising the two hundred Victorian rings. Four black velvet trays of ten on five.

Waneta examined the trays as though she were a headmistress searching for lice. She needed the rings desperately. Her last sale fell short of her quarterly estimate and she had to catch up quickly in order to meet her sales projection for the year. In order to get her bonus. In order to keep her job as head of the Antique Jewelry Department. "You do realize your terms are quite unusual?"

"Yes, miss." Little Vicky smiled. "My Bert always said I was an original."

"Mrs. Carr . . ."

"My late husband," she explained.

"I'm sorry."

"We had a good time, Bert and I. Lots of laughs. Well, you know. You have to in this business. Besides, it don't cost anything to laugh, he'd say. Good thing it didn't. Everything we had went back into spoons and rings."

"You had a shop?"

"Oh, no. We had a stall on Portobello. We did for years. Everybody knew Bert. They'd traipse from all over London to see him." She shrugged. "Well, not anymore they don't. I got a good price for his spoons. Except the Russian enamels. I'd never sell them. Never."

"Mrs. Carr . . ."

"My Bert was a real authority on spoons. He knew all about them. Tea spoons, caddy spoons, funny things like marrow scoops. He even wrote an article once, just like a writer. Everyone said he ought to have a shop on Bond Street. Can you imagine?" She put a hand to her mouth. "We had a good time on Portobello. The best." She began to cry. "He deserved a warrant," she pleaded. "It should have said right over the stall, 'By Appointment to Her Majesty the Queen'!"

Why me, God? Waneta thought. As though there weren't enough pressures. First, they expected her to be a goddamn archaeologist, digging up enough jewelry for three sales a year. Now she had to be a psychiatrist, too. "Would you like a tissue?"

"I'm fine, miss. I'm sorry. Sometimes it's hard to give things up."

Waneta raised an eyebrow. "Well, you're hardly giving them up, Mrs. Carr."

Cold, she was. Just like Timmy Matthews when she sold him the spoons. Why couldn't people understand? Not that she didn't want to sell them. But they were like her children! Every ring had a story, every last one had something nice to be said about it. Bert understood that best of all. Him and his Russian enamels. Having their ice cream at night with those grand spoons. As though they were the Czar and Czarina.

"How much, miss?"

Waneta shrugged. "Well, it's not as though we were a bank . . ."

"Oh, no. You're better than a bank. The bloody bank wouldn't give me tuppence ha'penny for my little dearies. But you know what they're worth. How much, miss?"

Little Vicky knew that the trays should bring close to seventy thousand. Give or take ten percent for aggravation. What Waneta knew was how hard it had become to find Victorian rings. And no wonder. Mrs. Carr owned them all! How in the world had a woman like that collected nearly *one hundred and twenty-five thousand dollars'* worth of rings? Still they were all in front of her. Ready to be added on to the projected profits for her department.

"Fifty," Waneta said.

"Fifty?" Coo, Little Vicky thought. If she's willing to do fifty, it's worth more than seventy. Got to be a hundred. A hundred? Is that possible? Must be. Must be at least a hundred. She shook her head No. "I don't think so, miss."

Waneta sat back. "Of course, I know they'll bring more than fifty, Mrs. Carr. But you're asking for credit. You're asking for an outright loan."

"I am. And I'm offering outright collateral. One hundred and twenty-five in collateral," she dared to say.

Waneta sighed. The only good client was a dead client. "If I do get this approval, and I'm not certain I will, I know it won't be for more than one hundred."

"Not more than one hundred?" Little Vicky said as though in a trance. "Dear me. Only one hundred thousand dollars?" she repeated.

"It's the best I can offer."

Wait until she told Bert! Soon as she got back she'd tell him. Little Vicky opened her purse. She took out a snapshot and held it up. "Look," she said. "My Bert."

It was a picture of a tombstone, across the top of which was engraved, "By Appointment to His Loving Wife."

56. **FABERGÉ SILVER-GILT, ENAMEL AND JEWELED ICON,** St. Petersburg, Workmaster Mikhail Perchin, circa 1895, the silver-gilt frames of the painted triptych in Rococo taste enriched with rose diamonds, cabochon rubies, emeralds, sapphires and pearls, enameled opalescent pink over guilloche fields. On the left panel is St. Princess Alexandra and on the right St. Nicholas. The central panel show-

ing St. Princess Olga to commemorate the birth
of their first child in 1895.
Height: 8¾ inches (22 cm).
Est. value: $125,000.

Harold Meisenstein slapped the palm of his hand noisily against his forehead the moment he saw the icon. He groaned with a sharp intake of breath. Then he groaned again.

"Harold!" Irv Goren, his accountant, considered Harold the most difficult of his clients.

"I must have it! I must have everything! I want it all!"

"Harold, you don't need them all," he said, as a mother to a child in a toy shop.

"Need, schmeed. I'm buying them!" proclaimed the man known as the King of 57th Street because he owned most of the real estate between Fifth and Sixth avenues. Harold had a skunk-wide streak of white hair that ran from his forehead like the tail of an exclamation point. He was tall, fiftyish, and wore a white turtleneck shirt and a white suit. His breath reeked of Turkish cigarettes.

"You're buying just to buy," Irv accused.

Harold grabbed hold of his arm. "Who decided I needed a social worker to go shopping? Did God decide I needed Mr. Plus and Minus along with me?"

"You're not supposed to be *shopping*, Harold. You're sup-posed to be *collecting!*"

"Bullshit! Collecting is a term invented by the goyim to ease their guilt for shopping. Jews don't have that problem. Shopping is the only thing we don't feel guilty about!"

"It'll cost you, Harold."

He shrugged. "So we'll take a second mortgage on Bendel. Big deal! What the hell do I care? The worst that can happen is I'll overpay. And if I do, I'll set a new world record so that everything I already own will go up in value. Don't you know yet by this time, Mr. Certified Public Asshole? It *never* costs me!"

6. **FABERGÉ NECKLACE OF GOLD, ENAMELED AND JEWELED MINIATURE EASTER EGGS,** consisting of a single strand of 150 egg-shaped pendants each approximately ¾ inch high, many depicting personal mementos of Alexandra Feodorovna, including one egg for each of the seven members of the Imperial family with their monograms and crown, one for each of the Imperial orders of knighthood, the Order of the White Eagle, and the Romanov griffin in gold and black enamel.
Est. value: $450,000.

"How unspeakably vulgar to decorate oneself with miniature dairy products. But then you know how inbred the Romanovs were. Surely there must be better ways to squander your money. Trust Aunt Magda."

Princess Magdalena Xenia had never really liked Delphina. Not that Delphina's side of the family was boring. One could pass a rather pleasant season with them, providing the champagne didn't run out. Greeks went well with champagne. Rather like Czechs, but unfortunately without their humor. Magda had hoped as Delphina matured they might have a truly meaningful princess-to-princess relationship. But all her hopes were dashed when Delphina went to work for Wyndham's. She disgraced the dynasty by becoming the first of the line to have a Social Security number.

"Aunt Magda," Delphina whispered, "you've got to come to Perry Falls. Charles won't let me bid because I work for the house."

"Delphina, you've brought all this upon yourself. I warned you about the sins of wages."

"But Auntie, I have something from practically everyone but Great-aunt Alexandra." Delphina stared into the case. "It's a necklace like no other. I'd die for it!"

"Which reminds me, have you still the brooch of Marie Antoinette's?"

"Oh, yes. And earrings from Juliana, the bracelet Albert gave Victoria, the pendant that belonged to Maud of Norway . . ."

"How unseemly to scavenge the royal vaults. In my day, virginity extended to one's jewels as well. We would no more have tolerated a used diamond than a . . . well, whatever. There are exceptions, I suppose." She smiled. "Notably the Hapsburgs. They were such wicked boys."

"Please, Auntie? You know how much it means to me."

"How will I ever get there?"

"I'll have a car and driver for you."

Magda sighed. "What kind?"

"A Rolls, of course."

"No, no. What kind of driver?"

Delphina smiled. "Aunt Magda . . ."

"I like them very young. Easily impressed. Nordic."

The two princesses embraced. "Thank you, Auntie!"

Magda pulled back and shook a finger at Delphina. "Don't count your eggs before they're hatched!"

3. **FABERGÉ CARVED AGATE PIG,** St. Petersburg, circa 1900, finely carved in striated agate, with gold-mounted diamond eyes, modeled seated, leaning slightly to one side, with curled tail.
Height: 3½ inches (8.9 cm).
Est. value: $25,000.

"Oh, Daddy!"

"Now ain't that somethin'!"

Mommy and Daddy traveled all year in the camper they called home. They worked antique shows up and down the East Coast. Their lives were devoted to collecting and selling Pig Art.

"We've got to have him, Daddy. I know just where I want him to be. We'll move Porky to the corner and put him right in the center of the table on a revolving mirror with that disco light right on his sweet little chops."

"Sure would be somethin'. You know what I would do? I'd frame the check to show how much we paid for him."

"Oh, Daddy, that is class with a capital K!"

Mommy and Daddy were doing the first annual "Flea-for-All" in the parking lot at Belclaire Raceway, where they slept in the camper. After washing his socks and underwear in the Men's Room at the clubhouse, Daddy was looking for something to read while he went to the "potty." He borrowed a catalog from a guy who sold military insignia. Daddy let out such a whoop when he saw the twenty-five-thousand-dollar pig that somebody knocked on the booth to see if he was all right.

Their business was called "The Pig's Pen." The stock included books, figures, coasters, decorated glassware, pins, watches, banks, key chains, and pictures of every important pig from the Three Little Pigs to Miss Piggy.

"Daddy," she whispered, staring into the case and speaking with reverence, "he's the most expensive pig in the whole world!"

"I just never figured I'd see anything like that. A twenty-five-thousand-dollar pig!"

"Daddy, we have those policies . . ."

"Mommy, we promised."

"I know. But you said it yourself. We just never figured we'd see anything like this. If anybody's got a right to him, we do! He belongs to us!"

"Lot of people looking at him."

"If you think there's a lot of people looking at him now, wait till they see him at the Route 19 Drive-In next week!"

CONDITIONS OF SALE
9. The auctioneer reserves the right to reject any bid. In the event of any dispute between bidders, the lot so in dispute shall be immediately put up again and resold. The auctioneer has the right to advance the bidding at his absolute discretion.

Coussac had everyone in his pocket, everyone except Denis Orlov, who walked into the Men's Room and looked around in amazement. "Surely you're joking!"

"You've known me long enough. I have no sense of humor."

"Then it's as I suspected ever since you paid that outrageous price for the Virgin of Smolensk. You're senile!"

They glared at one another with a hostility that had begun when their fathers worked in Fabergé's New Bond Street shop, and then flowered as the rivalry grew between Coussac et Fils (New York) and Orlov and Son Ltd. (London).

"I'm offering you the same terms as everyone else in the ring," Coussac said.

"How dare you!"

"I shall have them all," Coussac warned.

"If so, then you shall have them at a price they are worth."

"You will leave empty-handed. I promise you." Coussac was seething with unresolved anger. "It is that same British middle-class morality that made you such a bore as a child!"

"And you still buy your victories as though the world were your personal whorehouse."

They turned in surprise as someone came in and walked to the urinal. The two men stared at one another, searching for their youth. How old each thought the other appeared. Neither said anything until after the man had left.

"I have been paying everyone," Coussac said. "There is no reason not to pay you."

"The reason is, I have a client for whom I must bid," Denis said flatly.

Coussac hesitated, then cleared his throat. "I have heard things are . . . difficult . . ."

"That is no concern of yours."

Seething with frustration, Coussac asked, "Is there no way I can break through that servile mentality of yours?"

Denis smiled. "You surely cannot bribe your way through."

Coussac's lips parted in a smile. He laughed as he would do only with someone he loved. Then he nodded that he understood and locked his briefcase. The two men shook hands. Coussac asked, "The Queen?"

"Yes," Denis said. "The Russians?"

Coussac nodded and held on to Denis' hand. They looked at one another again, both smiling. "Two little boys," Coussac recalled. "Two little boys who once rolled enameled eggs in the back of a jewelry shop."

7. **"THE ST. BASIL'S CATHEDRAL EGG," A FABERGÉ GOLD, ENAMEL AND JEWELED IMPERIAL EASTER EGG,** St. Petersburg, Workmaster Henrik Wigstrom, 1906, of oval shape in the form of the Cathedral of St. Basil the Blessed, the eight onion domes each enameled opalescent white, with alternating swirled bands of rubies, emeralds, diamonds and sapphires reaching the pinnacles, each of the domes opening to reveal eight miniature painted icon "surprises" on cream velvet cushions.
Height: 5¼ inches (13.4 cm).
Est. value: $550,000.

Ben stared at the egg as though he had never seen it before. But he had seen it before. He just didn't know at the time that it belonged to him. All of it belonged to him. Everything on display was his. Hundreds of people were streaming through, staring at pieces of his life that he couldn't put together.

Ben stopped at the downstairs desk to buy a copy of the catalog as though he had never seen that before either. He was jostled by the crowd going into the elevator and then patiently waited his turn on line, although he could have identified himself and gone right through. His heart began to pound as the guard signaled him into the exhibition room. And then he thought it would stop when he looked up and saw a photograph of the woman who he now knew was his mother.

All he had to do was tell someone. He could have had the room cleared. He could open the cases and take the pieces home. They were his: a glittering jigsaw that didn't fit. They're mine! he wanted to shout.

Ben watched with fascination as a priest pushed a wheelchair from case to case. The old man seated in it was frail, hunched, blind. His gnarled fingers reached out hungrily to touch every piece. An icon. A box. A drinking cup. Each time his hands held something, the priest would whisper to him.

"He's a Romanov," someone said.

Ben stepped back as the priest wheeled the chair toward the St. Basil's Egg. The old man gasped with surprise as he was handed the piece. He began to whimper. His fingers traced the edges of the domes as though greeting an old friend. Suddenly, the old man began to wail—a thin, pitiful echo of his heart breaking.

Everyone in the room stopped talking. They stood frozen. The old man pressed his fingers into the enamel spires as though by causing himself pain he could recapture a life long past. Ben walked toward him. He reached out. But Father Kyril pushed his hand away.

"I want to speak to him," Ben said.

"He does not speak English."

"Will you ask him something for me?"

"No. He remembers nothing."

Ben pleaded. "Who is he?"

"Who are *you*?" Father Kyril asked. He saw the hesitation in Ben's eyes. Leaning over, he whispered again, "Who *are* you?"

Ben stared at Father Kyril. It was a simple question. He shook his head. "That's what I wanted to ask him."

It was raining when the buses left Manhattan, but along the New York State Thruway the skies had begun to clear. The clouds lightened near Kingston. An hour past Albany, the sky was blue and filled with a very yellow sun. Sy Sherman put up a sign outside his toll booth at the Adirondack Park Exit:

> PERRY FALLS   6 MI
> TURN LEFT THEN SHARP
> RIGHT AT DINER

The first bus was the press party. As the driver stopped to pay the toll, everyone applauded. It had been a long trip despite Ashanti's efforts to keep the reporters and photographers occupied. No sooner had they crossed the George Washington Bridge than the "borscht bar" opened, serving glasses of soup on the rocks, *pirozhki*, and, from a gleaming samovar, mint tea.

To accompany the elaborate press kit, and to kill time, Ashanti had arranged for experts to discuss Fabergé, estate laws, auction procedures and the fall of the Romanovs.

"What was the fourth daughter's name?" someone asked. "Olga, Tatiana, Anastasia and . . . ?"

But before Gregory could reply, a voice in the rear called out, "Sneezy!"

The bus had gone only a few hundred feet from the toll booth when the driver slowed down. There were dozens of kids lining the highway, holding signs that read, "Welcome to Perry Falls," "Mabel's Diner—2 Miles," "Gas Up at Wally's—Clean Rest Rooms." A few older kids had a toilet-paper banner that read, "Commies Go Home."

There were three state troopers on the highway outside Mabel's diner directing cars onto "Nickel Man Road." Mabel had a sign in front announcing

TODAY'S SPECIAL
CZARBURGERS ON TOASTED BUNS
FRENCH FRIES, 2 SLICES OF PICKLE

"Nickel Man Road" was lined with what appeared to be the entire town. People waved and pointed at cars with black windows into which they couldn't see. Some families sat on folding chairs, others lounged on blankets. People rocked on porches or leaned against trees or sat on fences. But one thing everyone did was take pictures of the first traffic jam ever in Perry Falls.

Dozens of police cars were parked alongside the road. Limousines, buses, cars, a few yellow cabs from Albany, and one pink camper with a bumper sticker reading "We Brake for Pigs" came to a standstill. For nearly ten minutes nothing moved as state troopers restricted entry to both the West Parking Area (formerly known as Farmer Brody's field), and the East Parking Area that surrounded the barn. The reason for the delay came from above.

Everyone looked to the sky, shielding their faces from the breeze, to watch the helicopter land in the middle of the highway. Father Kyril stepped out, his long black robes swirling as though he were the center of a tornado. As Rimski-Korsakov's *Russian Easter Overture* saturated the twilight from speakers all around the barn, he paused to bless the state troopers. Four bearded priests followed him as the music swelled. He walked along the bright red carpet that led across the grass.

The Nickel Man Barn had been freshly painted. It was illuminated on all sides by powerful klieg lights that made the scene resemble a Hollywood premiere rather than an auction. An enormous Russian Imperial flag with its two-headed eagle fluttered in the breeze. Security men in tuxedos stood under the newly canopied entrance.

Just inside the doorway Duffy was resplendent in her black velvet gown. More incandescent than the klieg lights, she welcomed everyone. Duffy shook their hands, thanked them for coming, and wished them the very best of luck. But she longed for someone to shout, "Hey Duffy, what's the story on this ruby picture frame?" "What the hell are you supposed to use this 1906 Imperial Easter Egg for?" "How cheap do you think that Alexandra Diamond is going to go?" But the city people barely nodded their heads, as though Duffy's greeting were an interruption. Even worse, the country people were self-conscious and confused.

Charles and Gregory flanked Duffy on the receiving line. They whispered important names to her.

"Jonas Longley. Director of the Metropolitan."

"Good evening, Mr. Longley," she said, reaching for his hand. "I'll bet a country auction is a new experience for you."

Jonas glanced at Charles, then smiled. "Sure is. And at my age I don't get too many of those anymore. Nothing crude intended."

Across from them stood the brothers and their wives. Emmett wore a new part in his hair and a satin-lapeled tuxedo. Rita was sheathed in silver beads, her long black hair swept to one side. Chip's heavy gold-link bracelet clinked as he fidgeted with the ruffled shirt that burst from his maroon tuxedo. Lorraine's hair was "New York" cut, severe and straight, above her one-shouldered hot-pink chiffon gown.

"First time we ever had a rabbi," Chip whispered as Father Kyril passed.

Emmett held tight to Rita's hand. "I feel like some kind of fool."

Lorraine was all aglow. "I feel just like it's graduation day."

"I hate what they've done to the barn," Emmett whispered. "I hate the way it looks. I hate the way we look!"

Duffy loved the way everyone looked. She loved the music, the carpets, the lights, the whole staff in evening dress. It was more than a sale that was being held, it was a performance.

Everyone had turned out to see The Divine Duffy count out loud, inscrutably acknowledge mysterious telephone bids, and artfully rap the famous ivory gavel. They came from all corners of the globe to be dazzled by a cast of millions in sterling, francs, yen, lira and rubles.

"What's going on with you people?" demanded Mrs. Davis. "I've been comin' here for more than ten years. Why do I have to park across there in Brody's cow patch?"

Duffy took Mrs. Davis' hand. "I'm so glad you came tonight. It's a very special evening."

"Hope that means you got something decent to sell!"

Gregory rolled his eyes and moaned. How much more could he take? What should have been his most elegant sale of the season had been launched by someone rushing up to Nemec and asking where the pie plates were.

Ben was the person Duffy most wanted to see. He stood in front of her, not even reaching out to take her hand. She leaned forward and kissed him. "I've been waiting for you."

He endured the kiss, staring at Duffy in her gown and Charles in his tuxedo. "You two look like you belong on top of a wedding cake."

"Whatever happened to birthday cakes?"

"Not this Saturday night. It's too complicated."

She took his hand. "It doesn't have to be."

Ben nodded. "But it is. It's both our birthdays."

Before Duffy could respond, Ben turned and walked inside. Charles poked her as two men approached. "Coussac and Orlov," he whispered. "VIP dealers."

"Good evening, Mr. Orlov," Duffy said.

Dennis nodded and smiled politely. "Good evening."

Duffy extended her hand. "Mr. Coussac, I want to welcome you to my barn." Coussac merely glared at Charles and walked inside.

Charles smiled. "He's a first-class bastard with the deepest pockets in town."

Duffy nodded. "And the other one?"

"He buys for the Queen."

"The Queen of England?" Duffy's eyes widened as Charles nodded Yes. She whispered to Emmett. "He's the Queen's dealer."

"What?" Emmett leaned forward. "I can't hear with that damn music."

Rita whispered to him, "He's a dealer from Queens."

"Well, I hope he's not hungry," Lorraine snapped. She stared accusingly at Charles. "There's nothing inside for him to eat."

Chip shook his head. "It's not fair. They changed everything. It's not our barn anymore."

The inside of the barn resembled neither the Nickel Man nor Wyndham's. It had a hybrid appearance that accentuated the worst features of both, an ugly woman after a facelift. The bleachers, kitchen and store room had all been ripped out, leaving a flat open area filled by some two hundred black folding chairs. The maze of ground cables was hidden under a false floor covered in red carpet. The walls were lined with cameramen, photographers, press, and staff. People were shown to their seats by tuxedoed ushers who were also security personnel.

"You're sitting in my seat!" Mrs. Davis accused.

"*Ich kann nicht Englisch sprechen*," mumbled Nemec.

"Don't you speak English? I told you, I sit in the front row. Every week."

Myra shook her head. "Look at that, Sophie. He took her seat."

"I never liked that man!"

Myra stood up. "There's a seat over there," she called to Mrs. Davis.

"I don't want to sit over there. This is where I sit every week. In the middle. Right under Duffy."

Duffy's pulpit was centered on a three-foot-high platform. On one side was a U-shaped bulletproof glass enclosure that held the jewels. On the other side were the tables on which the Bids Department kept their records and handled phone and absentee bids. Jonesy and Laura Clayton had their own tables from which to bid for special clients. Royce and Sondra shared a rostrum near Duffy. Every other inch of space was jammed with security people, spotters, and as many of Wyndham's staff as the buses could hold. Above them all, the currency conversion board announced

SALE 1758
GOOD EVENING

"Good evening, Mr. Rosenko." It was Kolmenkin.

As they shook hands in the crowded aisles, Gregory glared at him. "Comrade Director, I would have sent a car for you. Except no one had the courtesy to tell me where you were staying!" He squeezed Kolmenkin's hand angrily. "I will, of course, take care of your return trip."

"Thank you. But I have made my own arrangements."

Gregory hesitated, then leaned over and whispered, "Dmitri, what the hell is going on?"

Delphina's voice spilled over Gregory's shoulder. "Darling, who is that divine-looking man?"

Gregory was impatient as he began the introduction. "Comrade Director Dmitri Leonidovich Kolmenkin, of the Kremlin Museum."

Delphina, wearing white silk pajamas, laughed as she put her arms around Kolmenkin. "You bad boy, why didn't you call me!"

"Or me," Gregory muttered.

"You are very beautiful tonight," Kolmenkin said.

"Actually, I'm distraught. Someone has stolen Princess Magdalena Xenia. She should have been here by now. I sent a car and driver for her."

Kolmenkin spoke to Delphina as he offered Gregory an explanation. "I came by bus."

Delphina put a hand to her breast. "Thank God I'm not a Communist!"

Boris Shedlov was led to his seat by Charles. "It's good for everybody, high prices," Boris said. "It makes people greedy. Collectors get greedy enough to sell. Other collectors start peeing in their pants to buy."

Charles smiled. "I'm counting on you to put some of your best pieces in our next Russian sale."

"That depends on how many records you break tonight. Then, perhaps I will get greedy."

"Dmitri darling, I must try to find Aunt Magda." She kissed his cheek. Delphina rushed over to Laura.

"Another good-looking chauffeur, eh?" Laura sighed and handed her the phone. "Try the Holiday Inn."

"I want to be seated next to Coussac."

Gregory was surprised. "Dmitri, why?"

"I must be seated next to Coussac!"

John Parker was all dressed up. It was the first time he'd worn a tie since his mother died. He and his wife, Alice, sat directly in back of Father Kyril and his entourage. "Can you see?" he whispered.

Alice shook her head. "Not a thing! You think I can ask them to take their hats off?"

John opened the cooler and reached for two cans of beer. "You want the sandwiches now or later?"

"I haven't eaten all day," Duffy said. "That's the reason."

Rita and Ann Marie stood around her in the Ladies' Room while Mrs. M put a wet paper towel to Duffy's forehead. "You'll be fine."

"I've been afraid to eat. I thought I might not be able to keep it down." She smiled. "But now I'm so hungry! And I never think about food before a sale."

"Must be a death wish," Mrs. M said, putting another towel on her brow.

There was a knock at the door. "It's me," Lorraine called. Rita opened the door and Lorraine squeezed in. She put the tray down on the wash basin. "I got you the tea, and then I thought you might need a little something, so I made a delicious omelette with sour cream and lingonberry jam."

Duffy stood up as Lorraine showed her the plate. She put a hand to her stomach and began to moan. "Out! Everybody out!"

Kolmenkin paced nervously. He kept searching the faces in the crowd, not knowing for whom he was looking. He was waiting for someone to come up to him and say, "I am your contact. You will be safe!" While he waited, he thought of Marya's grave with the empty space for him that he would never occupy.

"Charles, I'm terribly worried about her," Delphina said, putting down the phone. "I've called every motel in the area and no one has seen a seventy-year-old woman with a tall blond chauffeur."

"Listen, my love. I've got an auctioneer with terminal nausea, and I've just been told the place is crawling with CIA. God knows why. So I'm not about to weep over Aunt . . ." Charles glared at her. "Delphina," he accused, "what the hell have you got her bidding on?"

Kolmenkin had taken nothing with him. A small suitcase. No tangibles of his life in Moscow. He dared not arouse suspicion at the airport. The only memorabilia to pass through Customs were those in his mind. His mind, a duty-free arsenal closed to inspection. His personal Kremlin.

Coussac, as always, sat in the first row and stared straight ahead like a blind man at a tennis match. It did not matter that Aldo and Neville sat to his right. He acknowledged them with a perfunctory nod. Nor did he care that most of the other dealers, like Denis, clustered in the rear in order to see who was bidding against them. All that mattered to Coussac was that he was going to win.

Kolmenkin thought of all the things he wanted to leave for Mikhail but could not. Money, books, paintings. Yet the most precious gift to give was nothing. No evidence. To be involved with a defector would have ended Mikhail's career. It was more loving to let Mischa feel betrayed than suspected. The constant worry of someone behind him . . . Kolmenkin jumped as he felt a hand on his shoulder.

"I am Father Lukyan," the priest whispered. He took an envelope and put it into Kolmenkin's hand. "The numbers on the outside are the lots you are to bid on for the Holy Father. Inside is the letter of credit and your payment as agreed to by the Patriarch in Moscow." He leaned closer to Kolmenkin. "The other priests are CIA. As soon as the last lot is sold, they will take you out by helicopter."

Kolmenkin's heart was pounding. Although he had never been to confession, he felt the need to explain. "Father, I have not done this for political reasons."

"Not again?" Charles asked. He knocked on the door to the Ladies' Room. "Duffy!"

She opened the door and let him in. He put his arms around her and said, "I love you."

"All Emmett ever said was 'sell one for Papa.'"

"I want to leave a bid with the auctioneer."

She put a finger to his lips. "Charles, the lot's been withdrawn." She kissed him on the cheek. "It hasn't been authenticated yet."

"It will be."

"How do you know?"

"I have an 'eye.' This is your sale, Duffy. By the time it's over you're going to be exactly what you want to be."

There was an angry knock on the door. Someone asked, "Are you ever coming out?"

"Myra, don't be rude!"

Charles handed Duffy the auctioneer's catalog. He brushed his lips against her hair. "Sell one for Papa."

"Good evening, ladies and gentlemen." The red lights glowed atop the video cameras. There was momentary feedback from the audio system. Flash bulbs began bursting. The conversion board clickety-clacked itself clear. The slide projector turned on with a whoosh-whoosh-whoosh and the title CZARINA appeared.

"Welcome to the Nickel Man Barn. We have for your competition this evening . . ." The words were coming out of her mouth, but someone else was saying them. She was a stranger standing in front of a room filled with other strangers. Hundreds of faces looked up without recognizing her. Where was Ben? She couldn't find him in the crowd.

Charles walked quickly down the side aisle and onto the platform. He stood next to Gregory and raised his eyebrows as if to say, "Here we go!"

"What are you doing here?" Coussac whispered as Kolmenkin sat down next to him.

"Good evening, Serge."

"Your presence will arouse suspicion. I don't want it known I'm bidding for your government."

"You're not."

John Parker turned to Alice. "Sounds like she's announcing a prize fight. What have we got?"

"Tuna and meat loaf."

". . . as printed in the forepart of your catalog, especially the condition which states that . . ."

"What catalog?" Mrs. Davis raised her hand. "Duffy, I didn't get a catalog. Nobody gave me one." She stood up and looked around. "Where's the man who tried to take my seat? I bet he took my catalog!"

Charles picked up a catalog and handed it to one of the ushers. "Quickly!"

Aldo looked over at Coussac. He caught sight of Kolmenkin and poked Coussac. "What's he doing here?" he whispered.

Coussac raised an eyebrow and shook his head as though apologizing for an unruly child.

". . . when the auctioneer says 'to the absent bidder' or . . ."

Chip and Emmett were standing against the wall. "You understand what the hell she's talking about?" Chip asked.

Emmett shook his head No. "Shit, I don't even know who that is up there."

"We start this evening's session with the Fabergé carved jade rabbit, Lot One." The presale estimate was twenty-five thousand dollars.

Luther held up the small rabbit in his white gloved hand as the slide flashed on screen. Jonesy and two of her girls were already on the telephone. Duffy took a deep breath and looked at her catalog. FIDDD. An order bid for $15,000. "Because of the great interest in this lot, I'm opening the bidding at ten dollars." People began to laugh.

Charles reached out to touch her. "Ten *thousand!*" he whispered, staring straight ahead.

Duffy felt her stomach turn over. "I'm sorry. The bidding will open at ten *thousand* dollars." Meisenstein raised his hand. "Eleven thousand," Duffy called.

"Yes," Emmett whispered.

"Yes," nodded Chip.

Neville bid. "Twelve thousand," she said. Then Meisenstein. "Thirteen." Neville. "Thirteen."

"I'm thirteen!" Meisenstein shouted angrily. "You did thirteen twice."

Duffy glanced nervously at Charles and caught sight of him wincing. She turned back to Meisenstein. "I have twelve, I mean, thirteen thousand dollars from the gentleman on my right." This time she didn't even dare to look at Charles. Instead, she turned to Neville. He nodded. "Fourteen," she said. Back to Meisenstein. "Fifteen." It was the worst thing that could happen to an auctioneer—she was more nervous than the bidders. Duffy had lost control and they knew it.

"Twenty!" Denis called.

Duffy hesitated. "We were at fifteen, sir."

"I am well aware of that!"

"Thank you," she said, feeling her cheeks flush. "I have twenty thousand. Twenty thousand dollars." Meisenstein. "Twenty-one thousand." Denis nodded. "Twenty-two thousand." Meisenstein. "Twenty-three thousand." Denis nodded. "Twenty-four. I have twenty-four thousand dollars." Charles was right. These people weren't there to enjoy themselves. There was too much at stake. They didn't need an auctioneer. They needed a five-star general.

"Twenty-five!" Jonesy shouted in frustration, while waiting to be recognized with her phone bid.

Denis nodded. "Twenty-six," Duffy called.

Jonesy shook her head No and hung up. She looked over at Charles and rolled her eyes in annoyance. Charles nodded that he understood.

"I have twenty-six thousand. On my left at twenty-six thousand." Aldo raised his hand. "Twenty-seven." Denis nodded. "Twenty-eight." Aldo. "Twenty-nine." Denis. "Thirty." There was a murmur. "I have thirty thousand dollars on my left. Thirty thousand."

Meisenstein yelled out, "Thirty-five thousand!"

Before Duffy could repeat the bid, Denis put his hand up and called, "Forty!"

"Forty thousand. Forty thousand on my left." Meisenstein shook his head in despair and turned the page in his catalog. "I have forty thousand dollars," Duffy said. She raised the gavel, waited and then slammed it down. "At forty thousand dollars, then. Sold!"

Charles took her hand. "It's all right. We went fifteen thousand over the estimate. The next one will be easier." Duffy stared at the ivory gavel. It didn't feel right. Nothing felt right. "Don't worry," he said, "you'll get used to it."

"Why did you stop?" asked Meisenstein's accountant.

"What are you, crazy? Forty thousand for some cockamamie rabbit?"

Forty thousand, Ben thought. It was his money. His forty thousand. All he would have to do was go to court. With his father. And his mother. And his son.

"Forty thousand!" Mommy whispered to Daddy.

"Rabbits always go high," he said. "Remember that Bugs Bunny mug in Atlantic City?"

Duffy took a deep breath. Her smile was forced. "Lot Two. The bidding will open at twenty thousand dollars." She tried to be charming and relaxed. The problem was the real Duffy Patterson was being held captive, bound and gagged by a black velvet gown.

Emmett had a pocket calculator on which he entered forty thousand dollars for Lot One. "Almost twice the estimate," Chip whispered. Lorraine entered forty thousand on her calculator, took twenty percent of it, and then divided by three. She showed the figure to Rita, who had a pad with lines numbered one through ninety-six. She wrote $2,666.66 at the top of the page.

"Twenty-seven thousand, on my right. Twenty-eight."

One of the ushers handed Delphina a piece of paper with the message, "Magda on 4." She rushed to the table and picked up the phone. "Where are you?" Delphina whispered.

"On a highway somewhere, across from something called Mario's Meatball! We broke down."

"Don't move. I'll be right there!"

"I'm at one of the emergency phones. It's a ghastly shade of green."

Delphina hung up. She whispered to Jonesy on her way out. "There will be a phone bid on the egg necklace. Princess Magdalena Xenia of Saxe-Weimar. She's clean!"

"Forty-six thousand against you." By this time, both Aldo and Neville had dropped out. Incredibly, the cigarette case was already nineteen thousand above its presale estimate. But that didn't matter to Peter Harms. He just couldn't stop now.

"Forty-seven." Denis nodded. "Forty-eight." Peter. "Forty-nine." Denis. "Fifty thousand dollars." Peter hesitated. This had to be his last bid. There was no way he could justify going higher to Eliot. He nodded. "Fifty-one thousand."

Denis wanted it desperately. But the Keeper of the Privy Purse had been specific. Fifty was Her Majesty's maximum. However, the pound had gone up. He sensed that fifty-one was the other bidder's last-ditch effort. He simply couldn't lose it for two thousand dollars. Denis raised his hand.

"Fifty-two thousand."

Peter had to go to fifty-three. Otherwise, regret would haunt him always. When would there be another case like it?

"Fifty-three thousand on my right." Denis had lost. He shook his head No. "Fifty-three thousand dollars, then, on my right. Fifty-three. Sold!"

"You've done it!" Charles said, beaming. "You've set a new world record!"

Peter was ecstatic. What a bargain! A veritable steal! He'd won over some of the most important dealers in the world! Wait till he told Eliot! "Excuse me," he said, getting up to claim his trophy.

Neville turned to Aldo. "Well, at least Denis didn't get it."

Aldo shook his head. "They are bidding like madmen." He smiled and shrugged. "I will have to raise all the prices in my shop. Otherwise, everyone will think I am selling fakes."

Lorraine took twenty percent of fifty-three thousand, divided by three, and showed the figure to Rita, who entered $3,533.33 next to Lot Two. She whispered to Lorraine, as though they were cheating on a test, "Let me see your subtotal!"

Fifty-three thousand, Ben thought. His stomach knotted as he imagined a front-page headline: BANKER'S SON IS REALLY BANKER'S SON.

Outside the barn, Delphina waved her arms frantically at Charles' chauffeur. They both ran toward the Rolls. He held the door open for her. "Where to, ma'am?"

"Mario's Meatball!"

Kolmenkin watched three of the priests get up. They whispered to one another and moved out of sight. Then, from the corner of his eye, he saw one priest edge toward the front door. The other two stood at the emergency exit near him. Kolmenkin took the envelope from his jacket pocket and glanced at Father Kyril as if to let him know he was ready. The first lot number was four. It was the same lot on which Coussac was to begin bidding.

"Lot Three," Duffy announced.

Mommy grabbed hold of Daddy's arm. "That's our little piggy!"

"We have a number of order bids on this piece. We'll begin at fifteen thousand dollars." The presale estimate was twenty-five thousand.

"Daddy!"

"That's not fair!" he whispered to Mommy. "They started the rabbit at only ten."

Denis raised his hand. Duffy acknowledged with "Sixteen."

"Seventeen." It was Jonesy on the phone.

"Don't worry, Daddy."

"Eighteen," Laura called.

"He's meant to be ours," Mommy said. "When do we bid?"

"Nineteen," from Aldo.

"Remember, we can only go to twenty-five," Daddy warned.

"Don't worry!"

"Twenty." Then Laura and Jonesy began conducting their own auction with lightning speed.

"Twenty-one."

"Twenty-two."

"Twenty-three."

"Twenty-four."

"Twenty-five."

Mommy moaned.

Laura shook her head No and sat down. It was Jonesy's twenty-five. She turned to Duffy. Duffy looked at Denis. He nodded. Duffy called, "Twenty-six." Meisenstein raised his hand. "Twenty-seven."

"Daddy?"

"Twenty-eight," from Neville.

"We never even got to bid!" she gasped.

"Twenty-nine thousand dollars."

"It's fixed!"

"Thirty thousand on my left."

"Thirty-one." Aldo's bid.

"Thirty-two on my left. On my left at thirty-two thousand."

Meisenstein's accountant threw up his hands in despair. "How come you're not bidding on this one? This one is going cheap!"

"Schmuck! Cheap? Thirty-two thousand for *traife?*"

"At thirty-two thousand, then. Anyone else? Sold!"

"They're all going well over the estimates," Charles whispered jubilantly.

Daddy put his arm around Mommy. "You going to be all right?"

Mommy blew her nose in the handkerchief and nodded. She leaned over and whispered, "Oink."

Ben remembered that day at the bank with Duffy and Charles. If only he could find an heir, he had thought. That would stop them. Instead, it had stopped him. BANKER'S SON IS REALLY MISS NATALIE'S SON. Will the real Ben Perry please stand up and claim his fortune?

"Lot Four," Duffy announced. There was an immediate murmur from the crowd. "The jeweled icon," she said, looking at her catalog. The presale estimate was $125,000. "The bidding will open at fifty thousand dollars."

Coussac cleared his throat. He took a pencil from his pocket. He looked up at Duffy for the first time. But then Kolmenkin whispered to him, "Do not raise your hand."

"What?"

Meisenstein waved his catalog and called out, "Fifty-five thousand."

"Sixty thousand in the rear."

"What are you saying?" Coussac asked.

"Sixty-five thousand on the phone," Duffy said.

"Do not bid."

Meisenstein waved. Duffy acknowledged with "Seventy thousand." And then, "Seventy-five thousand on the phone."

Coussac hesitated. "Then who will bid for you?"

"I will." Kolmenkin raised his hand.

"Eighty thousand to my left."

Gregory moved quickly to the pulpit. Why was Kolmenkin bidding instead of Coussac? "You can take his bids," he whispered to Duffy.

She nodded, then looked at Jonesy, who pointed a finger to signify Yes. "Eighty-five thousand on the phone."

Aldo nudged Neville and rolled his eyes toward Coussac. "He's not bidding. Kolmenkin is bidding for himself."

Neville smiled. "Looks like the Russians don't trust him any more than we do."

Charles moved close to Gregory. "Why aren't the other dealers bidding?" he whispered.

After Meisenstein shook his pencil in the air, Duffy said, "I have ninety thousand."

Kolmenkin raised her hand. "One hundred thousand. I have one hundred thousand dollars," she repeated.

"Where the hell are the bids?" Charles stared at Aldo and Neville. "Unless they bid we're not going to make it on this one."

"One hundred and ten thousand on the phone."

"I was paid to bid," Coussac said.

Kolmenkin raised his hand. "You were bought off. Just as you bought off the others."

"One hundred and twenty thousand."

"I was paid by your government to bid."

"You were paid by me."

"The bid is one hundred and twenty thousand on my left."

Meisenstein turned to his accountant. "What do they think, it's the last icon in the world?"

"One hundred and twenty . . ."

"For whom are you working?" Coussac said.

"For myself."

"Sold!"

Coussac started to rise. "I am leaving."

Kolmenkin pushed him down into his seat. "If you move again, if you cause any disturbance . . ."

Charles turned his back to the audience as he spoke to Gregory. "Why the hell is Kolmenkin bidding himself? Why isn't he using Coussac?"

Kolmenkin spoke softly. "Unless you do as I say, everyone will know the precise nature of your affiliation with the Soviet government. You will be ruined."

One hundred and twenty thousand, Ben thought. The stakes were definitely getting higher. More difficult to walk away from. Impossible to walk away from. After all, who understood money better than a banker's son? Ben felt as though he had been watching a movie in reverse. No, you weren't adopted. Yes, you are her son. How wonderful! How terrible! Congratulations! Shhhh!

"Lot Five," Duffy announced.

"And what of *your* affiliation, Comrade Director?"

"It is over."

Little Vicky turned to Waneta. "Here we go, ducks." She raised her hand.

"Thirty-one thousand on my right."

Little Vicky refused to give Wyndham's the rings until she knew the lot was hers. Waneta accompanied her to the sale. No one wanted Little Vicky to win more than Waneta, who was already planning her most successful Victorian jewelry sale ever.

One of the clerks signaled a bid. "Thirty-two."

"Thirty-two on the phone," Duffy said. Little Vicky nodded. "Thirty-three," Duffy called. She looked over at the clerk. "Thirty-four." Then she looked at Little Vicky.

"Oh, what the bloody hell!" Little Vicky said. "Fifty!"

Duffy smiled. "Fifty thousand dollars." The phone operator nodded. "Fifty-one."

Kolmenkin raised his hand. "Fifty-two."

Coussac turned to him. "It's Kyril, isn't it? You're bidding for the church."

The phone clerk nodded. "Fifty-three."

"This could go on all night," Little Vicky mumbled. She stood up and stared defiantly at the clerk. "Seventy-five!"

The clerk put a hand over her mouth as she spoke into the

receiver. She shrugged, nodded, smiled, and then looked at Duffy. "Eighty."

"Eighty thousand on the phone." Duffy looked at Kolmenkin. He nodded. "Eighty-one on my left."

"That religious fanatic thinks it all belongs to him," Coussac said.

"I have eighty-one thousand . . ."

Coussac grabbed hold of Kolmenkin's sleeve. "You are sentencing these pieces to oblivion. No one will ever see them in a church. They belong to the people!"

Little Vicky was still standing. "Eighty-five over here and going strong!"

"Your loyalty through the years has been admirable, Comrade Coussac." Kolmenkin raised his hand.

"Eighty-six on my left."

Charles walked quickly to Laura. "I don't care whose confidence you're breaking. Why isn't there more action from the dealers?"

"I don't understand," Laura said. "I know one of my people always bids through Neville but he hasn't jumped in yet."

"Ninety!" Little Vicky shouted.

The phone clerk shook her head and hung up. Meisenstein raised a hand. "Ninety-one." Then Kolmenkin. "Ninety-two thousand."

Meisenstein smiled smugly as he explained to his accountant, "There must be something wrong with it. None of the dealers are bidding. It's a good thing I know when to pull out."

"One hundred thousand dollars, miss!"

"Thank you," Duffy said. "I have one hundred thousand dollars."

Coussac whispered, "There is still time to save yourself, Comrade Director. I can make excuses for you to the Minister."

Kolmenkin raised his hand. "There is no excuse for me."

"One hundred and ten thousand," Duffy called.

Waneta slid down in her chair. There went her Victorian sale. Little Vicky whispered to her, "Listen, miss, we both know my rings are worth more than a measly hundred."

"You'll be bidding one twenty plus a ten percent premium!"

"Oh, you won't charge me a premium. I'm family by now."

"I have one hundred and ten thousand, then."

Waneta held her breath and nodded. Little Vicky stood up again. "I'm pleased to tell you, miss, you've now got one hundred and twenty thousand! But I warn you, that's my final offer!"

Kolmenkin stared straight ahead as he spoke to Coussac. "If it is of any consequence, Comrade Coussac, the Minister planned to destroy the pieces, to resell the stones."

"That is his privilege, I have never put my needs above those of the Party."

Kolmenkin bid again. Almost apologetically, Duffy announced, "One hundred and thirty thousand on my left." There was a murmur as it became clear Little Vicky had lost.

"You are not doing this to save the pieces," Coussac snarled. "You are doing this to save yourself!"

"Precisely."

"I have one hundred and thirty thousand, then. Anyone?" Duffy hesitated, giving Little Vicky a last chance to bid.

Coussac was enraged. He began to tremble. His eyes narrowed. He leaned over and whispered, *"Zhopoyob!"*

Kolmenkin stopped breathing for a moment. But the earth did not open and swallow him. He was not grabbed from behind and wrestled to the ground. People did not spit in his face or throw rocks. Yet, the very worst had happened. No, he thought suddenly. The very best had happened. He turned to Coussac. "Yes, Comrade Serge Pavlovich Coussac. Yes!"

"Sold!"

Little Vicky bowed her head for a moment. She patted the ring cases. "You know, I think Old Bert's been watching over my shoulder. I don't think it sat well with him, my wanting to give it all up. I still got a few years left. Something tells me Bert wants me to spend them on Portobello. That's where the happy times were."

". . . and so in view of the order bids for Lot Six, we'll open at two hundred and fifty thousand . . ." Duffy's voice trailed off. The audio system went dead. All the numbers went black on the conversion board. The light on the slide projector blew out. People began shifting in their seats.

As Duffy stepped forward to reassure the crowd, Charles shouted from behind the bulletproof enclosure. "I'm terribly sorry. We've had a temporary power failure. The engineers assure me it will be corrected within a few minutes. For your own comfort and safety, please remain seated."

Ben watched Charles take hold of Duffy and lead her outside past the security guards. He followed down the aisle and out the front door. "What's going on?"

"I had to stop it," Charles said. "I'm sorry, Duffy. But I've got to take over."

"You told me I was breaking records!"

"On the cheaper lots, yes. But not on the last two. There were no bids from Aldo or Neville or Coussac. Not even from Jonas, and I know he's desperate to build the Metropolitan's Russian collection. It's more than coincidence that they don't bid when Kolmenkin raises his hand. They've got a ring going in there!"

"Which ones are Aldo and Neville?" she asked.

"That's the problem!" he shouted. "You don't even know who the hell they are! I have no choice. There's too much money at stake."

She turned from Charles to Ben. "Is this a deal you two made? Let the kid sell a few lots to make her feel good and then pull the plug?"

"I didn't make a deal with him." Ben turned to Charles. "How do you break up a ring?"

"You can't. There's no way to force them to bid against one another. But I can raise the prices," Charles said. "I'll have to take bids off the wall."

"Not in my barn," Duffy yelled. "I won't have a crooked sale."

"You won't have any sale at all if you don't let me get prices up to where they should be."

"That's illegal," Ben said.

"I didn't start this. They did! I have to fight them any way I can. It's for the good of the estate, damn it! Listen, I'm trying to put more money into the bank's pocket."

"I won't let you call phony bids in my barn."

Charles grabbed her arm. "Let's get this straight. I'm the one who's getting screwed in your goddamn barn. I've got to come out of this with the highest prices ever paid for Fabergé! That's what my business is all about. Making money. Breaking records. Making more money. To hell with your moral outrage. I've put my reputation on the line. You've got nothing at stake!"

"I've got me at stake!" Duffy shook her head. "I thought this was the most important sale of my life. But it's just the most expensive, that's all. I'm not in the record business, Charles. I'm in the auction business. Every sale—in my goddamn barn—is important." She turned to Ben. "They were important before you came and they'll be important after you've gone."

"I don't care what the hell happens after I'm gone," Charles shouted. "All I care about is now. As of now this is *my* sale. If either of you do anything to stop me, I'll haul you into court for conflict of interest, and conspiring against the estate for your personal gain!"

Without saying a word, Ben swung his fist and hit Charles. He knocked him to the ground.

"What the hell's wrong with you?" Charles asked, rubbing his chin. "We're supposed to be on the same side." He started to get up.

"Stay right where you are," Ben said. "I have something to tell you and you might as well be comfortable."

By the time Ben finished it seemed as though no one would ever again have anything to say. The only sound was the flapping of the Imperial flag above them.

Charles sighed and got up. He brushed the dirt from his tuxedo and straightened his tie. "It's the ultimate nightmare for any auctioneer," he said. "The way an actor dreams about forgetting his lines. There you are, ready to bring down the hammer and someone rushes in and shouts, Stop! It's mine!"

Duffy took Ben's hand. "Why didn't you tell me?"

"What was I going to do? Call up and say, Hello, guess who this isn't? Guess who's the missing heir I was looking for? Guess who it all belongs to?" He paused. "If you had seen my father's face. He's terrified I'm going to make a shambles out of his life. And my mother's." Ben turned away. "The truth is," he said, "I'm terrified of making a shambles out of my own life. I don't know who the hell I am anymore!"

She kissed him gently. "Maybe you don't, but I do. Rubber bands north to south. Staples east to west. You're the same stuffy, rigid son of a banker you've always been. You're Ben Perry of Perry Falls, president of the Perry Falls Savings and Loan. That's who you really are."

"And now for the bad news," Charles sighed. "Why have you told us all this?"

"Because I won't let you take the sale away from Duffy." Ben cleared his throat. "I don't care about the ring or your percentage or mine. The contract says she's the auctioneer."

"Break the damn contract!" Charles shouted. "You've got a responsibility to the estate."

"I am the estate."

Duffy took Ben aside. "Why are you doing this? You could be throwing away a fortune."

"I'm not throwing it away. I'm giving it to you."

"Oh, Jesus! A born-again millionaire!"

"I can't let you do that," she said.

"I need you in my life, Duffy. And it looks like the only way that's going to happen is on your terms. I want you to have the sale. I want you to have the best auction barn in the state."

"You trying to tell me you're ready to be the auctioneer's husband?"

Ben smiled. "If you're ready to be the banker's wife."

"I now pronounce you crazy," Charles snapped.

"Either she continues or I stop the sale," Ben said.

"There's no sale in there," Charles argued. "It's a charity bazaar for the benefit of the ring."

"Tell them she's ready to start," Ben ordered.

Charles walked to the door. "I'll announce we're ready to continue." He hesitated. "As soon as I wipe the Imperial Egg off my face."

Ben put his arms around Duffy. He whispered his most secret thought. "I don't want to claim the money."

"Ben, you can't give it all up," Duffy said.

"I'm not giving it up. It doesn't belong to me. The money belongs to Miss Natalie's son. That's not who I am or who I want to be." He stared at Duffy. "Will you marry me anyway?"

"Yes."

"Then you'd better figure out how to break up the ring." He smiled at her. "At least one of us ought to come out of this mess a millionaire!"

". . . and so in view of the order bids for this lot, we'll open at two hundred and fifty thousand dollars. Lot Six, the Easter Egg Necklace."

Before Duffy had time to focus on the ring, a flurry of hands shot into the air. Meisenstein, Nemec, Denis, Jonesy, and Laura. And Kolmenkin. All three phone operators were busy. One of the calls came from the highway near Mario's Meatball.

"It's opened at two five zero," Jonesy said.

Aunt Magda sipped sherry as she sat inside one of the two Rolls-Royces parked on the road. Delphina stood on the highway, her white pajamas fluttering in the breeze as cars whizzed by. She shouted into the emergency phone, "Three hundred thousand!"

"I have three hundred thousand on the phone," Duffy said.

Nemec shouted, "Three twenty-five!"

Sophie looked at Myra. "I knew it! He wants my necklace!"

"I bet he wants it for his . . ." Myra hesitated, ". . . his mistress!"

"Myra!"

"I have three hundred and fifty thousand on the phone."

"Three seventy-five," Nemec called out.

Kolmenkin nodded. "Four hundred thousand on my left."

"Auntie, they're up to four hundred thousand!" Delphina shouted into the receiver, "Four twenty-five, damn it!"

Duffy went from Jonesy to Kolmenkin to Nemec. "Four hundred twenty-five. Four hundred fifty. Four hundred seventy-five." The bidding was going too fast for her to catch the ring in operation. She kept searching faces for a hint. Red had told her it was a business of faces. All she saw was Coussac's empty stare. She never noticed the movement of his pen. He kept circling the word "bid" on the title page of his catalog. And then, gently, so that Kolmenkin wouldn't notice, he nudged Aldo.

"Did you ever hear such a thing?" Meisenstein asked, turning the page. "They're belching twenty-five thousand dollars at a time. Good luck to them!"

As Aldo turned to him, Coussac motioned with his eyes. He was still circling the word "bid." Aldo stared at the page.

Duffy was waiting for Jonesy's phone bid, as she repeated, "Four hundred and seventy-five thousand dollars."

Myra thought the bidding was over. "Sophie, I think he got it!"

"Not again!"

"Yes! She's looking right at him!"

"Five hundred thousand dollars!" Sophie shouted. Everyone turned quickly in the direction of that frail voice.

"Sophie, what have you done?" Myra gasped.

"Five hundred thousand in the rear. I have five hundred thousand . . ."

Sophie held Myra's hand. "What am I going to do?"

"Five hundred and fifty!" Nemec called angrily.

"Thank God!" Sophie put a hand to her chest and sighed deeply. "Myra, did you bring the salts?"

"Auntie, I need more money," Delphina pleaded. "It's at six hundred thousand."

"It's where?" she asked as Ulrik refilled her glass.

"I need a few piasters, darling. Auntie, please!"

Aunt Magda slammed the door shut. Then she rolled down the window and said, "Six hundred thousand is a ridiculous figure."

Delphina waved the receiver in the air. "It's up to seven! I'll sell you the house in Biarritz!"

"Hang up, Delphina. You've crapped out." Aunt Magda rolled up the window. "Home, Ulrik!"

"Seven hundred and fifty thousand on my left," Duffy said.

Charles stood next to her. He watched Coussac's pen move in circles. He whispered to Duffy, "What the hell is Coussac writing?"

"I have seven hundred and fifty thousand dollars."

"It's no use," Charles said, "they won't bid against Kolmenkin."

"Sold!"

"Damn!" muttered Charles. "It should have brought double the estimate. They're really going to kill us on the next one."

"Lot Seven," Duffy said, "is the first of the Imperial Easter Eggs." She turned the page. "The St. Basil's Cathedral Egg." It was estimated at $550,000. According to her catalog she should open the bidding at $250,000. Instead, she kept her voice crisp and clear while announcing, "In view of the considerable interest in this lot, we're opening at six hundred thousand dollars."

There was an audible intake of breath from the audience. Charles, between clenched teeth, whispered, "That's the wrong figure. It's too high!"

Duffy held her breath. Ben had given her back the sale. Now it was up to her to make it pay off. She knew it was the wrong figure. But she hadn't broken any rules. The opening figure is always determined by the auctioneer. It was her sale. Her rules. Charles had told her that the very first day.

Kolmenkin raised his hand. Duffy breathed a sigh of relief. She had been afraid no one would bid. "Six hundred and twenty-five thousand."

Charles smiled. The country mouse had begun to stalk the city rats.

"Six hundred and fifty thousand on the phone."

Coussac brought his pen to the next paragraph on the page. Again, he circled the word "bid." He looked at Aldo and shook his head Yes.

Aldo leaned over to whisper, "You *want* me to bid?"

The country mouse pounced. "Excuse me, which one of you gentlemen is bidding? Is it you, sir?" Duffy asked, pointing directly at Coussac. "Or you?" She pointed to Aldo.

Coussac rose slowly from his chair. "How dare you?" he snarled. "I have nothing to do with him!"

"I'm sorry," Duffy said. "I just didn't want there to be any confusion."

"There is no confusion," Coussac said, taking full advantage of the situation. "He is free to bid as he chooses. He was merely asking me the time. This sale is taking a very long time." Coussac turned to Neville, as though by chance. "Why don't you ask *him* why he doesn't bid? He is free to bid on anything he wants. Just as anyone here is free to bid on anything he chooses. As for me, I choose not to bid."

Animated conversations sprang up all over the room. Gone were the hushed whispers. Everyone was talking at once. Kolmenkin turned to Coussac. "Your little charade is futile. I will still get the pieces."

"Perhaps. But now you will have to pay for them."

Duffy rapped the gavel for quiet. She knew she'd struck oil. "Ladies and gentlemen," she shouted, "the bid is on the phone at six hundred and fifty thousand dollars."

Kolmenkin raised his hand. "Thank you," she said, still rapping the gavel. "Six hundred and seventy-five thousand on my left." Charles was beaming.

During the confusion, Kolmenkin hadn't noticed that Jonas had sat down next to him. "It's a real shame," Jonas said.

Aldo shook his pencil, glancing nervously at Coussac. "Seven hundred thousand."

"Kyril's going to keep everything locked up in a church," Jonas muttered. "That's got to hurt a lot, Dmitri," he smiled. "Really got to hurt that curator's heart of yours."

Kolmenkin raised his hand. "Seven hundred and twenty-five."

"Seven hundred and fifty on the phone."

"Pardon my French, but let's cut the horseshit. I can do a lot more for you than the Heavenly Father."

Kolmenkin bid again. "Seven hundred and seventy-five."

Aldo whispered to Coussac as though asking for permission. "I am bidding again." He shook his pencil at Duffy and felt suddenly liberated. "And I'm not giving you back the money, either!"

"Eight hundred thousand." And then Duffy nodded at Neville. "Eight hundred and twenty-five. Thank you very much."

"I don't know what you're talking about, Jonas."

Jonas smiled. "Everybody thinks the CIA's got a tight lip. Truth is, they're just a bunch of yentas. No racial slur intended."

"Eight hundred and fifty thousand dollars," Duffy called.

"Better raise your hand, Dmitri," Jonas said. "I like eggs."

"Eight hundred and seventy-five thousand. On my left."

"It's no secret how much money you got from the church. Unfortunately, I'm not that well-endowed." Jonas smiled. "Moneywise."

"Nine hundred thousand on the phone."

"I got a real nice job for you, Dmitri. Head of our Russian collection. Better raise your hand again."

"The gentleman on my left at nine hundred and twenty-five."

"Now put your hand out, Dmitri." Jonas gave him an envelope. "I'm offering you that same helicopter ride out of here, but I'm throwing in a contract with the museum. A chance for you to make sure everyone sees the family jewels. If you know what I mean."

Neville sneered at Aldo and raised his hand. "Nine hundred and fifty."

"Listen, you bastard," Aldo whispered to Neville, "I want this piece." He shook his pencil furiously. "I bid on it first."

"Nine hundred and seventy-five. I have nine hundred and seventy-five thousand dollars," Duffy repeated, anticipating the magic figure that would come with the next bid. She looked at Kolmenkin, impatient to see his hand go up. But he was distracted by Jonas. It took longer than she expected. She hesitated, but her instincts took over. She shouted at Kolmenkin, "You're not going to lose it for another twenty-five?"

Charles stared at Duffy open-mouthed. Gregory covered his face with his hands. Jonesy shook her head. Laura gasped.

Kolmenkin was stunned. His hand shot up. Duffy called,

"One million dollars!" She wanted to say it as she had been taught. But there was no way to keep the excitement out of her voice. "One million dollars!" Duffy put a hand to her mouth, unable to believe the bid she had just announced. Her heart was beating so fast, so happily, the only thing Duffy could do was begin to laugh. She leaned over to the microphone. "Must have been a real rich chicken laid that egg!"

The entire staff at Wyndham's turned as one to look at Charles. They were astonished to see him laughing, too. People throughout the room began to smile.

Laura raised her hand hesitantly. "One million one hundred thousand on the phone." Duffy smiled at her. "I sure hope that isn't a crank call." She turned back to Kolmenkin. "All right, I have a million one. Where's the two?"

Emmett was grinning from ear to ear. He pushed his way down the aisle, dragging Chip behind him.

"Thing is, Dmitri, you've got to give the church their money back first if you're going to fuck 'em." Jonas smiled. "It's the American way."

Kolmenkin handed Father Kyril's envelope to Jonas. The two men shook hands.

"I got a million one. Where's the two? Make it two! Bid the two!" Kolmenkin nodded at Duffy. "Got the two!"

Emmett and Chip stood beneath the pulpit. "Yes!" Emmett shouted.

"Yes!"

"One million two hundred thousand!" Duffy turned back to Laura. "I'm looking for a million three. Should be!"

"Should be!" Emmett yelled.

Laura nodded. "Got it!" Duffy shouted. "One million three hundred thousand dollars!"

"Yes!"

"Yes!"

"Got the three. Where's the four? Bid the four. Make it four!" Duffy smiled at Kolmenkin. "Afraid you're going to have to come up with some more egg money, mister!"

Kolmenkin raised his hand. "Yes!"

"One million four!"

"Yes!"

"Yes!"

"Anybody?" she called. Laura shook her head No. "I got one million four from the man with a big smile on his face. He knows he's making a good deal. Is that it? Folks?" She slammed down the gavel. "Sold!"

The room burst into applause. Emmett and Chip reached up to shake Duffy's hand. Through the tears in her eyes, she saw Ben. He stood on his chair applauding.

Duffy turned to Charles. "You were right. I've become exactly what I want to be."

The inevitable had happened. There was no way to stop her. He kissed her on the cheek. "We could have made such beautiful money together."

Duffy opened the drawer and took out Red's gavel. "We got to keep moving, folks. They tell me it's getting late in Tokyo." She banged the gavel hard, hoping somehow Red could hear her. "Next thing we have coming up is Lot Eight, the ruby double-heart frame." She leaned forward. "Folks, I know what it says in your catalog about this piece." Every eye was on Duffy. "But there's something else I want to tell you." There wasn't a sound. "It's real pretty."

❧

Red waved goodbye and drove the truck onto Indian Creek Road. "Nice lady," he said.

Duffy sat cross-legged on the front seat. She smiled and held up half a cookie. "She makes good cookies, Papa."

He laughed. "You ever see so many cookies? Can't imagine who she was expecting."

"Maybe she has lots of children, Papa."

"Children? She's not even married. She lives in that house all by herself. Has for years." He smiled. "She must have baked six kinds of cookies!"

"You should have bought something from her, Papa."

Red turned to his ten-year-old daughter and asked with wonder, "You hear somebody say somethin'?"

Duffy sighed and pursed her lips. "No, Papa. I didn't."

He reached over and tousled her bright red hair. "Say, how about a cookie for the old man?"

She looked around wide-eyed. "You hear somebody say somethin'?" As Red began to laugh, Duffy deepened her voice. "All right, folks," she said, imitating his patter as she held up a cookie. "We got ourselves a brand-new cookie here. It's round, and with all its original chocolate chips. Who'll start the bidding at five cents?"

"I will," Red squeaked in a playful falsetto.

"I got five. Where's the six? Gimme six. Bid the six. Should be!"

He reached for the cookie. "Should have been," he said, eating it in one bite.

"Oh, Papa. I wanted to say 'Sold'!"

"You're my daughter, all right. Nobody's ever gonna question that."

They rode in silence, Duffy eating the last of the cookies Miss Natalie had given her. "You know, Papa, you should have bought her books."